THE SUMMER SOLDIER

"Plenty of action to satisfy any suspense and spy novel buff."

—CINCINNATI ENQUIRER

"An engrossing cat-and-mouse chase story."

—MILWAUKEE JOURNAL

"The ending of the book is suspense at its best."

—SACRAMENTO BEE

"An extremely well-crafted chunk of suspense . . . razor-perfect pacing."

—KIRKUS REVIEWS

"Superior, straightforward, compelling."

—LIBRARY JOURNAL

"Guild is a welcome addition to the genre with a masterful portrait of a man on the run."

—BOOKLIST

THE SUMMER SOLDIER

NICHOLAS GUILD

A JOVE BOOK

Published by arrangement with Seaview Books

Printed in the United States of America

Library of Congress Catalog Card Number: 77-27125

First Jove edition published October 1979

10 9 8 7 6 5 4 3 2 1

Jove books are published by Jove Publications, Inc., 200 Madison Avenue, New York, NY 10016

To Joanie, from one who loves her

THE SUMMER SOLDIER

I

FROM WHERE HE was standing on the driveway, he couldn't see much evidence of fire. Of course the roof and front wall of the house had been pretty thoroughly hosed down and one pane of glass in the dining room window inexplicably broken, but the kitchen, which occupied a rear corner, had sustained all the real damage.

They had even hosed down the garage door, which you would have thought well out of reach of the flames. He swept a hand over its beaded surface to leave a glistening smear. His palm, he noticed, came away covered with a milky film.

Louise had never really liked that color.

"Well look, if you think it's that bad I can take it back. I'll just tell the guy it doesn't look anything like what he showed me on the sample card."

Twisting around from his crouch by the lower left-hand panel, careful to hold the paintbrush so it wouldn't run out onto where the cement wasn't covered with sheets of newspaper, he had caught sight of her standing on the sidewalk, just at the edge of what, God willing, would sprout into their front lawn. She had peered through the blinding early afternoon sun, shading her eyes with one hand as she rested the other, tucked under at the wrist, on her hip. It was a characteristic attitude.

"No, forget it. I can live with it. And you'd have to repaint the whole door." He remembered how the hand shading her eyes had dropped suddenly, falling loose and despairing at her side. "Oh, Ray. What the hell."

"Mr. Guinness?"

Someone from behind had taken hold of him, just at the base of the triceps, and without thinking, Guinness snapped his arm forward to free himself. It was nothing more than a reflex, the kind he had once honed carefully but had thought long buried and forgotten, so when he stepped back it wasn't to drive his elbow into anybody's larynx. He even smiled, feeling slightly embarrassed at the expression of surprise on the face of the man behind him. The guy was only doing his job.

"Mr. Guinness," the man said again, recovering himself almost at once. It was the earnest-looking young detective with the tightly curling, sand-colored hair—a nice kid, about twenty-six or so and working very hard on his professional dignity. "Mr. Guinness, I'm afraid we won't be able to let you into the house. Can I take you anywhere? Some friends, perhaps?"

Ray Guinness didn't answer immediately. Instead he glanced down at the driveway, touching an eyebrow with the tips of his first two fingers, as if to make sure it was still there. He must have looked puzzled.

"For the night, Mr. Guinness. You'll have to have somewhere you can go for the next several days. Our laboratory people will have to keep the house sealed for some time. Until they've had a chance to sift through everything. There will have to be an arson investigation as well. We'll bring you out any clothes or personal effects you need, but I'm afraid we won't be able to allow you inside. I'm sorry."

The young man seemed almost to be pleading with him to understand, as if he expected torrents of abuse.

But Guinness understood. Yes, it would be dark in another hour and he would have to begin thinking about a place to sleep. A hotel. He couldn't think of anyone who was a good enough friend that he could ask them to put him up, not under the circumstances. At least not anyone he wanted the cops knowing about. No, it would have to be a hotel.

The place was crawling with police. It looked like every plainclothesman in the Bay Area was on his planter box of a front lawn. They stood around in little knots, talking quietly among themselves like guests at a party that hasn't yet quite gotten itself off the ground.

"When can I see my wife?"

Curly didn't much like that. He too glanced down at the cement, his face hardening with worry.

Everyone was being very cute about Louise; no one would tell him where she was or precisely what had happened to her. Except that she was dead.

The police had brought Guinness home. They had come and fetched him from his office, where he had been patiently working his way through a seven-inch stack of sophomore term papers. Just as he had finished the first reading of one comparing Troilus and Sir Gawain as courtly lovers, there came a light tapping on the glass upper panel of his door. The door had opened before he had had a chance to respond.

"Mr. Guinness?" It was Curly, standing with only half of his body across the sill. "Mr. Guinness, would you come with me please," he said softly, holding out his gold badge. "I'm afraid there has been an accident."

He wasn't told that his wife had been killed until after they had gotten him there. But he had guessed. Curly—was his name Peterson? He thought so, yes it sounded right—Detective Peterson had been very reluctant to say much. He gave the impression of having been ordered to keep things dark, or maybe he just didn't fancy his charge getting hysterical on him at forty miles an hour. Anyway, he was acting the way people do when someone is suddenly dead.

They had parked most of a block down from the house, and as he got out of the car Guinness had caught sight of a man in white coveralls stepping into the rear of a police van and closing the double doors behind him. For just a second the inside of the van had been visible, and there was what looked like a litter on the floor and on the litter was something covered with a black plastic tarp.

Had that been Louise?

So when he had finally been told, it hadn't been much of a surprise. But death had stopped being much of a surprise a long time ago.

A Sergeant Creon had been the one to break the news, if you could call it that:

"There was a body found in the house. Female, Caucasian, a hundred and ten to a hundred and twenty pounds. About five foot four, with dark-brown hair worn to the shoulder. Wearing a printed cotton house dress, dark tan with pictures of fruit on it. We assume it to have been Mrs. Guinness. That sound about right?"

We assume it to have been Mrs. Guinness. Guinness swallowed hard and nodded. He had been married to the woman for five years, and now she was just a series of identifying characteristics.

"Sorry," Creon responded nervelessly, not even bothering to look up from the little pocket book in which he was making notations. A few seconds later he closed it and sauntered off without another word. Guinness watched him go, measuring his back for an appropriate-sized bullet hole. Not a gent you warmed up to right away.

Could that really have been Louise? Five feet four in a tan dress. Yes, that was her. It had to be her. Still, it was hardly possible to think of her as a corpse.

Sadly, it would no doubt become easier. It always happened that way.

"They might be able to let you see her tomorrow," Peterson answered finally, apparently having made up his mind that it would be safe to risk that much. Creon must have been a real peach of a guy to work for. "They will have finished the preliminary examination by then, and there will have to be a formal identification. I should think by tomorrow, but you had better check with the sergeant."

The hell with the sergeant. He would be seeing Louise soon enough in any case. What there was to see.

When had been the last time—breakfast? No, lunch.

He had come home for lunch. He always came home for lunch on Thursdays, and it was a Thursday. Somehow it seemed important and strangely difficult to keep such things straight.

Yes, he had come home for lunch. On Thursdays he had two hours between his morning and afternoon classes, and so there was time to come home.

Louise had been wearing that dress. She called it her French dress because all the little printed apples and onions were labeled underneath and the labels were in French. She always wore that dress whenever she planned to do a lot of dusting. He hadn't the faintest idea why.

So they had had lunch together, or at least she had served him his lunch. She didn't eat lunch very often, saying it was hard on her waistline, but she had sat at the table in the little breakfast nook off the kitchen and had kept him company while he ate. That had been—when? Not quite seven hours ago. He had had a ham and cheese sandwich and a glass of iced tea.

Had they talked? Not precisely, no. She had talked and he had eaten, putting in a yes or a no as the situation seemed to demand. She had been after him to do something, but for the life of him he couldn't remember what it had been. Would it be important later that he should remember? What *had* she been talking about?

Yes, of course; it had been something about the venting for the clothes washer in the basement. It was backing up, and she had thought perhaps one of the hoses was clogged and wanted him to check when he got home from work. He couldn't do it right then because he would have had to change out of his slacks and jacket and there hadn't been time.

No, he couldn't imagine that it would be important to remember that.

They had sat there like that for maybe half an hour. Him eating a ham and cheese sandwich, thinking with one half of his mind about how that afternoon and evening and the next and the whole fucking weekend were hostages to his sophomore term papers, and with the other half helping her worry that perhaps it might be something major with the washing machine, something he wouldn't be able to fix with a pair of pliers and a screwdriver and a straightened clothes hanger. He would have liked to have stayed and seen if he couldn't have taken care of it right then and there, just so she wouldn't have to spend the whole afternoon tormenting herself over it.

And now she was so much cold meat in some locker in a police morgue.

A light-blue Chevy sedan, identical except in color to the half-dozen or so police cars parked along the street in both directions, pulled into the curb in front of the driveway and stopped. On the driver's side the front door opened and a man with black hair pared down to a crew cut got out and slammed the door shut behind him. He wasn't very tall, so it wasn't until he came around to the trunk of his car and bent over to open it with a key that his slate-gray suit appeared to be a couple of sizes too large for him.

Out of the trunk came a small black satchel, and the man with the crew cut and the baggy suit carried it into the house, amiably waggling his free hand at Creon as he passed. The good sergeant wasn't wasting any time in getting his sifters out on the job; probably by morning they would have collected enough fingerprint cards and samples of carpet fluff to keep them all out of mischief for a month.

Accident hell. Louise hadn't had any accident. Nobody dies in a stupid little kitchen fire, not in a kitchen from which there are two exits and which isn't much bigger to begin with than a good-sized bathroom.

Something was going on here that nobody was telling him about, and he didn't like it. Louise hadn't simply set fire to the place and died. Louise didn't have accidents, she wasn't the untidy type.

She even kept a small fire extinguisher, shaped like a can of whipping cream, in a drawer on the left-hand side of the sink. No, Louise wasn't the type to have accidents.

Guinness took a handkerchief out of his trousers pocket and used it to wipe his hand of the cream-colored paint dust from the garage door. When he had done the house, shortly after he and Louise had moved in, they had told him at the hardware store he would be smart to use an oil-based paint; the powdery film it left on the surface when it dried was supposed to keep it from blistering. What it really did was come off on your clothes every time you ventured near it.

He did not like the idea of the police poking around in his house. All of this business was an exercise in futility; they would never find out who had murdered Louise. Settling that score would have to be his own private concern.

Murder. It had been murder all right; of that, suspicion had hardened into certainty. The working axiom of Guinness's adult life had been that nobody dies until he's murdered.

No, the police would only muddy things up. And, besides, there were things in the house it wouldn't do for them to chance across—the evidence of older crimes than this one.

Of course they never would, would never think to rip up the carpeting in his study and find where he had cut through the width of three slats in the hardwood flooring. Why should they?

The slats could be lifted away to uncover a metal tray he had had to go under the house to screw into position between two of the floor supports—his little hiding place. They would never find it. In five years Louise had never found it, never even suspected that it was there to find.

But it was there, under the floor in his office. A locked steel box containing a little over eight thousand dollars in fifties and hundreds, a wad of bills wrapped tight in multiple thicknesses of Saran Wrap to keep out the dampness. If it worked for Bermuda onions, why not for money?

It wasn't the money that mattered, though. It was the notes. His working notes, carefully preserved from all the little jobs he had done for MI-6, all the little problems he had taken care of for them so that all the frightened little undersecretaries in the Foreign Office could sleep at night. Among his notes, and his memories, Guinness would find his answer, but it wouldn't be an answer that would be of any service to the police.

The stupid cops, what the hell were they doing here anyway? Why couldn't they all just buzz off, like good little tykes, and leave questions of retribution to the grown-ups?

Well, that wasn't likely to happen.

Across the lawn, with the broad tan back of his suit jacket turned to Guinness, Sergeant Creon stood on the walkway to the front door, smoking a cigarette. His nibs looked perfectly at home. Finally, with proprietary calm, he took the cigarette from his mouth, dropped it on the cement, and ground it out with his heel. Guinness watched him through narrowed eyes, and the hand that held his handkerchief slowly tightened into a fist. Just where did the sonuvabitch think he got off? Police investigation or no, the name on the mailbox was still Guinness. It was still his house, his and Louise's.

It made him feel naked to think of some clown like this boorish constable pawing over the contents of his dresser drawers and constructing elaborate theories about Louise's sexual behavior. The law would pick its sordid way through their private life, subjecting his wife to a personal indignity only a very little less degrading than murder itself, and then come up with nothing.

Well, not nothing. They would develop a theory; she had startled an intruder perhaps, or been killed by a faceless lover. (Did Louise have any lovers? It didn't seem likely; but that might just be his own vanity and, anyway, it was no one's business.)

They might even nail some poor innocent schmuck, but what of it? These kinds of murders simply didn't happen in Guinness's set—after all, he had been in the business himself.

"Mr. Guinness, is there anywhere you would like me to drive you? We'll take your statement in the morning; there's nothing you can do here now. You must want to rest. I'm sure this all must have been a terrible shock for you. Is there anywhere at all you'd like to be taken?"

Guinness looked up from the driveway in astonishment, having forgotten that the younger man was standing so close beside him. He smiled as his fist unclenched and he refolded his handkerchief and put it back in his pocket. Curly seemed to be a nice kid, but he was working awfully hard to get him the hell out of there. It made you wonder why.

The hell with Curly. Curly could wait.

When this thing was over, he would have the kitchen put back together—hell, it was insured—and then he would sell the place. Get a couple of rooms somewhere near the school and sell the place.

He had bought the house a week before their wedding. Paid cash for it, twenty-eight thousand. Louise had asked him where he had gotten the money; after all, twenty-eight grand was a lot for an assistant professor of English to have just tucked away in an old sock.

"I've been rolling a lot of drunks lately."

And she had laughed and not asked again. It was one of the things he liked about her, that she knew when not to ask again.

So that was where the money had gone, most of it. An inauspicious beginning for the House of Guinness, to be paid for with the money the British had paid him for services rendered. There was even some left, under the floorboards in his office.

As if it were something in which he had not the remotest personal interest, he wondered how much the place would bring today.

They had done a lot with it in five years. A whole new inside just two years ago, with wallpaper in the dining room and new carpeting everywhere on the ground floor. He was still paying for it—that much, at least, had come from legitimate sources.

And Louise's kitchen was almost new. That had been their first priority, to get rid of all that antique junk the place had come with and to put in all new appliances. A side-by-side refrigerator and a self-cleaning oven, even a fancy blender with the motor built right into the counter top. Louise had loved that kitchen with a passion that might have moved another man to jealousy.

He wondered how it happened that it was there they had found her body. It would have to have been Louise, but why just in the kitchen?

Yes, of course. The fire. He was being stupid. The fire was supposed to cover everything. A stupid business.

Did he have any stupid enemies? No, at least not ones who would have thought to murder his wife. All of those were dead.

But it had to be an enemy of his—who would want to murder Louise? It was all aimed at him somehow, and Louise had merely gotten into the line of fire.

What was the matter with him? It used to be he could smell trouble, could feel it coming the way some people can feel bad weather. This had caught him totally off his guard.

Aware that he was in danger of losing control, Guinness took a deep breath, sucking air into his lungs until they ached and then letting it out as slowly as he could. He repeated the process, three, and then four times, until his perceptions narrowed down to the patterns of the water drops on the garage door and the noise of the blood pounding in his ears. It made him feel faintly ill, faintly giddy, the way one did sometimes after coming up out of a chair too fast; but that was better than breaking into angry, hysterical weeping in front of a lawnful of homicide detectives. To hell with them too, his emotions were his own business.

The sun had dipped low enough to turn the sky a grimy orangeish color above the ragged edging made by the darkened buildings of his neighborhood. With a kind of visual pop the street lamps came on, creating long smears of shadow that ran across the lawn from the feet of the few huddled detectives who remained, like slicks of blackened water.

"I think I want to get out of here."

Peterson was only too eager. He sprang the rear door of his unmarked police car, waving Guinness into the back seat. Settling in, Guinness noticed with distaste that he was behind a cagework grating bolted into place over the driver's backrest. The back doors didn't even open from the inside.

The car pulled out, and he glanced back through the rear window to watch his house recede and darken as they left it behind.

II

GUINNESS'S WAITRESS WAS much practiced in that art they have of avoiding your eye when you want to ask for something, so he gave up and returned to a close study of his eggs. He had requested them scrambled hard, but what did that mean? At the moment they were hemorrhaging all over his plate. As it cooled, the pale yellowish mass seemed to sweat forth tiny droplets of what was probably cooking oil, giving the impression that it was dying in unspeakable agony.

What he wanted now was to order another cup of tea, but perhaps it was just as well. With about a third of one of their little containers of ersatz half-and-half stirred in, his last cup had still the approximate color of dead grass.

Anyway, for the day ahead he really didn't want very much on his stomach.

The physical texture of life without Louise. He had awakened several times during the night, each time feeling cold and peculiarly desolate, as if his bed had been quietly transferred to some moonscape.

Nothing more than the disruption of established habit. It was just that he wasn't used to sleeping alone anymore. There was no point in getting melodramatic about trifles; he would have the hang of it again before long.

Finally the waitress flew by of her own accord, stopping only long enough to slap his check down on the table. She was an enormous, energetic blonde of about forty-five, and as she charged away her buttocks pounded jerkily, like steam pistons under her black rayon skirt.

An English muffin, orange juice, two scrambled eggs, and a single cup of tea. Two forty-five, plus fifteen cents tax. Guinness slid a precise 15 percent under the rim of his plate, picking up the tiny paper receipt form between his first and middle fingers as he rose from the table.

Passing from the coffee shop, past a busboy's cart burdened down with clotted breakfast dishes, he took a few steps down a corridor that led in one direction outdoors to the swimming pool and in the other to the main lobby, and pushed open the door to the men's room. As it usually did when he ate away from home, breakfast left him feeling slightly sticky.

There was a balance scale in the men's room—"your true weight, no springs"—so Guinness climbed up on the little platform, dropped in his nickel, and watched the numbered band spin around until it came to rest as just a shade over one hundred and eighty-six and a half pounds. Well hell, he was fully dressed and it was right directly after breakfast, so at six-one it wasn't a calamity.

He washed his hands with the tiny rectangular wafer of soap that he found half-dissolved on the edge of the sink and splashed a little cold water in his face, and, as he was patting it dry with a paper towel, he looked up at his reflection in the mirror and frowned.

Bluish-gray eyes, hair that over the years had darkened from red to brown, a few dim freckles dusted over the bridge of a rather blunt nose—at thirty-eight still the face of a slightly seedy Eagle Scout.

Useful when you wanted to play the harmless bucolic from America's heartland—possibly having such a face had once or twice saved his life—but not a face that reflected much about its owner. It always gave Guinness the uncomfortable feeling that he was conducting his life from behind a mask.

Which, of course he was, and had been for as long as he could remember. How else could he have gotten by?

But you can't fool everyone. In the back yard behind their house was a small, hypochondriacal maple tree that was always threatening to come down with some exotic new deficiency-disease if you weren't out there every minute pounding spikes of plant food down among its roots, and during the winter, when all the leaves were gone, there were almost always a few tacky-looking birds sitting disconsolately in its naked branches. It didn't take very long before Louise decided that they had to be starving to death, although how a bird would contrive to starve in the San Francisco Bay Area Guinness couldn't begin to imagine. Anyway, she went right out to buy a five-pound bag of birdseed.

By turns they would each go out in the morning and sprinkle handfuls of birdseed around the base of the maple tree. At first, the instant either of them came out, all the birds would flutter up into the telephone wires to wait until the coast was clear. But eventually, with Louise, they would be satisfied with the next branch up, just out of reach, and finally they would come down to the ground while she was still outside. Had she survived another season they would probably have been fighting each other to eat the stuff out of her hand.

But toward Guinness their feelings never changed. The second he opened the back door, it was into the telephone wires. You don't ever really get to reform, and birds know a predator when they see one.

In the lobby there was a cutesy clock over the front desk, with the numbers replaced by the letters of the hotel's name and two dots to separate the two words they made. The minute hand was between the *D* and the *A*, and the hour rested firmly over the *H*, making it about seven minutes after nine.

The police, in the person of their sympathetic Detective Peterson, had arranged to pick him up at 10:00 A.M.; thus there wouldn't really be time enough to take a cab back across town to the campus, where his car was still waiting for him in the faculty parking lot. Still, he felt the need of something to keep his mind occupied, so he lifted a copy of the San Mateo *Times* from the top of a stack of them on the front desk, dropped a quarter in its place, and sat down in one of the two rather moth-eaten light-gray wing chairs that stood on either side of the main entrance, facing into the lobby like genteel, disapproving sentinels.

A quick rip-through didn't turn up any mention of the fire or the discovery of a body, which was disturbing. Belmont was a small town by relative standards, where disasters were rare enough to be reported with something almost amounting to civic pride, and a good death-by-fire would normally have been worth at least two columns on the front page of the local news.

But the editor was very likely to be Creon's Rotary brother or something and, in any case, more dependent on the good will of the fuzz than would be usual in Los Angeles or even San Jose. The paper's silence could only mean that the police were sitting on the story.

It was easy to imagine why; they hadn't quite made up their minds and they wanted time. Time to decide how to play it. It wouldn't do to start shouting homicide until you were absolutely positive, and perhaps not until you had someone to collar for it.

If he worked it right, Creon could come out of this case looking like a hero. And like something less if he blew it.

Guinness closed the newspaper, refolding and smoothing it down against his knee. He closed his eyes for several seconds and tried to reestablish himself somewhere over the tumult of thought and feeling, to slow things down and bring them into some kind of order.

It didn't seem fair somehow. It was too much all at once, too many demands from too many different directions. Out there somewhere was somebody who planned to kill him, who had already killed Louise, and Guinness would have to stay on his toes if he wanted to do that somebody full justice. Merely to keep on breathing would require his undivided attention, and in the meantime he would have to fence with the god damned police.

And just where was it written that there should be no time to mourn? After all, his wife, who had not yet been dead for twenty-four hours, had some small claim. As it was, if he stopped to think too much about her he might end up dead himself, and when finally there would be time—if ever there would be time—well, probably by then he'd be used to it. The strangeness would have worn off, and it would be too late. You do, in fact, get used to it. You can get used to anything.

It wasn't fair, to Louise or to himself. Because he also needed time, time to say a decent goodbye. People had a right to be human beings and to suffer through their sense of loss in peace, but apparently it had been decided somewhere that the Guinnesses should constitute a special case.

Poor Louise. He couldn't say he had provided her with much of a husband, but probably every fresh widower thought something like that. Widower—funny sort of word, applying with equal force to Bluebeard, Raymond M. Guinness, Henry VIII, and Sidney, 1st Earl of Godolphin.

Still, he couldn't expect to get off scot-free. Wasn't feeling guilty, after all, a part of the pattern?

And there had been enough to merit a little guilt; it wasn't precisely as if he were martyring himself on the cross of his own sensibility.

Just for instance, it wasn't as if their marriage had been founded upon the Rock of Truth.

Not that he had lied, precisely; but one can easily lie by omission. There had been so much silence.

Of course, one couldn't come right out with an exhaustive history of one's lurid past, and one didn't choose to lie. So one simply did not discuss some things. Not entirely honest perhaps, but then how many successful marriages could be built on that kind of honesty? What kinds of people would even want to try?

What the hell, people didn't have to ooze through one another like rainwater through a plaster roof in order to be happy. Other kinds of unions were possible besides the hideousness of the American Happy Marriage, and no one would suffer if the two of them hadn't contrived to be Ozzie and Harriet.

Live for the moment, that was the plan, and try to create the impression that you did not have too many specific memories. Why should the past have been different from the present? Why indeed?

There had been, he remembered, a cigarette machine in the coffee shop, just opposite the cashier's desk, and at that moment Guinness was dying for a cigarette. A cigarette—yes, he decided, the very thing. He hadn't had a cigarette in over four years, not since Louise had wheedled him into giving them up.

"Come on," she had whispered, her breath warm against his ear as she put her arms around his neck, sliding into his lap from the arm of his reading chair. "It won't be so very terrible. I won't let you suffer. We'll find other ways to gratify your base animal nature." And she had been as good as her word.

So he had stopped. Thus easily can one yield to the preposterous notion that one might live long enough to make lung cancer something to worry about. At any rate, events had cured him of that illusion.

Guinness reached into his jacket pocket and pulled out his change. Two quarters, three dimes, and a nickel—plus about seven pennies. Plenty.

Still, he didn't get up from his chair, and after a moment he returned the coins to his pocket. It could wait. It would have been like a betrayal.

Louise, poor Louise. Louise and the domestic virtues. Always so worried about his health, and then she had been the one to end up dead. Poor baby. He wondered out of how many years he had cheated her.

She had made it the business of her life to see to it that his clothes were pressed and his health sound, that he was comfortable and content and well loved. He had had everything he could want from her, even friendship—and the touch of her hand to lift the stray wisp of hair away from his brow when he was unhappy and would not say why. She wouldn't ask him. She would be content to understand without understanding.

But had it been enough for her? It had occurred to Guinness to wonder from time to time. It occurred to him now, to wonder and to hope that somehow it had been. Louise was dead and there would be no more time now, no more chances, so he hoped she had been happy for their five years.

Perhaps not happy, perhaps not that. Because who in this world gets to be happy? One mustn't ask for the moon.

But he hoped she had had whatever it was that she had been after. There would be no more of anything now, so all he could do was to hope.

Guinness glanced up at the wall clock over the front desk and checked it against his own watch. They agreed on nine twenty-eight.

He was to identify the body that morning and make his statement. Why in that order? he wondered. Perhaps they had some idea of shaking him up, of jolting him enough to start a few cracks in his story.

What the hell for, didn't they have any more imagination than that? Aside from the policeman's treasured axiom that the husband is always your best suspect, nothing pointed to him.

And it had been a long, long time since the sight of anybody's cadaver had managed to reduce him to quivering helplessness. No, it was a little late in the day for that.

It would be amusing to see how they would try breaking him down. He could imagine the scenario: being played off between Good Cop and Bad Cop, between his very own oh-so-sympathetic young Detective Peterson and Creon the Unkind. After a few hours of the sergeant's rough tongue he would be expected to come all unglued and open up to his "friend," who of course would see everything entirely from his point of view. You could watch it five nights a week on reruns of *Dragnet*.

Perhaps not really very amusing, but at least he would know how to behave, having already been through it once before. Not in Belmont of course, or even in the United States. In Yugoslavia, in the summer of 1965.

An apparently insignificant party official had suddenly fallen down dead, pitched right over onto the sidewalk on his way to lunch, the way a puppet will when suddenly you let go of the strings. It was small wonder, actually, because a 9 mm slug had just entered his brain about an inch above and behind his right ear. When they dug it out, it was resting against the back of his left eye, and it had done quite a lot of damage on its way across.

Suddenly the whole district was alive with police in olive uniforms, sweeping the area for anybody who didn't look as if he had been born on the spot. They picked Guinness up as he stepped out of an elevator in a building across the street from where the body had collapsed on the pavement. In the same building they found a 9 mm rifle, with a shooting stand and a pair of neatly folded black leather gloves resting on the ledge of a second-story window. It looked pretty bad.

They measured his hands and found that the gloves were a size and a half too small, but they grilled him for two days straight anyway. Who was he? What was he doing in that building? What was he doing in Belgrade? Who was he *really?* On and on. Finally they decided that there wasn't any evidence, that probably he didn't have anything to do with their precious assassination, and that they didn't dare hold him any longer unless they were prepared to go the whole distance and notify his embassy that he was being officially detained in connection with the murder of Janik Shevliskin. So they let him go. The gloves had saved him, and the fact that his story hadn't melted under pressure.

The gloves had been a last-minute inspiration. He always liked to leave a red herring of some kind against just such an emergency, and he had picked them up in a Parisian department store an hour and ten minutes before his train was due to leave. The label on the inside indicated that the gloves had been made in Poland, which was a nice touch.

The gloves he had actually worn to shoot with were

cheapie plastic jobs, the kind that come on rolls of a hundred, and had been flushed, one at a time, down the handiest john.

When he got back to London, he told the British that if they wanted anybody else axed in Yugoslavia they could find themselves another boy. This time had been a trifle close, thank you, and he couldn't risk being arrested twice.

The paper was still over his knee when Peterson came through the lobby doors. He walked about a quarter of the way into the room before he stopped and began looking around, turning back toward the entrance as Guinness cleared his throat significantly.

"Good morning, Mr. Peterson. You're early."

Peterson smiled suddenly, as if caught in some vague indiscretion, which perhaps he had been, and put out his hand to shake as Guinness rose from his chair. Probably there was no tactful way to greet a man whom you are taking to see his freshly dead wife.

Guinness, his lips compressed in a mirthless, ironic smile, took the offered hand and held it just a moment longer and in a grip just a shade tighter than the acquaintance warranted. His eyes searched the other man's face, as if he were considering something unpleasant.

The policeman was almost as tall, and probably had the advantage in weight, but he didn't attempt to disengage himself. Perhaps he was simply being polite—he certainly was a very polite lad. Perhaps he was thinking about Dion O'Banyon. Perhaps his education didn't extend that far.

When Guinness's hold relaxed, and the handshake ended, he had the definite impression that he had lost his friend at court, which was okay. Perhaps that way they wouldn't waste a lot of each other's time on the psychological niceties.

Instead of the police station, as he had expected, Guinness was driven to the county hospital. It hadn't occurred to him before, but the local police wouldn't have the facilities for a forensic autopsy. They probably didn't even have a morgue.

He and Peterson had little to say during the drive, and they exchanged only whispered monosyllables in the hospital itself. Peterson guided him into the basement, where he swung open a heavy, pale-green door, bidding Guinness enter with a gesture of his open hand.

The room was perhaps twenty feet square, with a ceiling high enough to be lost in shadow and massive doors at either end. Linoleum tile of some indistinct pale shade covered the floor, and the walls, like the doors, were a pale frosted green, giving one the impression of standing in the center of an enormous ice cube. It took several seconds before Guinness located with his eyes the camouflaged fixtures that made the light seem to seep in from every direction.

There was a heavy smell of antiseptic, and the room was perfectly empty except for a gurney table in its precise center. The table was covered with a sheet, and under the sheet were visible the outlines of something that had once been human and female.

Peterson seemed to hesitate, as if embarrassed, so Guinness took the few short steps to the head of the gurney and lifted back the sheet just enough to reveal the head and shoulders of all that was mortal of Louise Harrison Guinness.

It wasn't as bad as he had imagined it might be. There was the faintest odor of burnt flesh, and he could see where the hair had been singed along the back of the skull, but her face was unmarked.

Death was always an undignified business; her jaw was slack and her eyes half open. In life her eyes had been almost black, but now they were too glazed over to make it possible to pick out their precise color. Seeing her like this seemed a hideous intrusion.

He reached down and gently closed her eyes with thumb and first finger, and an emotion like nothing he could have expected or prepared for flooded through him. He brought the sheet back up to cover her.

"Can you identify these as the remains of your wife?" Peterson's ritual question, whispered though it was, sounded in the hushed room like a pistol shot. Guinness nodded and allowed himself to be led away.

He remembered that the first time he had ever seen Louise's face it had been bent over a typewriter. She styled her hair longer then and tied back, and the glasses that she wore only to read with had slipped down to rest on the saddle of her nose, giving her the appearance of some substantial, ferociously midwestern schoolmistress.

That had been almost six years ago, the summer before the first year he had taught at Belmont State. Louise had just started on her M.A., which was the only advanced degree offered in English, and was making a little pocket money and generally ingratiating herself by working parttime as one of the three assistants to the department secretary. Guinness needed a voucher signed for moving expenses, and Miss Harrison was the only person in the office. She took the form, smiled one of those automatic secretarial smiles, and said she would give it to the chairman when he made it back from lunch.

It was hardly love at first sight. Guinness simply noticed her existence, filed it away for future reference, and then went about his business for the next several months.

He got settled into his job and pursued other passions, and then one day at the beginning of the spring term he leaned across the vast composition-board counter top that separated off the inner sanctum of the typing pool, into which no member of the teaching staff was ever supposed to venture, and asked for a date. It had been as simple as that.

They had dinner at a little German place in San Mateo and went to a movie at the Palm Theater and then stopped back at her place, a little walk-up apartment over a jewelry store about three blocks from the campus. They were lovers before eleven that evening, there having been only a single feature, and she had moved in with him within a couple of weeks.

Toward the middle of the summer they made a quick trip to Las Vegas, lost two hundred and thirty-two dollars at the blackjack tables, and got married. In retrospect, they were both a little astonished at how casually their relationship had developed. Anyway, within reasonable limits, it had worked well enough.

Louise had been twenty-seven at the time, having returned to school out of boredom with clerking for an insurance company and making the rounds of balding salesman types with shiny faces and closets full of checkered sports jackets. Life seemed to have been leading nowhere, and she had a vague idea that she might enjoy teaching Jane Austen in some semirural junior college. So she set about getting the necessary credentials and, at least in theory, was still a graduate student even up to the time of her death. In the drawer of her night table the police discovered the typescript of an unfinished thesis on *Persuasion.*

Perhaps that had never been what she really wanted. Perhaps her spiritual destiny all along had been to find an agreeable, unattached male who didn't own any checkered sports jackets, tie the knot, and honorably retire.

And Ray was agreeable enough. It wasn't a bad life. It was steady enough, certainly; he seemed to place a high value on orderliness and predictability. He liked to be told in the mornings, before he went to work, what dinner would be; and, barring an act of God, they went to the movies on Monday evenings.

By common consent, the race-and-chase adventure flicks were the best. Ray said they had moral clarity.

She had married him—oh God—perhaps only because he had asked without seeming to assume that the suspense was killing her. Just a contract between two consenting adults who happened to strike a few sparks for one another, no big deal. Not quite a simple tax arrangement; there was more to it than that. But not Tristram and Iseult, not breathless and ethereal passion either. And it was something to his credit that he had the decency to refrain from pretending that it was.

And after all the other men she had known she was ready to give him a little credit. I'll be this, baby, or I'll give you that—just you wait and see. Promises of excitement or distinction. The Great Life, oh so very different from this one, always just perceptibly ahead. A few years, a change of jobs, a lucky break. Somewhere in the distance. And all the time they knew and she knew that the future would be precisely like the past, a reality too insipid even to allow you the privilege of ignoring it.

But not with Ray. He had a habit, when he didn't seem to be thinking about anything, of taking hold of her little finger and curling it up so that as he held it he could easily have crushed the joint under the pressure of his thumb. They would sit together—he would seem a million miles away, in some private existence of his own—and her heart would pound like a tom-tom.

Of course he never did it. She had never seen him harm any living thing—probably he never had, never would; but not perhaps because it had never occurred to him that he could. Somehow, in his very insistence that his life be uneventful, he managed to suggest that it might have been different had he chosen.

Once, to celebrate the publication of one of his papers, they had gone out to dinner in San Francisco, to a fish place on the Wharf, where the little square tables at which they seated couples were so close together that you couldn't have slid a book of matches between them. The man at the next table had left his cigarette untended—apparently he had forgotten about it completely—in a little tin ashtray, and the smoke was drifting remorselessly into Ray's eyes.

He had only just recently given up cigarettes himself and tended to be a little touchy on the subject, as if sensitive to the injustice of anyone being allowed what he was not. Finally he turned to his right and, very politely, asked if the gentleman would mind putting the damn thing out.

The gentleman was about ten years older, at least twenty pounds heavier, and none the better for a number of vodka and tonics consumed while waiting for his lobster claws. And just to make everything perfect, he was there with a woman quite obviously not his wife.

One gathered from the expression on his face that he did mind, but he stubbed out the cigarette anyway. Ray thanked him and went back to his Manhattan chowder. The matter seemed closed.

But it wasn't; a second later, apparently having thought the thing over, the gentleman at the next table started to flick Ray noisily on the sleeve of his jacket with the first two fingers of a pink, fleshy hand. It seemed there was a point of etiquette that it was imperative to have settled.

"Listen, Mac. When somebody does you a favor you should smile when you say thank you. That was a favor I just did you, so why don't you smile?"

Louise wasn't perfect, and she knew it. She shared with most women a morbid curiosity to see how her husband would behave under fire, what he would do when the bully at the beach kicked sand in his face. So she sat very quietly, torn between a certain guilty excitement and her dread over the prospect of a scene. She tried very hard, however, not to give the impression that she believed he had anything to live up to.

Her husband did, in fact, smile—a friendly, open relaxed sort of smile—but it was directed at her. He covered her hand lightly with his own and for a moment she thought he was simply going to ignore the whole stupid incident. But, of course, it wasn't something he could ignore. Drunks don't often allow themselves to be ignored.

"I think, pal," he said finally, turning only very slightly in that direction, "that I've already expressed my gratitude. I'd settle for that if I were you—I really would."

She didn't know—there was something in the very calmness of his voice, something not precisely of menace, that Louise, at least, found far more intimidating than any implied threat in the words themselves.

It amounted, almost, to a hope that offense would be taken, taken and acted upon. It almost seemed as if Ray wanted the man to pick a fight, as if that prospect somehow appealed to him. But of course that was impossible.

Fortunately, just at that moment the waitress came and brought the slob his dinner, and he took it as an excuse to let the matter drop. Of course the evening was ruined; they were all miserably uncomfortable together at those two little tables, silent and humiliated.

Except for Ray—he went on talking and eating as if he had forgotten the whole thing the moment it ended. Perhaps he had.

It wasn't until they got home that the reaction set in. He sat up in bed while she brushed out her hair, staring glumly at the lump his feet made under the blanket. When she mentioned it, all he said was that he couldn't be responsible for every middle-aged Lothario who had a little too much to drink. It seemed to make him angry.

"What would you have done if he'd called you out, Ray?" It was only a playful question. "Would you have gone out back in the alley with him and hammered away until one of you said uncle?"

Ray apparently didn't think it was funny and indicated by that impenetrable reticence of his that he wished the subject dropped.

"He didn't call me out."

So that was it. He was simply that way sometimes. Men were whimsical creatures, Ray no more than most; but when he did not choose to discuss a subject he did not discuss it.

Had that man in the restaurant upset him? Was he afraid of death, or a black eye, or the prospect of turning forty? When it suited him he was as silent and as fast as a stone wall. It did no good to pry.

Perhaps he had painful thoughts. Or perhaps it was the vagabond in him, she couldn't tell. She had lived her whole life within a few hundred miles of the hospital in Yuba City where she had been born, but Ray had traveled, had lived in England and had been all over Europe. Perhaps things had happened. Perhaps it had given him a sense of being a stranger everywhere. Perhaps that was it.

Sometimes he would talk about such-and-such a place in London, or what the train ride was like between Munich and Amsterdam, but he would only talk about the place or the thing, as if he were merely a pair of impersonal eyes. As fast as a stone wall. The past, she had the feeling, was served up in carefully edited versions.

But if the past did not, the present belonged to her. Their life together was to her taste; Ray was a good man and seemed to love her. She didn't mind housework, especially in a small house, and Ray made her feel that he was pleased with her, that she was to his taste too and that their relationship was enough for him.

At least he wasn't clamoring after her to have babies.

Why should he? After all, he had been married already once and had had a daughter, aged about nine now, whom he never mentioned or visited but whose picture, she happened to know, he carried around with him in an inside flap of his wallet. She didn't think he owned a picture of Kathleen.

Aside from one brief mention of her existence once when they were still Living in Sin, he never talked about his first wife. Things hadn't worked out, was the way he had phrased it. She had apparently left him, but nothing was said about what her motives might have been. It had all happened while he was abroad.

Did he think about her? Had he loved her with more of himself than he gave to his poor little Louise? Another area that wouldn't bear probing.

Well, let him have his past and his memories in quiet. She didn't mind. She had him now and would keep him as long as there was breath in her. And, after all, everyone was entitled to his little secrets.

With Peterson still tactfully leading the way, the two men came out a side door, directly up a little stairwell from the basement into the parking lot, where the dead sunlight was bouncing off of cars and the pavement and tier upon tier of hospital windows. It made you flinch away, as if some great hand were closing painfully over your eyes.

Guinness hoped she had been happy, that he had been able to make her happy. He hoped five years could somehow be counted as an atonement in advance for the way she had died. He was responsible for her death, just as surely as if he had murdered her himself.

The how and why were still uncertain, but they were only details. He had killed her—or rather his past had, which came to the same thing. Something had come up out of that silence he had imposed on it and her, and had killed her. That much it was pointless to try evading.

Mea culpa. Mea culpa. Mea maxima culpa.

III

FIFTEEN YEARS AGO there had been no sun. That day when it all started it had rained all morning long, had rained in rhythmic sheets that came and went every few seconds like the crackling of static on a radio. People were hurrying to get out of it, running with their heads folded forward and their hands in their pockets as they splashed along over the undulating sidewalks on their ways to some place dry.

Guinness tried not to notice. Instead he followed with his eyes the droplets wriggling down one of the front windows of a tea shop half a block off Bond Street. Between his hands he was nursing a mug of pale Darjeeling, almost room temperature by now. Once in a while he would take a birdlike sip—not too much, because he would have to leave when it was gone and he didn't have anyplace else dry he could go. Even his raincoat was up the spout, pawned the day before for five shillings. Minus the ninepence for the tea he was supposed to be drinking, it was all he had left, and he couldn't think of anyplace he could spend the night on that kind of money.

He had read once in Orwell, his literary hero and guide to the morality of poverty, about places where you could rent a chair by the fire for three and six, but he supposed all that was dead and gone. Swept up in thirty years of Social Progress. He couldn't even sleep on the benches around Trafalgar Square, not in the middle of February. Not in the pouring rain he couldn't. Well, perhaps by then it wouldn't be raining. But the bobbies wouldn't let him sleep there anyway; they hadn't let Orwell.

No, tonight would be another night of walking and hiding out in doorways and walking and walking. And tomorrow he would have to turn himself over to the American embassy so they could ship him home. It was all over, the whole fucking thing. Finished.

It had begun toward the end of his senior year in high school, a week after he had recieved notice that he had been accepted into the following year's freshman class at Ohio State. They would waive tuition and give him a scholarship, enough to cover most of his expenses, the assumption probably being that his parents would pick up the slack. What a laugh.

Anyway, a week after the good news, Guinness dropped a dime in a pay phone and called up the margarine plant where he worked five nights a week as a swamper and told them he had the flu. They believed him, and twenty minutes later he was in the Reserve Book Room of the university's main library, sitting in front of a stack of graduate school bulletins.

They were all there, all the luminous names. Harvard, Yale, Chicago, Berkeley, Oxford, Columbia, Princeton, Cambridge, Stanford. But the one that really made his fingers sweat was the University of London.

To be sure, it wasn't Oxford, but then Guinness wasn't George Lyman Kittredge. Bright, yes—good enough. His scholarship proved that much. Not even OSU, however, was scattering rose petals in his path.

But London might just be within reach, with a lot of crust wiping over the next several years. And wouldn't it be something to live in London.

A little after nine-thirty, when the only people left at the long study tables were those few who had set up shop for the evening and would be there, huddled over their math books, until the closing bell rang, Guinness began reshelving his catalogs. At the last, stepping into a deserted alcove for cover, he stuffed the University of London in under his belt, pulled down the back of his nylon wind-breaker to cover it, and walked out. It was the first directly criminal act of his life.

For the next four years the catalog was his holy book, his sustenance. He read it over and over, until he had it practically memorized, until so many of the pages had come loose that it was necessary to keep it held together with a rubber band.

His entire undergraduate program was based on a series of elaborate deductions about what D.Phil. program would require in the way of prerequisites. Lots of languages, especially Latin, so Guinness took a double minor in Latin and German. French he cobbled together on his own, working from a copy of *French for Reading Knowledge* that he had picked up used from the Salvation Army store.

Money, of course, was the real problem; it would take a lot of money. Seven thousand dollars would cover his passage and perhaps see him through as much as a year and a half, but how was he going to get his hands on seven thousand dollars? How else but the hard way?

So it was a good thing he had stolen the catalog—over the next four years he had need of sustenance. After his freshman year the university somehow got wind of the fact that he was holding down a full-time job and decided to regard him as in violation of the terms of his scholarship. It came down to a choice that was really no choice at all—give up the scholarship or give up the job. He gave up the scholarship.

Hell, what did they expect? He couldn't live, let alone save anything, on the money they gave him. They had even made him live in one of their damn dorms for the first year, even when he knew from experience that he could live on less on his own—he'd been doing it long enough.

So for the next three years he worked full time and went to school full time, even during the summers. He took light loads, as few courses as he could without them yanking his tuition waiver, but it wasn't often he managed more than five hours of sleep a night.

And anything he could do to save back some money, he did it. Once he lived for a month off a thirty-pound bag of rice he had picked up when the restaurant he was working for went out of business. Very economical if you don't die of scurvy.

So two weeks before he was due to show up at Russell Square to register for classes, Guinness quit his job as a packer with the Indianola Tool & Die Company, packed a bag, bought a bus ticket to New York and a tourist-class seat on a BOAC flight to London, and was on his way. When he landed, he still had $5,720 in traveler's checks—the goal of a $7,000 bankroll had just managed to elude him—and a little over $40 in cash. It was to last him for almost seventeen months, the best seventeen months of his life.

A little over two weeks before he figured his money would run out completely, Guinness went to his embassy. They weren't very sympathetic. The officer he eventually got to talk to, a puffy little man whose eyes seemed almost totally buried in his pink face, apparently entertained some permanent grievance against anyone who wasn't suffering from hardening of the arteries. He peered at Guiness through his gold-rimmed spectacles, loving every minute of giving him the bad news.

"I am very sorry, Mr. Guinness, but I'm sure you can understand that there's very little help we can offer you. Your difficulties about a work permit are entirely a matter between you and the British government. All we can do is advance you the money to book passage to New York, which of course you will be required to repay as soon as you can find employment there."

"Look," Guinness wheezed, running the palm of his hand over his hair, "all I need is maybe a year in this country, one lousy year, and I can at least have my course work done and go home. Surely you must have enough drag to get me a work permit for that long."

The clerk frowned and shook his head. No he hadn't that much drag, he said, implying that if he had he certainly wasn't going to dissipate it on some punk of a college kid who had probably just blown his grant money buying an abortion for some skinny little peroxide blonde with bent teeth. Not him, no sir.

He picked up a black plastic ball-point pen from a desk set just at the corner of his leather-rimmed blotting pad and began making precise, tiny notations in the margin of a page of typescript. "Good day, Mr. Guinness," he went on, without bothering to lift his almost invisible eyes. "Come see us again when you have made up your mind to accept the assistance of your government and go home."

So that was that, the Great World was indifferent to his fate. Hardly a paralyzing surprise to one whose own mother had thrown him out of the house two days after his sixteenth birthday because, as she put it, she was sick of the sight of him and had her own life to lead.

It was a cold day, and Guinness turned up his collar and thrust his fists deep into the pockets of his raincoat as he tramped angrily down the street toward an underground. As he walked, the fingers of his right hand began automatically counting out his change; it was something he had caught himself doing a lot lately.

Just at the entrance to the underground he stopped for a second and then went round the corner and began moving quickly off in the other direction. Fuck it—he would walk home and save his money. He had the time.

Fuck them all, every last fucking one of them. From his mother to the clowns at the Labour Ministry to this latest sleek little shithead, his fellow countryman. All the bureaucrats and the university administrators and the bosses who had paid him next to nothing simply because they knew he couldn't do without the work, what he would give to have them all together in one place so he could put a bomb under them, except that at the moment he couldn't afford the blasting powder.

Oh how he had loved it, this place, this way of life that he would have to leave behind him now. In England he had been officially a gentleman; not just a grubby little college kid with dirt under his fingernails, but a gentleman. He had been just as poor as in Ohio, but what difference did that make? He had been working on an advanced degree in literature, which did not in this country mark you off forever as a constitutional failure. You could be a gentleman and poor in England. You could forget, at least while something wasn't thrusting it in front of your eyes, that you were locked in combat with the whole human race. Perhaps that, in the end, was what undid you.

Well, in two weeks he would be on his way home, and there he would have less trouble remembering.

More for form's sake than anything else, since he had gone through it all already, Guinness spent the last two weeks making the rounds of all the places he thought might hire him even without a work permit, but every where the answer was the same. Britain, it seemed, was in one of her cyclical recessions. We must all pull together and to hell with the bloody foreigner.

Finally, when his money was almost gone and his room rent was due, he packed his suitcase and checked it in a locker at Paddington Station and moved out to continue his endless walk.

After a while he wasn't even looking for work anymore; he was just walking, trying to exhaust his demon. He pawned his raincoat—it was a dry day, hell, and he wouldn't need it after they had thrown him out of England; anyway, he was sick of carrying it—and he walked. He walked all over the town: down to the Tower and then along the river as far as Chelsea, and then over near the Victoria and Albert Museum and then along the edge of Hyde Park and then down to Buckingham Palace and then up again to Oxford Street. He followed Oxford Street until he was sick of the crowds of evening shoppers.

Finally he reversed his route, walking on into the night. And to a degree the program worked; hunger and cold began to replace bitterness, and to limit the horizons of his imagination to the next hundred yards of pavement, the next time he could dole himself out something to spend on food. He tried to see how long he could go without feeling shaky.

Toward morning it began to rain, and the rain made

him stop walking. That was fatal. After a few hours of standing around under store awnings he capitulated and went into a tea shop.

The tea was the cheapest thing on the menu, so he ordered a cup and sat down, thinking how restored he would feel after he had drunk it. But as he sat at the window and watched the rain he drank less and less. After all, what's a little discomfort in the old GI tract compared to a good case of pneumonia?

He sat there—weighing one evil against another and thinking how in a few hours he would have to turn himself over to the embassy for shipment home—for perhaps three quarters of an hour. The tea had long since ceased to make him anything except faintly nauseous when MI-6, in the soon-to-be-familiar person of Mr. Byron J. Down, made its move.

Guinness always liked ol' Byron J. He was, indeed, a likable man, not the sort at all you would expect to be running a stable of assassins. He looked exactly like what in fact he had been before the war had given him the opportunity to discover where his real genius lay—a professor of linguistics, in fact a specialist in deep structure syntax with three degrees from Cambridge University.

He must have been in his early fifties when Guinness first met him. A heavyset man with a placid, rather dreamy face set off by a pair of heavy, black-rimmed glasses. His hair was brownish and thinning, and he never wore a hat, no matter what the weather, on the theory that the hatband would cut off the circulation in his scalp and hasten the balding process. He had a nice smile, ol' Byron did, and he smiled it as he sat down at Guinness's table and offered him a nice thick wedge of apple pie. He slid the plate across the table with the tips of his thumb and first finger, as if it weighed nothing.

"Here you go, young man," he said in a caressing voice. "You have a bit of that. You look done in."

Guinness glanced up at him suspiciously as he picked up the fork and started eating. His first thought was that the guy was probably a fairy on the hustle, but what the hell. He was starving and a slice of pie doesn't bind you to anything. It hardly seemed an occasion in which to display one's outraged manhood. That could wait on events.

Down must have divined his thoughts—he had that knack—because the smile died.

Neither one of them said anything for perhaps as long as five minutes. Guinness was being careful, famished though he was, not to rush through his pie. He tried to make each piece about the size of his thumbnail, and he chewed carefully. It was ice cold and lovely, even with that hideous lardy crust the British favor, but he didn't want to appear to be enjoying too much. Regardless of what Chubby had in mind, he didn't care to appear too terribly hard up. It was bad psychology—people always want to kick you when you're down.

"There now," Down began at last. "That's better. You don't look the sort of lad to go to the dogs from long-standing habit." The pleasant smile reappeared slowly, and Guinness thought he noticed the faintest trace of an Edinburgh burr stealing in behind the words. "And you don't look the type to turn down an honest offer of employment—how would you like to make a round thousand quid all in one lump, hum? That would tide you over for a while, now wouldn't it?"

A little quick mental arithmetic made that out at about twenty-five hundred dollars. You could live a long time on that kind of money. Seven, maybe eight months if you were careful. Yes, Guinness would have to agree. Twenty-five hundred dollars would solve all of life's immediate problems quite nicely.

"Who do I have to kill?"

For the next six years, until Down fell over dead from a heart attack in the billiard room of his club—it was a real heart attack; Guinness checked and Byron's arteries were hard enough to pound through a tree—they always laughed about that unintentionally appropriate question. *Who do I have to kill?* It became a kind of in-house joke.

Poor ol' Byron, dead and buried lo these many years.

Very much alive for the moment, Down smiled even

more broadly, made a little sound that came out about halfway between a cough and a chuckle, and patted the air between them with his palms to indicate things were going too fast.

"You rush me; allow me to introduce myself." He pulled his wallet from the inside pocket of his heavy slate-gray jacket and produced an official-looking card that identified the bearer as Major Thomas Cruttwell, placing it on the table in front of Guinness. Cruttwell, as it later turned out, was Down's brother-in-law and the owner of several hop farms in Kent. The picture was right, though.

What in God's gracious name had put this dude on his tail? It was a question that plagued him vaguely until finally he asked Down over lunch once in one of the series of squalid little government offices in which their business contacts were usually made.

"Oh that," he said abstractedly, holding his claret up to the light. "Well, you came very highly recommended."

It seemed that the man at the embassy who had interviewed Guinness was a member of Down's London club. He had had such an amusing story about the young freeloader who had come to see him that morning; he was quite proud of the firmness he had shown.

"Maybe it'll help to shape him up when he realized that the world isn't his oyster." And then he had laughed softly. "But when he left my office, he looked like he wanted to kill someone."

Down had done a little checking to discover whom the man had been talking about, and then a little more checking to satisfy himself as to just how hard up Guinness actually was, and then he had tracked him down.

"It wasn't easy." Down took a tentative sip on his claret, made a face, and set it down on the desk. "What with that hike you set out on, you really ran my people ragged."

So that was how—a chance remark between two middle-aged clubmen and the whole direction of his life was changed. No, that wasn't fair. He had had some hand in changing it himself.

Guinness slid the card in toward himself with the ball of his thumb and looked it over without picking it up from the table. After a few seconds he slid it back.

"So big deal," he said blankly. "You're in the army. Are you after me to enlist?"

"Not precisely." Down's smile compressed a little, becoming kinder and perhaps a trifle sad. He was used to dealing with frightened and desperate people, and the experience had given him compassion. "I haven't actually been on active service since the end of the war. I have a position with the Home Office these days; it involves some aspects of military security—you might say that our interests have points of contact—but we tend to be emphatically civilian. I simply wish to identify myself to allay any suspicions you might have been harboring. There's no question of smuggling or male prostitution, nothing like that. Would you care for some more tea?" he asked, his hand going up before Guinness had a chance to respond. "Waitress!"

The girl was there in a second to take his order. That was another of Byron's talents he had always envied.

"But it is illegal," Guinness said after she had come and gone. "Am I right? For that kind of money it just has to be illegal."

Down sifted about half a spoonful of sugar into his tea and set the spoon down on his napkin, where it left a pale tan stain. He looked genuinely surprised that so obvious a point should even be raised.

"Naturally it's illegal, but that isn't the aspect of it that presents the difficulty." He picked up his cup and set it back down again, untasted. "If it were merely illegal I could arrange to have it taken care of for a good deal less than a thousand pounds, I assure you. The world is knee-deep in criminals." He picked up his tea again, tasting it this time, and his eyes rested on its surface when he set it down. "I will concede, however, that it does involve an element of risk."

Now we come to it. Now we see where all the fancy patter has been leading. The man was beautiful in his way; he made it all sound so devastatingly simple.

"How much risk?"

"Considerable. Why? Does it matter?" Down's eyes were steady on his own now, as if the question were a challenge. Which, of course, it was. Guinness simply smiled, eventually forcing a smile from Down.

"It depends."

"Look, young man," Down began, in the manner of someone making an incontrovertibly obvious statement, "we have been watching you very carefully since you were brought to our attention. We have checked into your background, and I mean from the day you were born; research is one of our strong points. And you look the type to do the kind of work we have in mind, and believe me when I tell you that we know the type."

He picked up his cup again, and his manner seemed to soften with his voice.

"Besides, I have an idea you'd like to stay in this country. You came over here to study, didn't you? Well, we can see to that."

"Just exactly what was it you had in mind?"

Down smiled his magic smile again and reached over to pat Guinness on the arm.

"That's the lad."

The rain had let up for a while by the time Guinness paid his check and left. Down, who was a good psychologist and knew that starvation is the handmaiden of fear, had given him two one-pound notes so he could think things over on a full stomach. Two pounds—just enough to keep him comfortable through tomorrow, but not enough to fill him with unreasonable hope. Well, he wasn't going to waste them on little cream cakes and watery tea. He felt the need of some protein and had plans with reference to something like a chophouse.

Down had made it sound like the most obvious thing in the world, just the sort of thing any well-brought-up young American would do in an instant if he suddenly needed a few bills to tide him over. *Facilis descensus Averno.*

"There is a man who for various reasons which need not greatly concern you has made himself objectionable to a certain department of Her Majesty's government.

We would in fact, as you so cleverly divined, like you to kill him for us."

"Are you kidding?"

"Young man, I never kid about such matters."

"Who is he?"

"For the moment that needn't concern you either. You'll be told everything you need to know if you decide to take the job, and until then the less you know the better. You should, however, in all fairness be warned that he is very dangerous; it won't be at all like robbing little girls of their sweet-shop money. It will require planning and intelligence."

Down sipped his tea as calmly as if he were discussing Georgian furniture. "You will, of course, be paid in advance, and you will have five days, no more, in which to do the job."

"What would keep me from just taking the money and cutting out?"

Down's eyes narrowed. No, he wasn't kidding. And, no, he wasn't discussing Georgian furniture.

"Young man, I have very unpleasant friends all over the world, any one of whom would do a number on you just as a professional courtesy. It's a kind of rule we have: Human life isn't worth very much, almost nothing in fact, but money is sacred. Everyone has to get full value. If you have any notions of welshing, I suggest you just forget them. As I said, research is one of our strong points—we're frightfully good at finding people."

So there it was. He was given a number to call if he decided to go through with it, and he had until eight the next morning to decide.

"Don't be shy, lad. You just call any time you like. I live alone and I'm a light sleeper."

The sky was still the color of mud and looked like it might break loose again any second, so Guinness made his way back to the shop where he had pawned his coat and redeemed it for six and six. He also stopped in at a chemist and bought a razor for half a crown. There was no reason he should go around looking like a vagrant, even if he was one. In the men's room of one of the big department stores on Oxford Street he used wads of paper towels to give himself a kind of sponge bath from the waist up, and he used the liquid soap from the dispenser over the washstand to shave with. It was the most uncomfortable shave of his life, and his face itched like the devil for an hour afterward, but at least he looked decent. He could walk into a restaurant without the waiter automatically trying to pitch him out onto the sidewalk.

Dinner consisted of a fried cutlet and fried potatoes, with surrealistically green peas. He had heard someone say once that the English used baking soda in their cooking water to get their vegetables that color, but who cared. What with the tip, he was left with about three and a half shillings; he wouldn't even try to find a place to sleep for that.

To kill a man, Jesus. Could he do that? Was it possible to just walk up to some guy you didn't even know, and then simply kill him?

Yes, he thought so. He could plan it out and do it—it might even be sort of fun. Merely the idea of it excited him. And he could use the money—that much money would take care of everything. All he had to do was to pull it off—and survive—and he could have everything he wanted. Presented to him, for once, on a silver platter.

But to kill a man. He didn't know, he just didn't know.

The food made him realize how long it had been since he had slept. Walking around afterward, he felt as if his arms and legs were in iron braces and his head were stuffed with cottage cheese. He had to find a place to lie down.

A few short blocks took him down to the Thames. It was a nice part of the city, and the retaining walls under which the river could be heard rustling by were lined with benches. He picked one and lay down, throwing the curve of his arm over his eyes. He was asleep almost instantly.

How long was he out? He couldn't say precisely, but it was pitch black when he was awakened by something on the side of his skull. It was a night stick, the other end of which was attached to a policeman who in the dim penumbra of his flashlight beam looked about fifteen feet tall. He had a pencil-line mustache; that was all that made him human.

"Come on, now," came a murmur in heavy cockney. "You can't sleep 'ere. These benches isn't for sleepin' on. The river ain't no hotel."

Guinness worked himself up into a sitting position. The cop had been reduced by then to nearly a human scale.

"Come on, now. You move off down the way there, and be about your business. Come on, now."

Without speaking, too tired to be anything but obedient, Guinness submitted to the Law's womanish nagging and began to shuffle off. He stayed by the river until he was sure the cop was out of sight, and then sat down again on another bench. He was awake enough now to be angry.

He didn't have any business to be about, that was the thing. He couldn't just keep on walking forever. He had to help himself somehow—he had a right to do that much.

Fully awake now, he continued on the bench for perhaps five minutes more as his anger and his despair ran together and hardened into a single idea.

Yes he did. He had business to be about. Yes, by God, it was time he was about his business. With a vengeance he'd be about his business.

Outside a pub that was closed for the night he found a telephone booth.

"Major?"

"Yes? Who is this?" The voice at the other end of the line didn't sound like that of a light sleeper.

"Major, I'm signing on."

IV

ACCORDING TO THE single-spaced, typewritten instructions he had received with his money, the victim-elect's name was Hornbeck. Peter W. Hornbeck. Five feet eleven, one hundred and sixty-five pounds, dark-brown hair, brown eyes. Age, forty-seven. Never married but no known homosexual tendencies. Address: 23 Ellerslie Road, Shepherd's Bush—a respectable middle-class neighborhood given to semidetached houses faced with stone or dark wood and white plaster. Hornbeck was listed on his tax returns as an "import consultant" and his business seemed to be almost exclusively with Eastern European countries.

Under the heading "REMARKS" there were two compound sentences, set off from each other as separate paragraphs.

"Hornbeck is an agent for the East German government, functioning primarily as a courier but sometimes as a masher or dipperman; he is usually armed when working, preferring small-caliber automatic pistols, and should be considered dangerous at all times.

"Hornbeck will be leaving for Yorkshire (precise destination unknown) on the evening of the 16th; he usually travels by car."

Guinness could imagine what a masher might be, but what the hell was a dipperman?

The sixteenth. Today was the morning of the twelfth, so the sixteenth was the deadline for taking care of Hornbeck. One could wonder what was going on in Yorkshire that they were so anxious Hornbeck should never make it there alive. The man didn't sound terribly formidable; certainly not formidable enough that Her Majesty's government should budget a thousand pounds toward having his lights turned out.

Well, this wasn't his line of work. He didn't have any idea what its rules and priorities were. Perhaps it was just policy to deal with small-time couriers and muscle-men as they became visible and troublesome. Somehow, though, he didn't really think so. It didn't sound very practical.

Yorkshire. The last place God made. What the hell could be going on in Yorkshire?

There was a photograph stapled to the upper right-hand corner of the instruction sheet, the head and shoulders of a middle-aged man who looked like he had a lot of difficulty keeping his weight down. It was obviously posed, probably for a passport.

Hornbeck certainly didn't look like a spy. His ear-lobes stuck out at peculiar angles and his eyebrows were so bushy they gave the impression that the photo must somehow have been blurred. Those eyes didn't look like they had ever registered fear or cruelty, or much of anything else. They were the sort of eyes you would expect to find in the man behind the ribbon counter at Woolworth's, certainly not staring down at you from behind a small-caliber automatic pistol. "Should be considered dangerous at all times." Well, Cruttwell's people must know what they're talking about.

How does one assassinate a ribbon clerk? The major hadn't been terribly specific.

"It doesn't matter, really. As long as you don't cut him in half with a shotgun blast in front of the rush hour crowd at Selfridge's, we'll arrange to have the best possible face put on it—suicide or a stroke or something. It would be nice if you were able to give us something to work with, however."

Something to work with, something to work with.

Guinness used the edge of his thumb to fan out the stack of ten-pound notes lying next to him on the bed-spread. Now *there* was something to work with. Ninety-seven of them, the other three having gone toward getting him back into his hotel room.

Jesus, he was tired; he could feel himself sinking into the box springs. The sun would be up in just a few hours, but friend Hornbeck would just have to wait until after the troops had had a short siesta. Guinness wrapped his money back up in the sheet of instructions, slipping that back in lengthways through the torn-open end of its envelope. Without bothering to get out of his shirt and trousers, he turned off the table lamp beside his bed and dropped into a profound sleep.

The afternoon found him stepping off the underground at the Shepherd's Bush station. He walked west on Uxbridge Road, turning up on Bloemfontein until he was past the point where it intersected with Ellerslie. There were some school buildings on the corner and an enormous athletic field beyond them. Hornbeck's house would be across the street.

Ellerslie Road, as it turned out, was only about three or four blocks long, and Number 23 showed itself to the sidewalk as a rather handsome leaded-glass window that took up the whole of a narrow second story. You couldn't see in because the drapes were drawn, and the first floor was cut off from view by a high, well-trimmed hedge. The entranceway consisted of a narrow arch through the hedge that opened from an alley running off from the main street. The alley was narrow enough that two pushcarts wouldn't have been able to pass one another. All in all, it looked like the perfect house for someone who liked his privacy.

It was a quarter to three, and on a Monday afternoon Hornbeck wouldn't be anywhere except at work. There wasn't a soul around, not even on the playing field on the other side of the road, so Guinness decided he would have himself a look.

There was a second-story door up a flight of white stucco steps—it had a brass mail slot about a foot and a half from the bottom and looked like the main entrance—and another opening off a small back garden. That one was less visible from the alley and looked as if it would spring with a hard look, so Guinness settled on it.

In college there had been a rule that all freshmen had to be in their dormitories before 2:00 A.M., when they locked the doors. A lot of the time this conflicted with Guinness's work schedule, and try as he might he couldn't persuade the head resident to give him a key. Thus, as a matter of pure necessity, he became something of an expert on the subject of window latches and door locks. This one was a cinch; twenty seconds with a hairpin he had had the foresight to bring along and he was inside the storeroom of Hornbeck's kitchen.

The kitchen itself was small and rather dark, with wooden counter tops all the way round on three sides. It didn't give the impression of having been used much recently, and Guinness passed through it quickly to the narrow stairwell that led up to the second floor.

There was a small foyer behind the main entrance, opening onto what must have been the living room in the front and the dining room in the rear. He went into the living room.

With the curtains drawn it was very gloomy, and would have been gloomy even if they hadn't been. The walls were paneled in dark wood and the furniture was mahogany—late Victorian in style, and covered with a dark-blue material that looked like velvet but probably wasn't. The fireplace mantel and four or five tiny tables scattered around the room were covered with porcelain figurines, each about six inches tall and most of them dressed in eighteenth-century costume. It was a fussy, overcrowded room, the kind in which you would expect to see seated an eighty-year-old widow from Putney.

The bedroom was a little better; at least it looked more lived-in. The bed was unmade and narrow enough to give the impression that Hornbeck didn't entertain much.

In one of the bottom dresser drawers Guinness found a .25 caliber automatic of Portuguese manufacture. The finish on it was dull with age, but it was well oiled and clear of rust. Guinness cleared the chamber so he could look down the barrel. It was perfectly clean, a timely reminder that its owner was not the grandmother his home might lead you to expect. Guinness wondered how much of all that shit out in the front room was to Hornbeck's actual taste and how much was protective coloration.

There was a set of car keys in the right table drawer, on a ring decorated with a Jaguar emblem. The house didn't have a garage, so Hornbeck's car must be in a public parking lot somewhere. That would figure. A Jaguar didn't really go with the Victorian bric-a-brac stands and the lace doilies and the Dresden shepherdesses; those would be his working wheels.

Guinness looked at the alarm clock on the dresser. Three twenty-seven, time to get the hell out before the lord and master decided it was time to come home. He had been careful to wipe off everything he had touched, so he was back out on Ellerslie Road within a minute and a half.

There were a couple of adolescent boys in dark-blue gym shorts kicking a rugby ball back and forth between them on the playing field. They took no notice of the solitary figure who passed quickly down toward the road that led back to the underground platform.

Should he have stayed, he wondered, and taken care of friend Hornbeck the second he stepped in through his front door? No, he thought not. Who could tell when Hornbeck would come home? Guinness didn't think it would have been all that good an idea to try making his escape when the whole area was clogged with schoolkiddies on their way home. Regardless of the major's assurances, he didn't particularly want anything tying him into this mess.

And besides, he didn't know enough about the man's habits to risk it.

But then, where? And when? Some place where there wouldn't be mobs of people around, all of them just dying to serve as crown witnesses. Some place away from London, yes. And Hornbeck was leaving London in just a few days, now wasn't he? He was going to Yorkshire on business in just four days. Guinness remembered the set of keys he had found in Hornbeck's night table.

It took about three quarters of an hour of cross checking between a street map and the London telephone directory to assemble a list of all the parking lots within walking distance of Ellerslie Road. There were four of them, and on the third one Guinness hit pay dirt.

"Hello."

"Hello, is this the Frithville Gardens Garage? This is Mr. Hornbeck. I wonder if you could tell me whether I'm paid up through the end of this month? I'm taking a little trip, you see, and I don't want to lose my space while I'm gone. Could you check that for me please?"

"What did you say the name was?"

"Hornbeck."

Over the telephone cable he could hear the rustling of pages. He wondered if this guy would have recognized Hornbeck's voice; he wondered how successful his British accent was. He wondered if the guy would ask him the damn car's color.

"What kind of a car was that, Mr. Hornbeck?"

"A Jaguar."

"Yes, sir. It's paid through the month."

"Thank you."

Well, now he knew where Hornbeck kept his car. He looked up the advertisement for the Frithville Gardens Garage, and they were open until two in the morning. Give the nightman half an hour to lock up, and make it quarter to three before he paid his visit. That gave him nearly nine hours.

Guinness took a shower, dressed with care, and walked over to one of the big hotels ringing Hyde Park for a roast pork dinner. From there he took a cab to the Garrick Theatre and watched a performance of *She Stoops to Conquer*. It was a good performance, very roughhouse and bawdy. Afterward he dropped in on a pub just off Leicester Square and nursed a gin fizz through several dart games with the actor who had played Diggory.

He was enjoying it all enormously, he discovered. And not just the roast pork and the play and the dart games, either. He was getting a big kick out of getting ready to nail this guy. It was fun, as if friend Hornbeck had suddenly become all those legions against which it had been the business of his life to conduct war. He was getting his revenge, and, as the Italians say, revenge is a dish that tastes better cold.

At ten minutes to three he was around the back of the garage. There was an exposed iron stairway up to a locked door on the second story, but beside it was a saloon-door window held together in the middle by an old fashioned clasp lock. By hanging way out from the top of the stairway, keeping hold of the railing with one hand and one foot, Guinness managed to work the lock open with his knife blade. He thought sure he would fall and break his neck swinging over to crawl through the window, but he managed it in one piece.

It was dark as a tomb inside, and noiseless. Every football sounded like an explosion in a cave.

There were no less than twelve Jaguars. It took half an hour to find Hornbeck's, a black 3.8 not more than two years old. It was a nice car, the kind spies drive in the movies, but perhaps in England they didn't have that special aura.

Guinness checked the gas tank—it was right up to the top—and then emptied in two handfuls of sawdust from a trash can he had found near the back door. That would do it. In ten minutes he was walking with studied casualness back to the underground station.

Now all that remained was to wait, to wait and to find out as much as he could about his quarry, about Mr. Peter W. Hornbeck.

Of course there wasn't very much he could find out. Not about a man like that, not in any kind of safety. Hornbeck seemed to be a good agent—hell, he would have to be; nobody puts out a thousand-pound bounty on a punk—and a good agent would have a sound grasp of the laws of probability and a memory for faces. If the same one turned up just once too often, he'd know he was being hunted. No, the very last face Hornbeck would ever see would have to be one that was utterly strange to him—otherwise Hornbeck's might turn out to be the last face he ever saw.

So there was no thought of tailing the man. Guinness allowed himself just one look at Hornbeck in the flesh, and that a quick one. On the day after breaking into the garage he waited in a pub across the street from where Hornbeck worked, waited most of the afternoon for him to quit and go home.

What he saw wasn't much help. Hornbeck wore a hat that covered most of his face, as who wouldn't in the middle of a London February?

He was a larger man than Guinness had expected and he walked with a heavy stride, throwing his shoulder forward when he took a step. There was something less fierce than sullen about him, about the way he carried his umbrella far down on the handle as if it were a club. This was the man whom Guinness had just two days to kill. He looked dishearteningly durable.

And there was something else. Somehow it made it different to have seen him like that, just walking down the street, fighting the wind like a thousand other guys. It might have been himself.

Before, the whole thing had been like a game, just dangerous enough to be sort of exhilarating. But the end move would be to snuff that heavy shape, and it wasn't any game.

Well, he was committed to it. Either he went after Hornbeck or all those little nasties who worked for Cruttwell would be coming after him; and if it had to be Hornbeck or Guinness, it was going to be Hornbeck.

Maybe it was just as well he had seen him. If he was going to get the queasies, better now than when it was time to make the score. He couldn't afford any second thoughts then. No, then they might get him killed.

The only other information he could come up with was that Hornbeck was indeed going somewhere that Friday. Guinness phoned his office on Thursday afternoon, pretending to be an Irish importer whose tongue was hanging out over the market possibilities of cheap Balkan wines. He asked for an interview with Mr. Hornbeck for late Friday afternoon to discuss brokerage terms, but the reedy-voiced secretary asked if he couldn't make it the middle of next week because Mr. Hornbeck would be out of town on business Friday.

Guinness went ahead and made the appointment for the following Wednesday. What the hell, Mr. Tyrone would be happy to see Mr. Hornbeck. Mr. Tyrone didn't exist, but what did that matter? By Wednesday one or the other party would be dead anyway.

On Friday morning Guinness rented a Morris Minor and took up his vigil two blocks down the street from Hornbeck's garage. He had studied his map and had come up with the route he would have taken if he had wanted to get to Yorskhire and wasn't interested in the scenery. It was the obvious way to go and Hornbeck had no particular reason to start being devious right away, so one could hope.

According to those maps, the city of Hull was 168 miles from the center of London, well within range of a tanked-up Jaguar. Wherever else he was going in Yorkshire, Hornbeck probably wouldn't feel compelled to buy gas before Hull.

Any time after the Jag's tank was half empty, say after a hundred miles or so, all that sawdust floating on the surface could be expected to begin clogging up the fuel lines. Guinness would follow along, keeping at a discreet distance, and wait for that to happen.

At about twenty minutes past four in the afternoon, Hornbeck's car pulled past and along the way anyone would take to connect up with the highways leading north.

Guinness let him establish about a two-block lead and then started squeezing into the flow of cars behind him. It wasn't easy. The London rush hour was just beginning in full earnest and traffic looked like it had been pasted together in impenetrable walls. It was necessary simple to take it on faith that Hornbeck was out there in front somewhere.

All the way through the city, just once did he catch a glimpse of him. The Jag pulled off into the Ealing Road and was visible for just a second, but that was enough. Hornbeck was going in the right direction, so it was enough to wait until they both got clear of this damn jam jar.

In the dark of the turnpikes, as they cut through mile after mile of the flat British countryside, Guinness began to worry that something might have gone wrong. He hadn't seen the Jag in nearly two hours, not since just after they had cleared London. What if he had misread everything? What if Hornbeck were meeting someone well before he got to Yorkshire, or had switched to another car?

Then there it was, parked outside a roadside tavern, where Hornbeck had apparently stopped for a little eye-opener. Okay. Let him have it. He hadn't stopped for gas—Guinness would have seen him—and it was only a matter of time before his fuel pump shut off and left him stranded.

It happened in what had to be the world's most perfect spot for an assassination. About four miles north of a little village called Deeping Market, Guinness sighted the car. It was pulled over on the shoulder of the road with its hood up, and Hornbeck was standing beside the engine, patting his upper arms to keep warm. There wasn't a light on the horizon and not one car in five minutes on the road. Perfect. You couldn't ask for more.

Guinness pulled off behind the Jag and climbed out of his Morris. He was nice and noisy about it, slamming the door for effect. Everyone automatically trusts a door slammer. Obviously, a door slammer is a man with nothing to hide.

Everyone, perhaps, except Hornbeck. At Guinness's approach his hand went into the pocket of his coat and his eyes narrowed.

"Can I give you a hand?" Guinness almost shouted, smiling his best boyish smile. "This is a hell of a place to be stuck on a winter night."

You could almost watch the debate going on behind

Hornbeck's eyes. He needed help or he would never make it to wherever he was going, but he didn't like being caught out in the open like this. For just a second Guinness wondered whether Hornbeck might not just decide to burn him where he stood and take off in the Morris. It was a relief when the eyes relaxed and the hand came back up out of the coat pocket, empty.

"I don't know what happened. It just died on me." The voice was thick and harsh, as if all that nice frosty night air was beginning to make itself felt. "I don't know much about cars."

Hornbeck smiled suspiciously.

Again his will, Guinness experienced a surge of compassion for the poor bastard. This was a shitty thing to do to somebody—it made him feel like a real heel. Here the guy was, asking for his help . . .

Then he remembered the gun in Hornbeck's pocket, and what the major had said about everyone getting full value, and he decided he had better reserve his finer feelings for a more appropriate time.

Guinness reached back through the window of his car to get his little set of crescent wrenches and flashlight and then walked around to where the other man was standing. He squatted down and let his light rest on the tiny glass globe that housed the gas filter. The globe was only about a third full, with the gas line just at the bottom of the filter.

"Well, there's your problem. You aren't getting any juice. You've probably got a bad pump." He used one of the wrenches to loosen the induction line, and then went around to turn the key over. "Is anything coming out?" Hornbeck shook his head sadly.

Guinness came around again to retighten the line, going on all the time about how a friend of his had had a lot of trouble with the fuel pump on his Jaguar, and trying all the time not to think about the .25 caliber automatic that Hornbeck doubtless had his thumb on. It wasn't easy.

"Let's see what the pump looks like," he said brightly.

Guinness unscrewed the little panel in the right wall

of the Jag's trunk, telling Hornbeck to turn the key just to see if the pump wouldn't click on. It didn't, and as he flashed his light over it, Guinness could see a particle of sawdust in one of the lines. That car wasn't going anywhere.

They fiddled with it for some time. Guinness banged on the pump with one of his wrenches while Hornbeck worked the key, and gradually Hornbeck began to defrost. He became more talkative. He was beginning, without even being aware of it, to trust the helpful young Yank who seemed to be having such a good time tinkering with his fuel system. It was a mistake, the mistake Guinness had been counting on.

"Here, come have a look at this," Guinness called out excitedly from the front of the car. "Look at that, that right there. No, a little further down. That's it, right there. See it?"

A week later, staring out of the same tea shop window at what might have been the same rain, Major Byron J. Down, who had by then dropped his alias and come at least partially clean, found it hard to keep a rein on his enthusiasm.

"It was lovely," he said, his voice low but fervent as he vigorously stirred sugar into what might have been the same cup of tea. "You dropped him like a poled ox. The other side's Number One iceman for the whole of the British Isles, a man with twelve confirmed hits on his ticket, knocked over by a twenty-three-year-old college boy. Son, you're a natural, a born killer. You have found your true vocation, your true self."

Guinness wondered if he perhaps wasn't being put on. No, the guy was serious. It was scary.

"You might have told me who the hell he was."

"I might have, but would you have tried it if you had known?" After a moment of silence, Down turned up his open palms and smiled. "My point precisely. I'm sorry, son, but we were in a hole. We needed to get rid of Hornbeck; he was giving all the nancies in the Foreign Office palpitations, and he was making our organization look bad. We couldn't use any of our own men—Hornbeck's been around and would have spotted them in a minute. It was a job for the gifted and lucky amateur."

There were, of course, still quite a few things that Down wasn't being entirely candid about, things Guinness would eventually figure out for himself, after he had gotten to know more about how The Business was run.

Such as the fact that Down probably hadn't expected him to survive, that he had probably had in mind some sort of sacrifice play. Probably he had hoped to nail Hornbeck in a nice legal way for murder, his murder.

Down knew too much. It was almost as if there had been a tail on Guinness while Guinness was tailing Hornbeck. Had they been there, watching the whole show from a comfortable distance, hoping to rush in and catch Hornbeck with his hands covered in Guinness's fresh gore?

Well, this didn't seem a business where you could afford to resent such things. And, in any case, it hadn't worked out that way.

Guinness had stood up slowly while Hornbeck was still stooped over, trying to see just what it was that was so interesting under the hood of his car. Guinness came down hard on the back of Hornbeck's neck, driving home with the heel of his fist. It worked in the movies, and it worked then—Hornbeck went down, after first bringing his head down with a thud on the Jag's fender.

But he was still alive; out like a light, but alive. Guiness put his head on the man's chest and listened to the heart beating. After a few panicky seconds of considering what to do, he took off his coat and pressed it down against Hornbeck's nose and mouth. He waited five minutes, the longest five minutes of his young life, and then once again put his ear down against Hornbeck's chest. There was nothing. Hornbeck was dead.

Even in the winter cold he couldn't bear to put that coat back on. He simply threw it in the trunk of the Morris and fled. All he wanted in the world was to get away from there, and in his haste he nearly collided with a vegetable truck that was carrying a load of Valencia oranges to the good people of Humberside.

And now the protectors of all things democratic and humane had arranged his future for him. First he would be carefully trained—three months at an unspecified location in Western Scotland to study weapons, tactics, the personnel and administrative structures of the other side, everything he needed to convert him into the finely honed instrument of Her Majesty's revenge.

And there were other things. A part-time job teaching in a public school in London, a school the headmaster of which MI-6 had in its pocket. And his employers, the ones who mattered, could be counted on to be generous, generous and tolerant. After all, he was a valuable property.

And all he had to do was once in a while a little job of work for Mr. Byron J. Down.

"You'll do the work, son. I haven't a doubt in the world that you'll work out just fine. We're enough alike, you and I, that I can read you like the lettering on an eye chart, and this sort of thing is quite your line of country.

"Oh, you'll spend a few more weeks feeling sick and shaky over this little episode—it's always that way with the first job—and then you'll be back."

Down leaned toward him over the table, his fingers digging into the tablecloth like a hawk's talons into the flesh of its victim, and his eyes were round and bright.

"It's the hunting. Not the killing so much, even if that is a part of it, but it's the stalking that takes possession of you like divine fire and makes you feel like the master of worlds. You against him, your life measured against his. It's what every man on earth was designed specifically to do, and you more than most. We have you now, boy; you won't be able to help yourself. It's in the blood, you know."

And he was right, of course.

V

BUT CREON WASN'T. He wasn't even close, the stupid bastard. Down would have loved talking to Creon; he ran so perfectly to type.

Apparently Down had had a lot of ugly dealings with the police and had developed, in addition to the instinctive dislike everyone in the profession entertained for the cops, rather settled opinions about how they should be handled.

"Basically, they all use the *a priori* method," he would say, comfortably crossing and recrossing his legs as he sat by a half-open window after one of his enormous lunches. He was always much given to theory during that part of the afternoon. "What they believe to be true is what you have to worry about, not what they can prove—after all, what do they care about proof?

"The policeman will always construct an initial view of things, sometimes within a few seconds of arriving on the scene, and the evidence, as it filters through to him, will be made to conform. God knows what the ingredients of that marvelous solution are likely to be—how he felt about his mum when he was five, or the quality of his wife's conjugal embraces—but the great thing is to give him a push in the right direction, or at least in some direction away from you, and allow him to chart his course on that.

"The analogy with bulls and red flags should be obvious."

Creon, it seemed, had the beginnings of a theory, and he was very busy fitting the world around it.

His office was a little partitioned-off cube on the second floor of the new city hall, and, although lacking the floor space taken up by a queen-size bed, it represented a shade more than 10 percent of the working quarters of the whole police force, which had to share the second floor with the comptroller's office and the Department of Youth Services.

There wasn't much in that cramped space to suggest the character of its occupant. Aside from the usual pale-gray metal desk, which was covered with half-filled-out yellow forms, nested chrome in-and-out trays, and of course the black plastic telephone with one red and five clear plastic buttons, there were only a metal filing cabinet and two chairs, both made out of metal and Naugahyde, both on rollers and both pale gray. There wasn't even the usual little clear plastic cube on the desk, filled up on five of its six sides with pictures of Mrs. Creon and her brood. Well, you couldn't fault him for that; perhaps he preferred to keep those parts of his life separate.

Still, as he waited there alone for the great man to come and take his statement, Guinness couldn't help but compare Creon's office with his own, which was twice the size, had furniture made out of real wood, and was decorated with four paintings—three watercolors and an oil—which he had bought at various times from students in the art department. It gave him a small psychological boost to think of the policeman grubbing out his life in this soulless little box.

Of course Guinness didn't have any pictures of his wife and daughter on his desk either.

As it always did, the thought of his daughter left him feeling faintly depressed. His hand crept up until it rested lightly over his right inside breast pocket, within which he could feel the slight bulge of his wallet. There he kept, almost as a secret from himself, the only photograph of her he owned: a snapshot taken when she was three months old. It was how he remembered her; he hadn't seen her since. He couldn't even be sure she was still alive.

Guinness had known a few bad moments on that score since all this with Louise had started. But no, whoever was zeroing in on him would have had to have done one hell of a lot of homework to have tracked down his ex-wife and daughter. Kathleen had probably remarried, human nature being what it was, and might be living anywhere.

He brought his hand back down on his lap and pushed the idea out of his mind. At the moment it was his own safety he should be thinking about. It was his own damn neck that was stretched out so gracefully over the chopping block.

But first there was this idiot cop to shake off. Guinness hoped he would hurry his ass up. He was tired of waiting for Creon to decide that Anxious Anticipation Time was over. Being sweated like this was such a bore; it almost made you nostalgic for the white lights and the rubber truncheons.

Finally it was over, and Creon came in to settle himself behind his desk. Somehow he looked taller sitting down; anyway, he looked solid enough. There were deep furrows tapering down from his cheekbones almost to the line of his jaw; they made his face look hard and immovable, as if it had belonged to some Polynesian idol carved in wood. It could have been a dead face except for the eyes. They were small and angrily blue and all the more startling for the fact that the eyebrows and lashes were blond to the point of invisibility.

"Before we begin," He said quietly, as if he were reading something prepared in advance, "you should know that this conversation is being tape recorded and that anything you say may eventually be introduced in evidence against you."

"Am I being charged with anything?" Guinness asked, more to throw Creon off his pace than anything else. He was gratified when the blond eyebrows pressed together in a slight frown.

"No. You are not being charged with anything at this time."

Guinness smiled pleasantly and crossed his arms loosely over his chest. "But I may presume, I suppose, that I am under suspicion?" The question was almost insolently polite.

"Mr. Guinness, in a case of this kind—"

"Yes, I quite understand," he interrupted, for the second time, making a relaxed pass through the air with his hand, as if to dismiss those legions of things he quite understood. "Please go on." For a few seconds the room was still enough to allow him to hear the sound of Creon breathing heavily through his nose.

"You have the right to remain silent," Creon continued doggedly, as though refusing to notice what Guinness might or might not understand. "You have the right to have an attorney present. Do you wish to have an attorney present?" Guinness simply raised his shoulders and smiled. "May I take that as a negative, Mr. Guinness?"

"For the moment, yes."

That was obviously not the reaction Creon had been looking for. He placed his hands, one folded over the other, on the desk and leaned forward solicitously.

"Mr. Guinness, I think it only fair to advise you that we have a homicide here. This is no light matter. Your wife was murdered, are you aware of that?"

When he didn't get a response, he pushed himself back into his chair. His eyes narrowed, and he was angry. He didn't like not being taken quite seriously—it offended his sense of decency. Guinness was guilty, that was obvious to him, and when he had himself a lousy little wife-butchering sonuvabitch of a "professor" on the pad, he wanted him to sweat some. He wanted him to quiver in his knickers.

"How was it done?"

The question seemed to catch him off balance. His eyes started open again, startled and blank.

"How was it done?" Guinness repeated, spacing the words with elaborate care. "By what means was she killed?"

"Oh," Creon answered finally. "An ice pick, we think." With the tip of his little finger, he touched the soft spot just behind the lobe of his left ear. "Here."

The gesture turned Guinness's intestines into ice water, which he assumed must have been the whole idea. Poor Louise, poor baby.

"At least we're pretty certain that was the cause," Creon went on casually. "We have a puncture wound that probes to a depth of two and a half inches, which is certainly deep enough to kill. We won't know for sure, of course, until after the autopsy is completed."

"Are you sure it was an ice pick?"

There was a wary narrowing of Creon's eyes, suppressed almost instantly in his elaborate calm. He was working very hard to convey the impression of being on top of everything, of being in perfect control.

"We assume that was what it was."

"But you don't have it?" Absurdly, Guinness couldn't help thinking that some kind of victory. Absurdly, because the weapon, had they had it, might have cleared him.

"No, we don't have the weapon." Creon riffled a stack of papers on his desk, perhaps unconsciously providing himself with an excuse to glance down. "It'll probably turn up, though—and, in any case, it isn't material."

Creon quickly switched subjects, and Guinness let him. But still, it didn't make much sense. It had always been Rule Number One: Leave the playthings behind when you're done with them. Why take a chance on getting caught carrying an ice pick, still hot and smoking with your victim's blood. Taking it away like that just wasn't very good tradecraft.

Unless whoever-he-was had some special use for it. But like what, for instance?

"Also, we know she wasn't killed in the kitchen. We found a sizable bloodstain upstairs, on the bedroom carpet, and traces on the stairway itself. We assume, therefore, that the kitchen fire was set after the murder, probably in order to cover it up. If that was the idea, it didn't work very well. The fire was started by pouring cooking grease over the stove burners and then turning them on, but the stuff smokes a lot and the neighbors saw the fire and phoned for help before it had had a chance to really take hold."

Creon smiled faintly, as if he had just scored one off. Guinness, it was obvious, was really a very incompetent murderer.

Well, let Supercop think whatever he liked.

Guinness couldn't remember Louise ever keeping anything that could be described as cooking grease—not Louise, not the original low-carbohydrate kid. Therefore . . .

So that was how it had happened. Someone had surprised Louise in the bedroom, killed her, and then dragged her body down the stairs for the little scene in the kitchen. Just the sort of dumb move everyone would expect from the amateur who is looking for a way to get rid of his wife. That someone, whoever he was, had set him up beautifully. Nothing like a murder that looks like a murder.

And then Creon wanted his statement. "I would appreciate it if you would describe all your movements, in detail, on the day of the murder. I want to know everything, no matter how small, and please remember that everything you say will be checked."

The statement took about five minutes. Creon didn't make any notes, thus confirming the existence of the tape recorder, and he asked no questions until Guinness was finished. Then the questions never stopped, not for two and a quarter hours—Guinness kept track. Over and over, the same questions. The same details, checked and rechecked. Finally even Creon got bored and said they were through for the day, but that Guinness should keep himself available. They would talk again.

"Would you like me to call you a cab?"

"No. Thanks," Guinness answered brightly. "I'll walk it."

What the hell, the campus was only about two and a half miles from city hall—perhaps a little less if, once you got past Crystal Springs, the local madhouse, you got off Ralston and took the shortcut over the hills. But he didn't think so today; he wasn't up to hills.

Even so, he could use the exercise. Also the chance to think.

It was a nice day. The sky was blue and cloudless and on every block, it seemed, someone was in servitude behind a lawn mower. Tomorrow would be Saturday, and on Saturdays it was his turn to cut the grass. On Saturdays, in the summer, he would get an early start so he could have it all finished while the morning was still cool, and then he would set out the sprinkler—a half-hour on either side—so the lawn wouldn't dry up and turn brown and ruin their standing in the neighborhood.

And Louise would put on her jeans and her canvas gloves and a kerchief over her hair and spend the better part of the day on her knees, locked in mortal combat with the honeysuckle vines or the broadleaf weeds.

"Oh the damned borders; I'll never get them completely cleaned out. Next summer I'm just going to let the place go to the devil. Who the hell cares anyway?" But she said that every year.

For the past two seasons he had been trying to persuade her to use mulch in the borders, but she wouldn't. She thought it was ugly, she said.

And the next morning they would sleep in. And about eleven-thirty, without having bothered to shave, he would go out and get the Sunday paper while she cooked French toast, and they would read the funny pages over breakfast.

Well, not anymore.

In another five weeks the spring term would be over and summer, with its pale sunlight and its odor of ocean salt and beer, would officially begin. They had planned to sneak away for a week or two and camp out up in the Sierras, and they wouldn't be doing that either.

Guinness was scheduled to teach three courses in the summer term: Freshman English, Survey of British Literature to 1780, and a graduate seminar on the Metaphysicals. God, Freshman English in the summer—what could possibly be worse? Full of mindless little twits, every one of whom would be guaranteed to have failed the same course at least once during the regular school year. He was bored in advance.

And the other two courses wouldn't be much better. There was something about the summer; nobody was really awake to anything except his own biological cycle. The students would all be padding down to the edge of the sea to spawn. Everything resting. There would be a general husbanding of strength, an expectant preparation, as it were, for the decreed series of ritual fornications. Waiting for night, or perhaps merely for the temporary privacy of a sheltered reach of shoreline, they would throw their Frisbees, play structureless games of grab-ass, and burn their bodies to a creamy, enticing brown.

The girls, often as not, would sunbathe on the campus lawns, coming to class in their bikinis. It happened every year. You didn't say anything—you couldn't, really, without creating an odd impression—and they would sprawl in the front seats of the lecture halls, all bosoms and bare, open legs. And when your eyes touched them, as they had to if you were human, they would smile luscious and alluring smiles.

Guinness resented it. It was one of the thousands of tiny grudges every teacher—probably everyone in daily and promiscuous contact with the young—harbors up over the years. He didn't like being practiced upon; he didn't like being reminded that at thirty-eight they already thought of him as an old man and therefore too far out of the running to be dangerous. One day he would like to rape one of the little yumyums, just stop right in the middle of droning on about some tedious patch of nonsense like the Medieval Lyrics and jump on her bones, just drape some foxy peroxide blonde over one of the front pews and rape the hell out of her, right in front of the assembled multitudes. It would serve her right.

And the fact that he knew he never would, would never even lift a hand to one, made him resent their unthinking displays of flesh all the more.

And finally, he knew he didn't so much resent them

as envy them. He envied them their youth, their blindness to consequence, their capacity to journey down to the sea, to lie on the sand and close their eyes. In that sense, he had never been young.

Unpleasantly, he recollected that he was thirty-eight and therefore no longer even chronologically young. In two or three years he would be emphatically middle-aged. And then after that, should he be spared, old. It wasn't the first time the idea had occurred to him—hell, everyone over thirteen is aware of advancing age—but somehow, while he had had Louise, it hadn't seemed so imminent. She had had that trick; she had made him feel that the two of them would go on together, more or less unchanged, forever.

Oh Louise, my solace and rest. Never more will I touch your face with my tired hands.

She had been dead only the one day. Guinness pulled back the sleeve of his jacket to check his watch. Not even one whole day. It was twenty-seven minutes after two, and she couldn't have been killed much before four in the afternoon. Not even one whole day yet.

He couldn't accept the fact that she was dead. He had seen her dead, and he still couldn't accept it.

Yes, he could, and he couldn't. He was conscious of living in a kind of fantasy, one part of his mind still conforming to reflex—wondering if Louise would worry that he hadn't come home for lunch, wondering if he should phone—with another part whispering that that was all nonsense, that Louise was dead and under a sheet in the basement of County Hospital.

He knew when he went home tonight he would expect to find her in the kitchen, making dinner. But he wasn't even going home tonight. His home was under police seal, and his kitchen was burnt out.

His wife was dead, and his life was a shambles, and he couldn't bring himself to believe any of it. What the hell was going on? Who was doing this to him?

The faculty garage was on three levels. That was all there was to it, the three levels and the cement pillars that held them up. There was only one entrance for cars, but the thing was open on all four sides; anyone could walk right in from any direction without attracting attention. It was something worth worrying about.

There was a little booth at the entrance, where a student would sit all during the day and keep the other students out. For this minor treachery the administration paid him one dollar and seventy-five cents an hour.

Today the booth was occupied by Jerry Freytag, a large amiable redheaded boy whom Guinness had nursed through English 100 and finally, on the basis of his conviction that the poor bastard had really tried, had awarded one of his conditional *D*s: I give you this grade on the understanding that you will never become an English major. Jerry had been properly grateful and always smiled and waved greetings whenever they came within fifty feet of one another. He seemed a nice kid and probably meant it.

"Hi, Dr. Guinness," Jerry bawled enthusiastically as he saw Guinness approaching. He was wearing the summer uniform, a colored tee shirt and a pair of khaki Bermuda shorts; his feet were stuck into run-down blue sneakers, and a green baseball cap was perched backward on his wiry red hair. He was sitting—if you could call such a posture sitting—on a bar stool, with his legs and back propped against opposite walls of the tiny booth. Resting between his thighs was a paperback edition of *Jaws*. "Read this one yet?" he said, picking up the book and displaying the cover with an enthusiasm he had never manifested for *Pride and Prejudice*.

"Jerry," Guinness began, ignoring the question, "you know what my car looks like, don't you? Has anyone been near it today?"

"Sure. A couple of cops showed up a little before lunchtime. They musta been pokin' around over there for close to an hour." Jerry's thumb was tapping unconsciously against the spine of his book; you could tell he was dying to inquire why the fuzz would bother to shake down his old English prof's wheels.

"Thanks, Jerry."

Guinness passed on into the gloom of the first level and opened the door to the central staircase. What could he have told the kid, that the police were curious to know where he'd hidden the ice pick he had used to poke holes in his wife?

It was reassuring, though, in a way. If the cops had done a halfway decent job, they would have uncovered any little surprises left behind by the real murderer. Probably there wouldn't be any cobras in the seat cushions or sticks of dynamite wired to the starter.

The car was a metallic-gray Fiat. Guinness had his key in his hand before he was out of the stairwell, and as he settled in behind the wheel he slipped it into the ignition.

Instantly his hand and half his forearm were engulfed in flame.

And then nothing. The fire disappeared as suddenly as it had appeared, having barely singed the hair on Guinness's knuckles. Except for the black smudge on the metal ignition disk and the heavy odor in the air of something like burnt gunpowder, he might have thought he had imagined the whole thing.

Nitrogen triiodide. In his college days it had been the staple of one of the favored parlor tricks among the chem majors. The substance was so volatile that you had to keep it stored underwater. While it was still wet you packed it into the lock of your best friend's dorm door, where it would dry in a few hours. Then, when your best friend came home, probably a little worse for spiritous liquors, and put his key in the lock—BAM! The Fourth of July. Lots of smoke, lots of fire, lots of fun, and nobody gets hurt. The friction of the key over the tumblers will set it off, and there isn't enough to do any damage.

Of course you scare hell out of the poor sonuvabitch.

Guinness fell back against his seat, sweating and listening to his heart pound. It took him perhaps as long as fifteen seconds to fully convince himself that he hadn't been spattered all over the rear window. Jesus.

It was a little demonstration, obviously. Somebody was making his little point—proving, lest any should doubt, that Louise's murder hadn't been the work of any junkie burglar caught with his hand in the cookie jar. Somebody wanted Ray Guinness to know that he had an enemy in the world, and that Ray Guinness had better start being afraid.

Message received and understood.

VI

So WHAT HAD we got? A crazy, that much it seemed safe to hazard. Who else but a crazy would go to all the trouble of setting your wife on fire and then booby-trapping your car just to let you know he doesn't love you?

What's to stop him from simply sending a letter?—that would have been a hell of a lot safer. Or what about the phone—what ever happened to that old standby, the whispered menace that wakes you from a profound and beautiful sleep at four in the morning?

Ray, old lad, I was planning to bump you off sometime in the next several weeks and decided it would be ever so much more sporting as the grand prize in a guessing game, so I thought I'd call. Good luck, and keep on your toes.

Or why go through all the elaborate preliminaries? Potential victims get very dangerous when they begin to realize that that is what they are; a sensible man would just walk up behind the mark of his choice and put a blade in his liver. Either that or, having gone to the trouble of tampering with his wheels, how much extra was involved in wiring a few sticks of dynamite to the ignition and thus producing a bang worthy of your efforts?

Guinness had seen a couple of people go up like that one time, and it still gave him bad dreams.

Well, what the hell; one mustn't complain. It was that kind of a world, and if attempts were going to be made against his life, Guinness would, on the whole, prefer them to be made by crazies. Crazies always want to talk, to explain everything and impress you with how devilishly clever they've been. This guy, whoever he might ultimately turn out to be, was going to a lot of bother, and before he pulled the trigger he would be sure to want Guinness to understand just what had made him worthy of so much attention. You could stake your stick on it.

And a crazy is almost always playing some sort of a game, and games, unlike real life, have rules.

That had been the other part of the message conveyed via the nitrogen triiodide in his ignition switch: Don't worry, pal. I'm not going to kill you while you're not looking.

A necessary precondition, because what else would prevent Guinness from simply taking off again? He was good at hide-and-seek; it wouldn't take him very long to dust a tail, no matter if it was Sherlock Holmes following him around, to bury every trace of himself and pick up anew as a toaster salesman in Paraguay. Whoever-he-was would have the devil's own time ever finding him again, and he would know it.

So we play by the rules. If whoever-he-was was going to have his way, if he was going to get to speak his piece before push came to shove, he would have to take his chance. Things would have to be so arranged that Guinness wouldn't be simply offering himself up for execution. Something had to keep him from simply disappearing down a hole.

Not that Guinness had the least intention of disappearing, not yet. It was all very nice that his nameless antagonist was being such a gentleman about it—that way there would be a little breathing time; perhaps enough to figure out an angle—but no matter what, if the guy came tomorrow with flame and sword, Guinness was sticking around until one or the other of them was finished.

He had made himself a little promise, had promised Louise, that she would have her revenge or he would die in the effort. It was a stupid business, he knew that—after all, nobody but he would be keeping score—but it seemed to him a hell of a lot more important that merely staying alive.

So, where were we? Guinness didn't know who was after him, which gave whoever-he-was the initiative. But who-ever-he-was was clearly just a shade on the flaky side, and flakes tend to get in their own way a lot. The two canceled each other out, which made Guinness's chances of survival about even money. A man could do worse.

It was the day of his wife's funeral. He adjusted the knot of his tie and, holding up in one hand the coat of his dark-green three-piece suit, picked a tiny fragment of lint from the lapel. It was the suit in which he had been married and was the closest thing he owned to mourning.

As he dressed, he worked out in his mind the ponderous calculus of his dilemma, his lips moving silently from time to time, as if he were rehearsing the speeches of a play.

In five minutes he would walk down the hotel corridor and knock at the door of another room precisely like his own. There, with any luck, he would find his father-in-law dressed and ready to leave, although there was no certainty about it. The old boy might just as easily still be sitting in his underwear on the edge of the bed, weeping as much from the exhaustion of grief as from grief itself. Murray Harrison was taking the death of his child very much to heart.

Had Louise been alive to arrange her own funeral, she probably would have hit upon some excuse for not inviting her father at all. One could not have said, at least not with any kind of accuracy, that she hated him. She didn't hate him—there was nothing so grandly tragic about their relationship—she merely avoided him with all the dexterity at her command.

In the five years of his married life, Guinness had seen him on only one other occasion. About a month after their nuptial trip to Las Vegas, they had been invited down for a visit to his house in a retirement village outside of Los Angeles.

"Do you really want to go?" she had asked. At the time they were still moving into their new house, and the floors were awash with sheets of crumpled newspaper and cardboard boxes; it didn't seem that they would ever get everything sorted out. She had pulled the letter out of a back pocket of her jeans as they sat on a packing crate in the living room, sharing dinner out of a box of Kentucky Fried Chicken. He remembered the way her face had puckered as she spoke.

"Sure, why not?" Guinness looked at the postmark and noticed a date of four days previous; she must have been keeping it to herself for a while. "He has a kind of right, doesn't he?"

"Aaaaaall right, but don't say I didn't warn you."

In any case, she was careful, without making a point of being careful, to arrange things for just before the beginning of the autumn term, so they couldn't under any circumstances stay longer than two or three days.

In the vague sort of way peculiar to people without families of their own—and for all practical purposes Guinness was alone in the world—he had rather looked forward to being possessed of in-laws. During his brief first marriage his wife's parents had been content to stay put in Washington State, so he had never met them.

Louise's attitude amounted almost to a grievance, as if she were trying to withhold something.

It was a strange experience, their visit. Sitting on the sofa in Mr. Harrison's front parlor ("My God," Louise had whispered to him the first moment they were alone, "this place, it's like a time capsule out of the Truman era"), his knees captives to a squat little blond coffee table covered with a succession of doilies, Guinness found himself being guided through a scrapbook tour of Louise's early life, of the life they had all lived—Louise, her father, and her long-dead, apparently much-loved mother—before the family had crumbled away and Mr. Harrison had retired from his stationery business in Chico and moved down to Southern California to cultivate a tan and a heart condition.

Guinness maintained a kind of bored, deferential attention, asking a question just often enough to keep his father-in-law's monologue going smoothly—he wanted the old boy to like him—but Louise was in agony. Occupying a chair in the opposite corner, next to a portable record player that rested on a brass stand, she was working her way through a pack of cigarettes she had purchased from a service station machine in Santa Barbara (Guinness couldn't remember ever having seen her smoke before), drumming her fingers and frowning. Her father didn't seem to notice.

It was out of character for her, but not inexplicable. She had a new husband and a father who was something of an embarrassment, and probably still some feeling that she was out on approval, so it couldn't have been a very pleasant afternoon for her.

After that she was better. She made dinner that night and the three of them played canasta until nearly ten o'clock. They went back to Belmont on the morning of the fourth day, and so that was that. There was a meager exchange of letters, perhaps two a year, and father and daughter never saw one another again.

Then, the day after Louise's murder, about three hours after he had inserted the key in the ignition of his car and received its gaudy warning, Guinness phoned Mr. Harrison and delivered the news.

The next morning they met at the San Francisco Airport and drove directly to Sergeant Creon's office on the second floor of the Belmont City Hall. Guinness had already decided he would prefer not to be present and waited in the car. He had seen the performance before.

Sitting behind the wheel with the window rolled down, listening to the birds chirp, he tried not to think about anything, but that was impossible. A couple of kids went by on bicycles (Guinness wondered for a moment why they weren't in school and then remembered that it was a Saturday) and a squirrel was carefully picking his way over the roof gable of the Episcopal church. The noon whistle sounded; Guinness checked his watch and frowned at the unrelieved ugliness of life.

After thirty-five minutes Murray Harrison came back out into the sunshine, and Guinness could tell by the way he walked that Creon had at the very least strongly intimated that he had a favorite suspect all picked out.

That evening, in Murray's room, Guinness twisted apart the seal on a bottle of Jack Daniels he had smuggled into the hotel in a paper shopping bag marked "Kepler's Books." He poured a good three fingers each into two stubby water glasses from the bathroom, and the two men sat together in the filtering twilight, silently drinking.

It wasn't until about two thirds of the way through the second glass that Murray began to cry. Small and birdlike, with his white hair falling down around his ears and his Adam's apple pumping up and down, he sat on the edge of the bed, rocking back and forth in time to the spasms of his grief.

"I dunno," he whimpered damply, "I just dunno who coulda done a thing like that." His eyes were on Guinness in a way that suggested he might be afraid of what sort of an answer he would receive. Guinness only shrugged and freshened the old boy's drink. After all, to him the question of who could have killed Louise was technical rather than moral; it contained no element of outraged surprise.

After a tentative sip, Murray brought the glass down to rest on his thigh and uttered a kind of wheezy groan. He took a couple of panting, carefully separated breaths and then, for a moment, didn't seem to breathe at all. "Well, at least she didn't suffer," he said at last. "At least we have that to be thankful for."

Guinness could think of no appropriate answer, or at least not one that he would care to give to a ravaged, half-drunk old man, so he simply made a small noncommittal sound that his father-in-law would be free to interpret as agreement if he wished. Anyway, Murray was probably correct from a medical point of view—an ice pick in the medulla oblongata probably wouldn't leave one with any time to suffer. But, God, what must have preceded it. It didn't bear thinking about.

But he did think about it. How could he help but think about it? Over and over, almost compulsively, Guinness had, like a man suffering through his wife's pangs, lived his way over Louise's final twenty minutes or so of helpless existence. It must have been horrible: the fear, the certainty of death, the crazy pointlessness. The stranger with his fingers buried in the flesh under her jaw, keeping her head straight as she knelt, bound hand and foot, on the bedroom carpet. Out of the corner of her eye, just at the limit of her field of vision, she must have seen his hand raised to strike.

Only a Murray Harrison, a man with no imagination, a man who had passed his life conducting inventories of his rubber-band stock, could suppose the absence of pain any kind of comfort. More terrible than pain was the prospect of pain, and more terrible still the prospect of death. Pain was nothing, just a fact of existence like passion or bereavement; it could be accepted and overcome. Fear was the final enemy, the crucible in which intelligence, dignity, any sense of oneself as a human creature were melted down into a numbed wretchedness infinitely worse than any mere anguish of the flesh.

"Do you know who did this?" Murray both sobbed and shouted, in a kind of capitulation from the comforting fact of death's painlessness. "Ray, do you have any idea who coulda done this?"

The real question, of course, the one he wanted to ask, was, "Did you do this?" There was something like an implied forgiveness if he would only confess and relieve an old man of his intolerable burden of uncertainty.

Guinness drained his glass in a single swallow, setting it down on the tiny circular table next to which he was sitting in a low armchair, the back and arms of which were a single curve of red Naugahyde, and with the same hand he poured himself another three fingers, holding the bottle by the neck.

"No, Murray, I don't know who could have done it,

but believe me when I tell you it wasn't me. I know what you're thinking, but Creon is full of shit." With a smooth, careful movement he reached across the perhaps four feet of space to where his father-in-law was sitting and refilled his glass.

"Here, you need this worse than I do," he said quietly, suddenly heavy with compassion for a sorrow that was no less real because it had been yielded to.

As if unaware of its existence, Murray took a sip of the whiskey. You might have thought the operation performed by some agency independent of the will. The drink had its effect, though, and with a slight shudder the angular, stork-like figure on the bed seemed to come back into focus.

"I never really believed you did it, boy; not really. But still it's a comfort to hear you say so."

"Yeah." Guinness rose to go back to his own room, leaving the bottle of Jack Daniels behind him. "Good night, Murray."

"Good night, Ray."

For most of that night Guinness lay awake, staring up at a ceiling hidden in darkness. He didn't even try to sleep; he was past that.

Instead of numbing him, the whiskey had produced a version of clarity all its own, difficult but persistent. He didn't drink usually, and now he could remember why: The stuff made you feel melancholy and self-pitying and at the same time left behind sufficient intellectual detachment with which to deplore such maudlin excesses. It was like being two people at once, and they didn't like each other.

Louise and her father. The shame of the clever child for the weakness of her parent, whose love is rather like conventional piety and chiefly operates at weddings and funerals.

Still, Murray wasn't a bad man just because his emotions had been patterned into clichés. Louise had been wrong to turn her back on him, even if he hadn't noticed.

But so what? It didn't matter anymore—Louise was dead—and who the hell was he to criticize? He hadn't himself been precisely what one would call a model son. He hadn't seen or had contact with his own parent in twenty-two years, not since his sixteenth birthday had ended her legal obligation to support him and they had parted with mutual relief.

Mother. At the time he had felt—what? Distaste, resentment, a whole series of confused, hostile sensations, no two of which fitted perfectly together. He had been glad to get away from her, to be on his own (that would pass soon enough), but angry that his mother should be glad to see him go. Somehow your mother didn't have the right to be tired of supporting you.

God, that woman; how he had hated her. She had been, at least at the time, the embodiment of everything he wanted to put behind him, of everything from which the effortless dignity of academic life would protect him. A dark-haired, bony vulgarian who made her living and his by tracing parallel lines in whitewash around the bells of crystal water goblets in a glass factory in an ugly little town named Newark, Ohio. The lines served as guides for the cutters and were washed off when the design was complete. She would place the goblet upside down on a little potter's wheel on the table in front of her, wet the tips of her brush that looked like a pair of navigator's compasses, fit the brush into its vise, and turn the wheel. Day after day for years, the same thing. It must have been maddening.

She was a woman who perceived her life—and perhaps rightly—as a series of unprovoked calamities, and of these her son Raymond was by no means the least. It wasn't that he was perverse or unusually stupid (she credited him with these failings, but they were not the source of her grievance against him); it was merely that he existed. In himself, by virtue of the fact that he needed to be fed and clothed and put up with, he was a burden she most emphatically did not need. He was expensive and a distraction; these were his sins. And she never forgave him.

Guinness returned the compliment.

He remembered her as a coarse-skinned, scowling figure with knuckles the size of golf balls, leaning against the refrigerator, holding a dark-brown bottle of unidentifiable beer delicately by the neck between her first finger and thumb. In recollection she was enormous, but that had to have been a carry-over from childhood; she couldn't have been more than five feet four, and even at sixteen Guinness would have towered over her. How old had she been then? Late thirties, perhaps—no more.

Of his father he knew nothing. He had been merely The Deserter, a figure of myth, and Guinness couldn't even be sure whether he and his mother had ever been divorced. Or even married, for that matter. Perhaps even she wasn't sure who he was. Perhaps, except in a purely chromosomal sense, he had never existed.

So that left Murray Harrison down the hall, mourning for his butchered child. Father and daughter had appeared little concerned with each other alive, although that again might have been nothing more than an impression, and Murray's grief was no doubt largely compounded out of a sense of propriety, but so what? It was there. It is the emotions that create one person's responsibility to another, and they are, after all, finally something more than the sum of their ingredients.

So, what the hell. Guinness slipped his arms into the sleeves of his coat and prepared to depart. Today he would bury all the family he had left in the world—except the mother and the daughter on whom, at various times, he had turned his back; and could they have been any less dead to him than Louise was now?—and then Murray would get on a plane and go back to his condominium and his pinochle games and his scrapbooks of life in Chico, and the whole issue would become academic.

He walked to his father-in-law's room and tapped lightly on the door with the joint of his first finger.

"Come on, Murray. It's time."

VII

IT WAS LAUNDRY DAY. Exactly a week had passed since the Belmont Police Department had packed his suitcase for him, padlocked his front door, and driven him to the hotel of his choice—and he was running perilously low on underwear.

Guinness hadn't been inside a laundromat since his bachelor days, but the only change he could perceive was that the washing machines seemed to take fifty cents now instead of thirty-five. Otherwise, everything was the same. The same long, narrow room with the washing machines against one wall and huge, vatlike driers built into the other. Even the molded plastic chairs where you sat transfixed before the drier windows, watching your clothes tumble past like the characters in some particularly repetitious television show, were exactly the same, linked together in groups to make it harder for aficionados of vulgar furniture to rip them off.

It wasn't a very entertaining way to spend time, but time was suddenly something Guinness had plenty of, so it didn't matter. He was officially on leave from his university—paid leave, which provided some measure of how badly they wanted him out of the way.

The day after Louise's death, just half an hour before he was nearly blown up in his car, he had found a note in his department mailbox that the dean would appreciate a word. Not the chairman, but the dean. In the six years of his tenure at Belmont State, Guinness could remember only one other private encounter with that august personage; a rather perfunctory welcome on his first day. Perhaps it was different in the prestige schools, but at Belmont State the deans were like gods, powerful and distant. You were thankful if in their brooding majesty they left you alone, because a summons from that quarter usually meant you stood in violation of some particularly serious tribal taboo.

The dean in this case was also a former chairman of the English department, an intimidating gentleman with spectacular gray eyebrows and an almost mandarin sense of his own personal significance. He drove a Mercedes, as befitted his position in the world, and had served his country faithfully and well during the Korean conflict as a member of the Military Police, making something of a specialty out of harassing enlisted homosexuals.

His office was on the highest floor of the Humanities Building, so Guinness took the elevator up and stepped into the dean's waiting room, which, like his office, was paneled in wood. His secretary picked up her telephone and whispered something into the mouthpiece, and within five seconds the dean stepped out smiling, his right hand extended in greeting. Guinness took the offered hand only to have the other clapped on his shoulder as he was propelled into the inner office.

"Sit down, Dr. Guinness," the dean said, sliding into his own chair. "Please let me express my own very sincere personal condolences on the tragic death of your wife."

Guinness muttered something that sounded like "thank you" and made a vague depreciatory gesture with his left hand, and for a moment there was a tight silence. As if to break it, the dean picked up a long yellow lead pencil that had been lying on some papers and began a nervous, rhythmless tapping of the eraser end against the sheet of glass covering his desk top. It must have made more noise than he had intended, because after only six or seven taps he stopped, stared at the eraser for a second or two, and then gently set the pencil back down. He kept his hand on it for just an instant, as if to make sure that it wouldn't begin to roll, and then settled back in his chair, letting his finger tips rest against each other and smiling kindly. They always smile at you like that just when they're getting ready to screw you.

"I suppose you must be terribly at loose ends," he said, still smiling and still peering over the tips of his fingers, "and you mustn't allow yourself to worry about things over here. I've always observed that in times of trial a university acts rather like an enormous family; we take care of our own. So please don't be anxious—your colleagues will be happy to cover for you during this period of personal crisis."

Guinness suddenly found himself wondering how his dean had heard about Louise's death. He hadn't told anybody—he hadn't even phoned her father yet. There hadn't been time.

It had to have been Creon. Probably that morning sometime. Probably while Guinness had been busy identifying the body.

What the hell else had the damn man said?

Probably nothing, at least not right out. A few hints would have been enough—college administrators had very fine antennae when it came to scandal and if there was any chance at all of Guinness taking the fall for his wife's murder, then he would have to be distanced as much as possible from the sacred centers of academe. After all, it wouldn't do for the police to walk in and arrest him in the middle of class. Think of the newspapers.

An enormous family, the man had said. What bullshit.

"It's all arranged. Jenkins and a few of the junior men will take over your classes until the end of the term. And I'm sure we can find someone if you decide you would rather have the summer off—what with the current Ph.D. market, we have no trouble finding people for short-term work. Even on such brief notice as this."

The dean smiled again, as if the thought of all those poor hungry bastards coming out of the graduate schools just made his day.

So there he was. Ray Guinness, the remittance man of Belmont State's big happy family. With nothing to do all day except watch his laundry go round.

Of course that wasn't all there was to watch. There was, for instance, the guy in the pale-green Chevy parked outside.

Not that Guinness particularly minded being tailed. He had grown accustomed to it over the past several days; keeping track of the hotel detectives and the police legmen had developed into a kind of game. When he had his lunch, there was always another party-of-one crumbling saltines into his chili just three or four tables away, and if he turned around on a city sidewalk he could count on spotting some dude suddenly twisting aside to look into a shop window or leaning against a building as he read the sports pages. If he took a drive, there was always a dark-colored hardtop about half a block behind.

They were always the same five faces. Like factory hands, they worked in shifts, and Guinness got so he always stopped some place for a cup of coffee when it was time for the Changing of the Guards. They weren't very good, and he didn't want to make their lives needlessly difficult.

Five—probably close to half the manpower Creon had in his whole department. It must have been making one hell of a dent in his budget for the month.

But this guy wasn't one of the regulars. For one thing, he didn't seem to keep a schedule; he didn't come on at nine in the morning and go off at dinnertime. He had simply appeared the day before yesterday and had been around ever since. He was just there—it was almost as if he wanted to be spotted.

The regular escort hadn't spotted him yet, but then they probably wouldn't have noticed him if he'd been riding a camel. Somehow it never seemed to occur to police that somebody might be watching right along with them. These guys never even turned their heads.

But he was there all right. And while he watched Guinness and Guinness watched his laundry, Guinness was trying to make up his mind what to do about him.

He was not a cop, of that much Guinness was sure. Murder not being a federal offense, Louise's death was purely a local matter. And there was no good reason why Creon should use two sets of tails. Besides, he didn't look like a cop.

And if he wasn't a cop, it would be worth something to discover his interest in this matter. Whoever he was, he would have to know more than Guinness did about what was going on.

So we bust him.

Guinness picked himself up out of the chair from which he had been watching his underwear dry and went over to the change booth. He really didn't need any change, but the booth was toward the front of the Laundromat and provided a better view of the parking lot.

He slid a dollar bill across the counter and the attendant, a skinny craggy-faced old gal with hair dyed to a violent henna that made her look like nothing so much as Abe Lincoln in drag, took a handful of dimes from the cash register and carefully counted out ten, arranging them in pairs on the counter until they made an orderly little two-by-five rectangle. Just to be on the safe side, she counted the ten dimes over once more before pouring what was left back into the till. Guinness pushed them off into the palm of his right hand, smiled a "thank you," and turned casually around to face the big picture window that took up most of the Laundromat's front wall.

What the hell, if you're going to watch someone who's watching you, there is no point in being cute about it. None of that over-the-shoulder shit; he'll spot that faster than anything. But a man who simply looks out of a window, without making an enormous production of it, could just be checking the weather.

The pale-green Chevy was still there.

Yes, this was a gentleman who deserved a few minutes of our undivided attention, provided he could be gotten off somewhere by himself. It would be necessary to shake the police, but that shouldn't present too much of a problem. Not for Raymond M. Guinness, social pariah and local master criminal.

Guinness experienced a decided thrill at the prospect. It would be good to be doing something positive, to be on the offensive for once.

He packed his laundry back into the small blue-and-white canvas suitcase he had owned since college, and he left. The Laundromat was only about ten blocks from his hotel, so he hadn't bothered with the car. It being a warm day, he slung his coat over his shoulder and set the suitcase down on the sidewalk in order to roll his shirt sleeves up to the elbows.

Two blocks down from the Laundromat was El Camino Real, until within living memory the main roadway north and south upon which the suburban towns of the San Francisco Peninsula were strung like beads. Now all the really serious traffic was on the Bayshore Freeway, but you still went to the El Camino if you wanted to catch a bus, and Guinness wanted to catch a bus.

He sat down on a bench on the west side of the highway and checked his watch. It was twelve minutes after one, and at that time of the afternoon the local buses ran only about once every half-hour. He couldn't see his police tail, although it was likely that if he turned his head fast enough he would spot a familiar face. The new man, whoever he was, wasn't being even that coy—across the street, parked in plain view at the head of the next side road up, was a pale-green Chevy.

The arrogant bastard. The sonuvabitch was just begging to be taken down.

Finally a southbound bus came along—Guinness didn't really care about the direction; he just happened to be on that side of the highway—and, after fishing around in his coat pocket for five of his recently acquired dimes, he got on and found himself a seat over the left rear wheel. Out of the back window, in the right lane so as to keep track of who got off at each stop, the green Chevy was clearly visible, and, about three quarters of a block further back, there was a very familiar-looking dark-blue Ford. Guinness sighed and shifted his attention to the Blue Cross ads posted over the side windows. Just once in his life he would have liked to be tailed by a hot-pink Cadillac convertible.

The bus made its painful way past the Pup 'n Hound diner, past a billboard announcing the current feature playing at the Carlos Theater, past a tiny bookstore with a Tudor bay window that Guinness had always had it in mind to investigate someday, and pulled in at the Redwood City Depot.

It wasn't much of a place—just a square building with a ticket booth and a concession stand against one wall and some coin-operated lockers against the other, with three long rows of slat benches in the middle. Guinness got off his bus and checked his suitcase full of underwear in one of the lockers. He hadn't eaten since breakfast, so he bought a hot dog and a small paper cup full of tepid Dr. Pepper at the concession stand and sat down on one of the benches to wait for the next bus going north.

The hot dog wasn't bad, but the Dr. Pepper made him faintly ill, and it occurred to him, as it did from time to time these days, that since Louise had died he had begun to live an awfully seedy life. Here it was just a week and he was subsisting almost entirely off of junk food. Louise would never have let him sink to a meal like this one. Hot dogs and Dr. Peppers, indeed.

Lately, he had taken to having his dinner at the McDonald's a block away from his hotel. Hell, it was fast and you weren't likely to pick up a social disease in the men's room.

Every night a Big Mac and a large order of French fries, every god damned night.

Louise had always been very careful about that sort of thing. "Fried foods will kill you," she used to say. "I don't intend to have you dropping dead on me so I can spend my middle years back clerking for some damned insurance company." She made sure he had a lot of chicken and fish, and she kept the starches down. If he felt like he just couldn't live another minute without a nice big greasy cheeseburger, he had to buy it on the Q.T. and eat it in his office at school.

Now his weight was up a good six or seven pounds and he went around all the time with an oily feeling on the roof of his mouth. All that garbage and he couldn't even enjoy it; not like when he could believe he was pulling off the crime of the century and knew Louise would put it right with a dinner of skinless chicken and green salad. Hell, he used to go to the Burger King across the street from the campus and feel like he was walking through the doors of a bordello. Shit.

A northbound local pulled in with an exhausted sigh from the air brakes, and Guinness fed another fifty cents into its coin catcher just as the bus closed its doors and started to pull back out onto the El Camino. With any luck at all, that would give him a tiny head start while Creon's man tried to pry open his rented locker to find out what exactly Belmont's Othello could be hiding in a bus station beside nine fresh pairs of his B.V.D.s. It was a temptation no cop in the world would be able to resist, and Guinness hoped this one wouldn't even try.

Within two blocks of the terminal he pulled the cord over the wundow, signaling that he wanted off, and was dropped at the next stop, where he turned off on foot into a sidestreet. After about four blocks, he was satisfied he'd shaken his official escort.

Not so for Green Car, however. He would be back there somewhere, and anyway we didn't want to lose him. No, we wanted to take him alive, alive and talkative.

Of course, there was always the chance that he might not feel chatty just that day. If he was the man who had killed Louise, there was even the chance that he would start shooting or something, although Guinness couldn't really bring himself to worry too much about that. No, the man who had stabbed Louise and had booby-trapped his car was a man with a message. He would want to deliver it before he declared war.

Still, he would be armed. He would be carrying a gun—they all did. It occurred to Guinness that he was going to have to break down and get one for himself sometime soon. It looked like the nice quiet days were over for a while. Maybe forever.

The green Chevy was nowhere in sight, but that didn't mean anything. Its driver would have left it somewhere, there being difficulties involved in tailing anyone on foot from a car.

After a few more blocks, Guinness caught sight of a familiar face reflected in a shop window. His new escort was across the street, leaning up against a building. Very cool he was, not looking like he was tailing anyone and not looking like he wasn't. He had "pro" written all over him; and not cop pro, but the only pro that mattered. This guy was in The Life, a ghost. Guinness knew the type.

He was wearing a dark-brown summer sport coat and what looked like khaki trousers and no hat, which was a relief. Hell, nobody wore a hat these days; it only passed for a disguise in police circles.

Dark hair, perhaps even black, with a little silver at the temples—that might or might not be real—but a youngish face. Not tall and with the build of someone who had wrestled in college. Put his age at around thirty-five.

In that instant, Guinness saw him reach up with his left hand to pull at where his belt was apparently pinching him in the side. The movement brought his elbow out akimbo, revealing that the armholes of his jacket were unusually loose and deep. Well, that was instructive—he was strapped into a shoulder holster.

It was nearly three before Guinness found what he had been looking for. A nice old-fashioned gas station with a nice old-fashioned men's room, the kind that has a latched window high up on one wall rather than a fan that operates off the light switch. He made sure to approach it from the proper angle, keeping his shadow across the street and where he would be able to see the door but not the window.

Once inside, Guinness turned over the open trash can into which you were supposed to drop your used paper towels and shinnied out through the window, skinning his rib cage and nearly breaking his neck in the process.

Jesus, it had been a while since he had had to do anything along those lines.

Outside, he stayed close to the corner of the building. It was only a matter of time before our friend with the shoulder holster would begin to wonder what the hell was taking so long in the fucking john and come across the street to investigate. When he worked himself up to coming in, he would see the turned-over trash can and the open window, making the obvious deduction that he had been spotted and that Guinness had ducked out on him, and then come back out through the bathroom door. As soon as he came back out—BAM! Right over the gourd.

But with what? Guinness considered for a moment the side of his horny hand—it would hardly have been the first time—but decided against it. He was out of practice, and you don't try to take a working agent barehanded when you're out of practice.

Ultimately, he settled for removing his left sock, sifting in a couple of handfuls of the heavy gravel that was lying all around the back of the gas station, and tying it off to make a perfectly serviceable little blackjack. He balanced it in his palm for a moment, estimating its weight and how hard a blow he would have to strike. After all, this yoyo wouldn't be any use to him dead.

Finally, he could hear the gravel crunch and then someone trying the bathroom door. It was locked, of course, and a gentleman would simply have walked away, finding somewhere else to take his leak. Not this baby—after a few seconds there were the sounds of a lock being picked and then the door opening.

Instantly the door closed again. Guinness raised his cosh, there were two quick steps on the gravel, and then they were on each other. There in the alley behind a men's room, two pros face to face.

Guinness took advantage of that inevitable instant of surprise and brought his weapon down against the side of the other man's neck. It was enough to stun him and he pitched around a quarter of a turn, instinctively bracing himself with his hands and forearms against the side of the building. One more blow to the base of the skull and he was out, first sinking to his knees, and then gradually, still pressed protectively against the building, he slumped to the ground.

Dragging him into the men's room, Guinness was astonished at his weight, but then an unconscious man always feels like he has been padded out with lead.

Once inside, a quick frisk was in order. Yes, Virginia, there really was a shoulder holster, and in it a lethal-looking 7 mm automatic of Spanish manufacture.

But the big surprise was in the guy's wallet, in the form of a small, plastic-coated federal identity card in a leather holder. Guinness leaned back against the bathroom door to drink it all in: He had just clobbered a member in good standing of the U.S. Secret Service.

VIII

Ernie Tuttle, for such was his name, emerged from the bathroom of his quarters at the Casa Belmont Motel holding a damp washcloth against the back of his head. He had taken his shirt off and on his right shoulder, just at its insertion into the neck, could be seen a large oblong reddish smear that promised to develop into a dandy bruise. In his free hand he carried two bathroom glasses, which he set down on the glass-topped chest of drawers in order to extract a half-empty bottle of Teacher's Scotch from the pouch of a folding suit bag that lay open on one of the room's two single beds.

"You want a snort?" he asked, holding the bottle up to about eye level of where Guinness was sitting in the chair nearest the door. "I'm sorry I don't have any ice."

"No thanks. I'm not the one who got tagged today."

Tuttle grinned, very much the good fellow, and took the washcloth from the back of his neck, tossing it back through the bathroom door and into the sink. For all his gray at the temples, it was a boyish grin, open and friendly. He had a certain animal liveliness of manner that made you think of a slightly decayed fraternity brother at a college reunion, still game for a few beery choruses of "The Sweetheart of Sigma Chi." The sort of man you trusted instinctively because he didn't give the impression of having brains enough to be devious, the sort of man it would be childishly easy to underestimate. It wasn't a mistake Guinness was much interested in making.

Tuttle poured himself about two fingers of the Scotch and set the bottle down next to the still-empty glass on the chest of drawers before allowing himself to sink into the other chair.

"Yeah well, most people would expect an apology at the very least. You really laced me, you know." He pulled a rueful face and Guinness laughed. Then Tuttle laughed—it was a big joke.

"Okay, so it might not have been very elegant tradecraft coming around a corner flat-footed like that, but I was beginning to think I was never going to get an opening. You sure as hell aren't an easy man to invite by for a drink and a quiet word." He took a sip of his Scotch and shook his head slowly, as if engaged in some lengthy meditation on how hard Guinness had been making his life lately.

"If that was all you wanted, I haven't precisely been in hiding. What's the matter with the phone?"

"Rule Number One—sacred." Tuttle raised one finger in a warning gesture. "Never unnecessarily involve the local police. The Company wouldn't like it." He looked at Guinness as if he expected some sort of reaction, but Guinness's face remained masklike. Suddenly Tuttle understood, and he grinned again. "Or didn't you know they've had your hotel phone wired?"

Guinness had not, in fact, known. The possibility hadn't actually occurred to him, a lapse of vigilance he found difficult to explain to himself. In the old days you had always simply assumed that someone was listening in. He must be slipping.

It wasn't the sort of thing he much cared to admit, however—although he would have liked knowing how Tuttle had found out; perhaps he had cultivated a source in Creon's office—so he picked up Tuttle's little plastic identity card from where it was lying on the table between them and held it up by a corner. "Is this your 'Company'?"

Tuttle shook his head and laughed. "The Secret Service? That band of fairy godmothers? Not likely. The card is strictly out on loan; it gives us something to flash at the cops if things go drastically sour. Sorry, pal—the people I work for aren't in the habit of advertising."

For an uncomfortable moment Guinness had the sensation of looking into some sort of weird retrospective mirror, of having reflected back at him his own insane hubris as a younger man. With perfect clarity he could recall the perverse egotism, the professional pride he had felt at being one of those who did the really nasty stuff, of numbering himself among the world's political garbagemen. Oh boy, the traps they laid for you.

"And besides," Tuttle went on, with a slow contemptuous wave of his hand, "if Uncle Sam has got business with a hit man of your particular distinction, what concern is that of some small-time cop trying to polish his badge on a little domestic murder?"

Guinness started to say something but then thought better of it. Instead, he picked himself up out of his chair and took a few heavy steps to the bureau to fix himself a drink. He really didn't care much for Scotch, but it wasn't the moment to be fastidious.

So they knew. They absolutely knew now who he was. In the end, as he had always realized they would be, all the elaborate precautions he and Byron Down had taken had been for nothing. He could almost see his dead patron shaking his head over the sad certainty of it. As if to say, I told you so. Well, he had.

"How did you find me?"

"It wasn't easy." Tuttle's tone of voice suggested a world of blind leads and wasted labor. He laughed shortly, as if at some private irony. "Man, you really know how to go about burying yourself; I don't imagine even the British have any clear idea of what became of you."

More by a kind of general relaxation than through any perceptible movement, he took on the attitude of a man settling down to begin some favorite story, the kind you would hear sometimes from people in The Business when they were tired and had had a drink or two more than was good for them and thought it might be safe to unbutton a little and recount some particularly significant and instructive personal triumph, or some disaster that after years and years still had the power to make them cringe. It was by definition a lonely and secretive line of work, and opportunities to brag or confess, or simply to talk openly, were rare enough to be enjoyed almost voluptuously.

Guinness prepared himself to listen, to nod and to grunt from time to time and to let Ernest Tuttle talk on for as long as he liked. People want to tell their stories on their own terms, and in present circumstances Tuttle's good will might be worth something. Besides, there was no hurry. And it was nice after all these years to have a moment or two during which he didn't have to wear his psychic disguise, when he could put off his sheep's clothing.

"I joined the Company in sixty-five," Tuttle began quietly, his eyes seeming to focus on some point behind Guinness's left shoulder, where he might have been reading the Book of the Damned. "I was in the CIA then; they'd recruited me right out of college and set me to field-work in Honduras. Jesus, sometimes it feels like I spent the whole two and a half years down there crouched all night in the middle of a damned banana grove, listening to some greasy little urban terrorist tell how for five hundred dollars and a Benrus watch he was going to sell me Che Guevara's ass.

"Anyway, that August a guy came around to the little office we were using in Tegucigalpa and asked if I wouldn't be interested in a transfer to another service. He said I'd be posted back to Washington at first, but that if things panned out for me I could expect to get in on some real action. Well, that time of year down there you can't see the wallpaper for the flies, so I said okay.

"For the first year I was in Research. They always do that; it gives them a chance to watch you for a while and teach you enough to keep you from getting your head plucked off, and also they can kind of break if to you gently that you haven't exactly joined the Boy

Scouts. Anyway, I spent the time putting together files on current operations being mounted by other governments, mainly so we wouldn't accidentally fuck up anything for our beloved allies, and on any new players our people might come across in their own games.

"D.C. isn't a bad town to play spy in. Every embassy had its own little gig going, so you kept busy; and if things got too dull you could always pull a black-bag job on HEW or something. Hell, we were burgling our own people more often than we ever did the Russians.

"And the women, you wouldn't believe. Every one of those government office buildings was about six deep in broads and they all have a weakness for bad guys. A man could die of turberculosis just trying to keep up.

"Anyway, about that time we were just beginning to get some rumbles that MI-6 had this new headhunter. We like to keep track of the talent in that field, so we opened a file and made a few inquiries, but there was nothing. Not a god damned thing. We never got a fingerprint or a photograph or even so much as a decent description.

"I mean it was embarrassing. All we had was a file full of assassinations we couldn't hang on any of the established pros, and that was about it. We couldn't even be sure all of them were the work of the same hand because the methodology kept changing. There were plenty of rumors, which we figured the British were probably spreading themselves just to scare the hell out of everybody. Just whispers, something that would float by one day in an internal memo we'd get a peek at, but nothing we ever had any hopes of being able to check.

"Anyway, we kept up the file. Nobody we cared about was getting zapped, but we like to stay informed. That way we know who to keep off the guest list for the State Department's Fourth of July party.

"All that cold meat. God, there must have been close to thirty hits in all and each one a tailor-made. The only thing they all had in common was a stylishness, a certain aesthetic polish to the work. Every time it was a very tidy job—no loose ends, no clues, no witnesses spilling their guts about the mysterious stranger in a tan raincoat. Somebody would just die.

"Word was that Byron Down ran things, but that wasn't much of a shock. Down held the strings on most of the British hit men, and he generally kept them out of the normal lines of command. Even then, most of the time we can come up with a name and a photograph and a pretty complete track record, but not on this one. Down was being extra-special careful, even for Down—I guess he knew when he had a good thing—so we were left with nothing.

"But you've been through all this already, haven't you, sport?" Tuttle punctuated his grin with a slow theater wink. "No need to tell you what a hotshot you were."

The hotshot might have been cast in bronze. If he was breathing, it didn't show. Finally, in an almost imperceptible movement, he began to shake his head and his eye fixed on Tuttle in a way that suggested he was not prepared to be joshed.

"Watch yourself, sport. If you want to tell stories, I'm prepared to listen, but don't try to hang things on me. I figure I don't have the patience to be suspected of more than one murder at a time."

Guinness shifted uncomfortably in his chair, wondering why the hell he bothered protesting his innocence. Habit, he supposed. They both knew perfectly well who he was.

"Sure. I keep forgetting you're just a harmless professor of poetry who wouldn't step on an ant." Tuttle smiled and got up to fix himself another drink. "Can I freshen yours?"

Guinness surrendered his glass and watched it being filled to about halfway. Then he watched Tuttle sit back down and take a long pull on his own glass before setting them both back down on the table between them.

"Okay then, have it your way. This for-the-moment unspecified gentleman was supposed to be an American, just like you and me. Anyway, he wasn't British.

"We kept getting worried memos, all the time. Why

weren't we getting a fix on this guy? That sort of thing. It made a lot of very respectable people very nervous that he might be a citizen; the thinking was that if he ever got caught, everyone would be only too eager to assume that he worked for us and there would be a big stink about how the nasty Yankee imperialists were sending out squads of murderers to prey upon the innocent commissars; that sort of thing.

"Also, it was voiced here and there that maybe we could steal him. Good assassins are hard to come by.

"So there was a plan developed. We would borrow him from MI-6, or at least get them to send him out after a target of our choosing—nobody really believed our trusted allies would just hand him over—and we could sort of keep an eye on things. We would know who he was after. We would even set things up so that the touch would be made under controlled conditions. Some nice little country like Greece or Portugal, where they were already paranoid about the Red Menace and we own the local intelligence service.

"We arranged a trade. I don't remember the details, but we were going to give them something we thought perhaps might amuse them, some new circuit design or something, and they were going to let us use their new secret weapon, this human meat grinder of theirs that had every spook in Europe crapping in his drawers.

"Everything was all set, and then Down says he won't allow his man off the leash. It made a lot of second secretaries very mad, but apparently Down had enough clout with his own service to get away with it. Or maybe the British really never had it in mind to trade and were just using Down as a graceful reason for saying no. Who's to say? They have a peculiar sense of tact over there.

"Say, I'm getting kind of hungry." By way of emphasis, Tuttle put his hand over his stomach. The contact seemed to remind him that he wasn't wearing a shirt, so he got up out of his chair and fished one out of the suitcase on the bed. "There's a hamburger place about a block down on El Camino. It isn't too bad. You want to go there?"

Guinness smiled tensely and shook his head.

"Not unless you want me picked up. I imagine Creon is a little curious by now about just where I took off to. This is his town, you know."

Within a minute Tuttle had put on his jacket and was on his way, with orders for a double cheeseburger, fries, and a strawberry shake. And within a minute and a half Guinness was busy turning over Tuttle's motel room. That, of course, had been the whole idea.

From Tuttle's point of view it made perfect sense. He knew that if Guinness had wanted him dead, he would have left him in the john of that gas station with a pill in his brain, and he wouldn't be dumb enough to leave anything behind that he would really mind having found. Everyone in The Business was always patting down everyone else's motel room, and the practice had developed a decorum of its own. So long as you didn't break the furniture and remembered to put everything back, nobody really minded.

After riffling through the suitcase and discovering Tuttle's deplorable taste in pajamas, Guinness turned his attention to the briefcase that was lying on the desk. Considerate chap, Tuttle hadn't even locked it. Inside was a well-thumbed passport with visa stamps that suggested Central Europe, from Switzerland to Hungary, as his main theater of operations. There was also a hard-leather case containing a syringe and three little numbered tubes of colorless liquid—a drug kit; Guinness wondered which number would put you away for keeps—and, in the organizer clipped to the inside of the briefcase lid, a folder with a red "SECRET" stamp across its face and the words "SUMMER SOLDIER" typed in capitals on the file tab. It was his very own dossier—his professional biography, or as much of it as the Americans had been able to piece together.

Summer Soldier. Just the sort of priggish witticism you might expect from the boys in Planning and Analysis, chubby little nerds who liked to play god from behind a memo pad and wouldn't dream of risking their own necks.

Summer Soldier. A pattern observation or a moral

judgement? Probably both. Most of his work had been in the summer months, the flood tide of espionage all over Europe, when you could scoot in and out unnoticed on the annual tourist inundation. Hell, in the winter the security police might arrest you just to fill up their quotas. Besides, Down had always been as obliging on that score as he could. He tried to keep his hands off in the middle of the term, although once Guinness had nearly flunked a seminar on the Anglo-Saxon lyric because of a rush job in the middle of April. Somebody needed killing, and it couldn't wait.

But there was no getting around it: All those patriotic career boys in their short hair and their three-piece suits kind of looked down their noses at you when they knew you did it for money. One should only commit murder for the most high-minded reasons.

It was all such bullshit—they were all in it for the same thing. The only thing that mattered was the action. After the first time, money never really had had much of a role. More than anything, it provided an excuse, a motive that made some sense. You did the work and the work was your living through school, but it wasn't a matter of cause and effect. You did it because doing it filled some need that had nothing to do with the paying the bills.

And then one day the need wasn't there anymore—or it got in the way of something you needed even more—and you quit. You packed it up and paid the bills some other way.

The Summer Soldier. What a name. What a pile of horseshit.

The file contained a lot of loose papers, not many of which seemed to have much to say, and there was a list of names and dates and places, with references to other files, pasted to the inside front cover:

Collins, Eugene; 23/7/63; Berlin; see 465943-C
Genik, Vasili; 1/9/63; Prague; see 759247-G
Kleutgen, Georg; 30/6/64; Liège; see 557523-K
Shevliskin, Janik; 15/7/65; Belgrade; see 968434-S

There were twenty-eight names in all. Some of them he recognized, some of them not. They had missed a few—more than a few—of his early clients and there were some that must have been the handiwork of someone else.

The only other item of interest was a photocopied page of typescript—a translation, it seemed, from the KGB's Bluebook, the list they kept of all the standing orders for execution: "The person or persons, not yet identified, responsible for the deaths of the following Soviet citizens." And then there was a list of about seven names, all of which appeared again on the American list. The date at the top of the page was November 1969. A quick check of the other sheets in the file didn't turn up any later Bluebook extracts.

Guinness replaced the folder and closed the briefcase, wondering who else had made the connection between Byron Down's Number One mechanic and a certain associate professor of literature now living in California. Byron had always been so careful, so meticulous. He had never used Guinness's real name, not even in internal correspondence, never allowed him to be photographed or fingerprinted. There had never been anyone else present when Guinness had received his instructions.

When Byron died, there had been a prearranged exchange of announcements in the personal column of the *Times*, and Guinness got a new handler: a tall, reedy Scotsman with a sandy mustache. His name was McKendrick. He had been Down's second-in-command for eleven years and continued his methods. He and Guinness had never hit it off.

Down had worked out a detailed escape route should Guinness ever decide he had to disappear. It involved four changes of identity and a circuitous series of journeys by plane and train that ended with entry into the United States via Canada. It was a secret not even McKendrick had been in on.

"It's very good, of course," Byron had said once, holding a cigar to his ear to see if it had the right crackle. "But don't ever think you can stay in this branch of trade for as long as you have and then disappear without a trace." With the little silver knife he carried on his watch chain, he made a delicate slit in the blunt end of his Havana. He had always contended that the Americans were little short of barbarians for having allowed a trifle like Castro's communism to hypnotize them into cutting off trade relations with Cuba. "If someone with the proper connections wants to look hard enough, he'll find you." A puff or two and Byron had broken out into a smoky smile. "But there's no getting around it—it is a very good plan."

Yes, it had been a good plan; it had worked for seven years. But somebody with the proper connections had decided to find him. The KGB? Did the KGB want to look that hard? Had they finally found him? They never forgot, those guys. They might wait for decades, but they never forgot.

Guinness dropped the file back into its slot in the organizer of Tuttle's briefcase, and his lips compressed into a hard, joyless little smile. Well, if after all these years they suddenly wanted to start playing rough, that was just fine with him. All comers welcome.

IX

"VLASOV. MISHA FEDOROVICH VLASOV. You weren't far off, though; until about ten months ago he was a member in good standing, but I wouldn't be the least surprised if right now the KGB would like to kill him even more than they would you. Recognize the name?"

Guinness set down his little waxed paper bag of French fries, which looked and tasted as if they had been carved out of bamboo, and nodded.

Game time was over, he had decided. Tuttle wouldn't be any more dangerous for having confirmed what he knew already; the room didn't show any signs of having been bugged and nothing he might say here could legally be construed as a confession anyway, and, besides, it isn't a very hot idea needlessly to antagonize a potential ally.

"Sure, I know him. I also know you're just begging for a coronary if you keep on eating like that—chiliburgers and Scotch, for the love of God."

Tuttle cracked a grin and wiped his upper lip with the hand still holding a last fragment of chiliburger. "You're trying to tell me that that strawberry gook of yours is any better?"

"How do you know it's Vlasov?" Guinness asked, opening up his cheeseburger and peering inside like a Roman augur examining the entrails of some sacrificial animal. "It's possible, you know, that he might not be the only one who thinks he has a bone to pick with me."

Licking chili sauce from his fingers, Tuttle finished his dinner and stepped into the bathroom to wash up. "You mean because you're such a popular fella?" He laughed over the running water. "Anyway, for the time being you can just take my word for it. It's Vlasov, and he's very interested in seeing you dead."

Tuttle sat down again, snagging the bottle of Teacher's off the dresser on the way in and pouring himself another three fingers. He was just reaching that point of drunkenness at which every movement appears to be the product of separate acts of will. The creases in his face seemed damp and thoughtful, as if he were laboring to keep his mind orderly and his sentences consecutive.

"He wants you dead, old man. He means to kill you, and he's a clever bastard. I can't say I envy you much." He shook his head slowly and smiled, and Guinness decided he could do without the compassionate side of Tuttle's nature.

"So he wants me dead. So what? If it's strictly a private matter, why should the government bother about involving itself?"

"That's a long story," Tuttle said quietly, setting his glass back down on the table. Having apparently realized that Guinness was no longer drinking along with him, he had barely touched it. "It's a long story, so bear with me. I can't guarantee a happy ending.

"Vlasov began to make a name for himself in the middle sixties; at least that was when he first came to our attention. What he did before then or what his background might be is anybody's guess. Anyway, at about that time he started running a very tidy little shop out of Italy. He lived in Florence with his wife, pretending to be an Aeroflot agent, although his office wasn't open but for two hours every Tuesday. Regular banker's hours.

"And he held the strings, so the story goes, on a man

in every major British consulate in Europe. He was a real star.

"The story might even have been true, because it seems that in nineteen seventy somebody tried to do a job on him. The Russians put a lid on the whole affair, so our information is pretty sketchy, but we do know that his wife was killed and that he very nearly was. As a matter of fact, we did think that he was dead, since he had disappeared from Italy. At least we thought that for a while.

"Then a year or two later he turns up again working as a strategist for Department V. They seem to like his work—he gets promoted to lieutenant colonel in seventy-three and then to full in seventy-six. He's a very bright boy, a real comer. We hear that the great Andropov himself has taken a personal interest in his career. Then guess what happens."

Tuttle leaned back in his chair, resting his chin in the angle of his thumb and smiling like a Cheshire cat, and Guinness continued stirring with a straw the half-inch or so of lukewarm strawberry milkshake that was left at the bottom of his paper cup. He seemed to be hunting for something just underneath the surface.

"He defected," Guinness said at last, his tone precisely that of an adult forced to participate in some singularly uninteresting children's game.

It didn't sound like the Vlasov they both knew and loved, but he had, as a matter of fact, guessed right. He could tell from the half-surprised, half-disappointed expression on Tuttle's face. Well, Tuttle didn't need to look so astonished—he was the kind of storyteller who telegraphed his punchlines.

The rest of the story, except for an ending which hadn't been played out yet, was at least in general outline fairly obvious. All that needed filling in were the details.

"Well I'm sorry if I've been boring you." Tuttle seemed seriously annoyed, which was all right. This whole clubby little trip he was on—espionage for the discriminating connoisseur—was beginning to wear on Guinness's nerves.

"No, go ahead. One likes to hear the gossip about one's friends." Guinness smiled and dropped his fingers down over the mouth of his whiskey glass. He didn't drink, didn't even lift the glass from the table, but the gesture alone served to confirm his willingness to be an attentive listener, a good fellow who could dispassionately enjoy the finer points of the game.

It seemed to work. Tuttle leaned forward in his chair, virtually crouching as his elbows came to rest on his knees. The story began almost visibly to retake possession of him, as if Misha Vlasov's treason had worked some sorcery and thus made anything possible, had cast a magic pattern into which Tuttle felt himself irresistibly drawn.

"Anyway, that was when I met him. As a reward for being a good boy and kissing all the proper asses in Washington, I got posted to Zurich. I was supposed to have something to do with coordinating American and Swiss pharmaceutical research, but the cover couldn't have been any more transparent if I'd run it out of a Christian Science reading room.

"Have you ever done any work in Zurich? It's a great place if you feel like playing a little knuckle-tag with the opposition—so long as you don't make a scene or do a number on one of the locals, the police are more than happy not to notice. Hell, they don't want to get caught in any wringers.

"But you can go crazy there. You get so you wish somebody would wire your toothbrush or put a tarantula in your bedroom slippers, just so you'd have something to do. When there isn't a job on, the time seems to go mainly to padding out your behind. Even the women are ugly, most of them, and the ones who aren't act like cataleptics in the sack. You have to go all the way to Vienna to get a decent piece of ass.

"I was there, oh God, for years. That part of the world was a territory I had pretty much to myself, unless trade got very brisk. The breaking into file cabinets and stuff was left to the CIA, and I was only brought in on what you might call a consulting basis. If it was likely to get nasty enough, if it was a question of riding shotgun on something they really didn't want ripped off, or of getting blood all over somebody's shirt front, then the matter was turned over to me. Otherwise, they didn't even want to be reminded of my existence. You know what that's like.

"So then one day about ten months ago, somebody in the local office has a personal little chat with somebody from MI-6, all very high level and hush-hush. It seems that Comrade Vlasov has it in mind to do a deal and for reasons best known to himself has decided to give the British the honor of acting as his brokers."

"The British?" Guinness leaned forward in his chair, suddenly very interested. "Why the British? Why the hell didn't he simply contact you himself?" He didn't like the sound of it, not one little bit.

Tuttle turned the palms of his hands upward and shrugged.

"Haven't the faintest idea, pal. All we knew was that he wanted to defect—to us. About that he was very specific. And he wanted the full treatment. A new identity, asylum in the U.S., a colonel's pension, the works. To top it off, we'd only been given six hours to make our minds, and if we liked the idea we were to have a car with Norwegian plates waiting to pick him up outside of Jelmoli department store before closing time. I guess he was worried that his own people might catch on that he was getting ready to rat; you can't keep treason a secret very long.

"Well. It's not the sort of offer you get every day, and sure as hell not from a dude like Vlasov. The man had a reputation as a True Believer and as far as we could determine, then or later, there was no trouble at home. Hell, they'd just bumped him to full colonel a few months before.

"It was a problem. And to more than a few untrusting souls it smelled for all the world like a setup. We couldn't even phone D.C. for instructions because Vlasov had dropped word that our local communications man was one of his plants.

"He was, too.

"Finally we decided to go ahead and grab him. I got

called in in case things got bouncy and because Vlasov was the man who planned a lot of Moscow's thuggery for them and it was thought I might be helpful in the initial phase of interrogation.

"Also, although nobody came right out and said so, I think they wanted somebody around who would know how to drop the hammer on Comrade Misha if it turned out he wasn't being entirely candid with us.

"It was the middle of summer, which was nice because at least we wouldn't freeze to death—I'm from Maryland myself, and I never have gotten used to that high-altitude cold. Anyway, we stole a car with the right kind of plates and took up a position outside the main entrance of Jelmoli. We waited for two hours, and we were beginning to think he had stood us up when, just as the whole downtown started to jam up with the big closing-time mob of shoppers, Vlasov opens the back door of our car and climbs in.

" 'What are you waiting for?' he says, whispering as if he was afraid the KGB would hear him all the way to Moscow. 'Drive off.' Well, you can believe we got out of there. We almost sideswiped some pudgy little middle-aged broad who was trying to get across the street so she could catch her trolley. I looked back through the rear window to see if she'd actually fallen down, and I don't suppose I'll live long enough to forget the expression on her face."

Deciding that the closeness of the tiny motel room had managed to give him a headache, Guinness picked himself up out of his chair and went to the door for a breath of air.

"You sure you want to do that?"

With his hand still on the knob, Guinness turned to see Tuttle smiling wanly back at him from where he remained sitting. Without bothering to answer, Guinness jerked the door open, letting it swing wide around until the drag from the carpet brought it coasting gently to a stop. He leaned up against the frame, where he would be silhouetted against the light from behind.

It was a warm evening and the air outside was only a little cooler than the room, but at least there was a slight breeze. Across the El Camino, in a distance he knew was filled mostly with machine shops and factories that would have been closed for hours, he could see the lights from the cars out on the Bayshore Freeway.

If Vlasov was out there, and he probably was, he would have a clear shot if he chose to take it. But he wouldn't. A man doesn't turn his back on cause and country just to plug some clown leaning up against a door frame. No, there would have to be more to it than that.

Vlasov would want to say his piece before he pulled the trigger, and that would mean that they would have to come to terms. He would have to set it up so that Guinness would be willing to accept the risks. Otherwise it would be right back underground, and Vlasov didn't have the time to go digging for another seven years; not with the KGB breathing down his neck.

So there was no immediate worry. There was plenty of time. Vlasov's revenge was likely to be a leisurely business.

The night air didn't seem to help much, so Guinness went back inside, into the bathroom, and prepared himself a cold washcloth. It didn't make his headache go away, but at least his eyelids didn't feel like they were glued shut anymore.

"So Vlasov defects," he said, sitting down again and tasting his Scotch. It was pretty nasty at room temperature and he made a face—who could tell, though, it might make his brains stop throbbing. "So then, how did he get from there to putting an ice pick in my wife's ear?"

Did Tuttle flinch, just a little? Yes, by God, Guinness thought that perhaps he had. Maybe it was possible for some people to make their living as government assassins and still be squeamish about words, unlikely as it sounded. At any rate, it would seem so.

"So we got him out of the country," Tuttle resumed after swallowing about half the contents of his glass—apparently he had decided drinking was safe again. "We took him out of Switzerland in the trunk of a car, and then from Germany we used a military helicopter to fly him to Orly and put him on the first plane to the States.

"That part was the hardest. The French were as nervous as cats, which might have had something to do with the fact that we wouldn't tell them what we were coptering in. It gives you some idea of the importance assigned to Vlasov's defection that it was felt worth nettling our touchy Gallic brothers over.

"Vlasov and I had gotten on pretty well, so it was decided that I should stay on as his handler during the interrogation phase. If he was horny, I got him a broad—but he was never horny, that guy—if his teeth hurt, I got him a dentist. For two and a half months I was never out of earshot.

"In all that time he never left the apartment we rented for him, along with the ones on either side and directly below and above—we weren't about to give anyone a chance to get near enough to give him a cold. The interrogators were brought to him.

"You know, usually in a situation like that you get to know a person pretty well. I mean, hell, it figures. A guy who jumps the traces has got to feel that even his new 'protectors' think he's a creep. They're a chatty bunch, defectors, very eager to have you understand what sterling types they are, how they really didn't have any choice but to fink on their own people. Usually by the end of the first week they've told you everything, every sordid little detail of domestic history. God, one time I had one of them tell me how he used to like his mistress to whip him with a clothes hanger.

"Besides, cooped up together like that for weeks and weeks . . . it doesn't matter if you hate each other like poison. Eventually you start to talk, if it's only for the sake of a little noise.

"But not Vlasov, not him. No lurid confessions from that quarter. I've never spent so much time with a man and understood him less. I didn't have the impression he gave one fuck what anybody thought.

"One time, though, he came unstuck, just a little. Just enough to remind you that he was human.

"Vlasov didn't like television, couldn't stand the

sound of one on in the apartment, so we spent a lot of time in the evenings sitting around reading newspapers. It was one of his permanent grievances against us that we couldn't get him the Paris edition of the *Herald Tribune*.

"So there we were one night, reading away. And suddenly Vlasov folds up his paper and comes over and sits down next to me on the sofa. The next thing you know he's got his wallet out and he pulls something from the card holder and hands it over to me.

" 'Would you like to see a photograph of my late wife?' You can bet I was surprised; in nearly two months it was the first time he'd ever said or done anything to indicate he hadn't been born in a KGB uniform. It was funny, but I felt kind of honored.

"It was only a snapshot, of a blond woman in a summer dress sitting in a lawn chair. I guess I said something to the effect that she was pretty and handed it back to him. He put the photo back into his wallet and the wallet back into his inside coat pocket; and then he shook his head and smiled, his hand resting on the bulge in his coat. 'No, my friend,' he said finally. 'She was an angel.' He never mentioned her again; it was as if the whole thing had never happened.

"She didn't look much like an angel to me—just a pretty woman with short blonde hair, a little too delicate for my taste. I was surprised she was as young as she was, though; Vlasov is fifty-two, and in that picture his wife isn't a day over twenty-five. Maybe that was what made her an angel.

"Anyway, I finally figured out that Vlasov must have had his reasons for showing it to me. I doubt if it was just a spontaneous gesture—he wasn't the type. No, he had his reasons, and I'll bet you could make a pretty good guess as to what they were. Hey, Guinness?"

Tuttle laughed, rather brutally, and Guinness decided that the booze must be making him careless. Some men were like that.

"But most of the time, oh Jesus, you should have seen him, just as cool and out of reach as he could be. He would sit in the front room all during an interview—away from the window, even though the shades were drawn; he was a very careful man—slouched down with his head back in an enormous overstuffed chair, his elbows on the armrests and his knees crossed, holding a cigarette between thumb and first finger and looking for all the world like a character out of a Fitzgerald novel."

It was an odd description, and no doubt would have been deeply shocking to a man of Vlasov's earnest communism—certainly he wasn't the sort you would expect to see lounging around the bar of the Ritz—but it made a kind of sense. The man Guinness remembered had been small and slightly built, with a finely molded, rather ascetic face. A hard little mouth under a curved, well-defined nose, and rimless glasses. Longish hair, astonishingly black and pulled straight back as if to emphasize the width of his brow.

Vlasov looked like what he was: an intellectual and a man of fanatic integrity, someone for whom it would seem perfectly natural to risk everything for something or someone he had given his life to. In a way, perhaps he was a kind of socialist Gatsby, if that didn't amount to a contradiction in terms.

But then he had defected, so perhaps he had never been what Guinness had thought him. After all, they had never met face to face, and having tried to murder a man doesn't really establish much of an intimacy.

"He gave us almost more information than we could handle," Tuttle went on, "but as much of it as we were in a position to check turned out good as gold. So when we were finished with him we kept our part of the bargain and started building him a new life.

"He said he wanted to live in Oregon, which was okay with us. We got him a new passport and constructed him a past, complete with records, and arranged for him to purchase a small nursery supply store. He said he wanted to be around living things, that that was what he had missed most in his old line of work; isn't that droll? That was about seven months ago.

"For three or four months after that, we kept a loose

check on him, just to be on the safe side, but everything seemed to be going ginger peachy. He was living his new identity to the hilt. He'd even become a registered Republican.

"Then a month ago he disappeared, just disappeared without leaving a trace. We went over his shop and apartment like we were doing an inventory of the dust particles, but we didn't find anything to suggest where he had taken himself off to, let alone why. Nothing.

"Then four days ago I got a special delivery package—it was mailed care of a drop address in Baltimore that we didn't think even the CIA knew about. Inside was a letter from Vlasov: 'Tell Raymond Guinness that he is a dead man. But first, before the end, he must die as I have died.' That was all there was to it, except for your address and one page torn from the KGB Bluebook, listing what they had against you. Where the hell he had kept that hidden during all the time we had him, I'll never figure out.

"A quick check of your movements during the sixties was enough to convince us that Vlasov knew what he was talking about and that you were the dude on whom we'd kept an open file all those years.

"Suddenly everything made perfect sense. It had been you the British had sent to kill Vlasov in seventy. Only you had fucked up for once and killed his wife instead.

"All those years he had spent tracking you down, running to ground one lead after another until he came up with the right name—Raymond Guinness. His own private little research project within the archives of the KGB, and they probably never even guessed.

"Then, when he finds you, he defects so that we can practically deliver him to your doorstep. He throws away everything, all those years of faithful service to the Party and the Cause, just for the chance to turn your lights out. You should feel flattered."

Tuttle raised his eyebrows and smiled. He looked like one of Guinness's students, waiting to be patted on the head after his conclusive demonstration that Beowulf had to be a faggot.

"So when we figured out what was going on, I caught a plane out here. We kind of thought we might have interests in common."

"You said a package. Nobody send a package with just a letter in it. What else was there?" Guinness waited, but his question elicited nothing beyond a tense silence. "Come on, Tuttle—you know you're dying to tell me. You've been building toward it all evening. What else was there in the package?"

With the air of making a concession—remember, baby, you asked for it—Tuttle lifted one hand to about shoulder level and inhaled deeply through his nose. It was more than just a little theatrical, giving the impression that he regarded himself as taking a risk.

"The weapon he used on your wife."

"Show me."

Tuttle got up out of his chair and went to the chest of drawers. Taped to the back of the bottom drawer was a plastic bag, the kind you see advertised on television as having a "zip-lock top." Inside, with the tip stuck into a small cork, was an ice pick with about a three-inch point; the blond wood of its handle, as well as the inside of the bag, were melodramatically smeared with blood that had dried flaky and almost black. It was a color you read about a lot in Aeschylus.

Tuttle set the bag down on the table between them and sat down again. It was a horrible thing, the most horrible thing Guinness could ever remember having seen, and yet he couldn't take his eyes from it. In a way nothing else had, it made the issue between himself and Vlasov personal—no doubt that was what Vlasov had intended.

"There is a very clear set of prints in there," Tuttle said quietly. "Part of a thumb on the metal collar of the weapon itself and three fingers in the blood on the inside of the bag. There's no disputing it's from Vlasov."

"What do you want from me?" Even to himself, Guinness's voice sounded hollow and far away.

"What do you think we want?" Tuttle, it was clear, was embarrassed. "We want you to kill Vlasov for us.

He defected to us, and now he's defected from us—it makes us look bad.

"What are we supposed to do, launch a national manhunt? Put him on the FBI's Ten Most Wanted list? This is not a stupid man we're talking about, and that's what we'd have to do to get him back, alive or dead. Quite frankly, we can't afford the publicity, not the way the intelligence community is on everybody's shit list these days. And we don't want the Russians to get wind of it either; nobody in Washington much relishes the thought of them laughing up their sleeves at how we got suckered. We can't go after him and we can't afford to leave him running around loose either.

"So you see, you're the only answer. He'll come to you. He wants to kill you so bad, he can taste it, and that gives you the only chance there is of nailing him."

"And if he comes, and if I get him first, what then?"

"Then we want him to disappear." By way of emphasis, Tuttle noiselessly snapped his fingers. "We want him dropped down a hole, a very deep hole, so that neither the Russians nor anybody else will ever be sure what happened to him, so that for all the Kremlin knows he could be happily climbing up the corporate ladder at IT&T. We'll even provide the hole if you'll just take care of him in some nice anonymous way.

"And if you do that for us, then we'll get the police off your ass. They will be told, quietly but firmly, that their suspicions are groundless, that the real killer is dead, that you are just the nicest, most nonviolent person who ever drew a breath, and that their government would much appreciate their simply dropping the whole matter. We'll even show them the ice pick and the fingerprints we took from it, although they won't be told whose they are. And you will be one hundred percent clear of all this."

Guinness smiled weakly; he had the distinct sense that his viscera were gradually hardening into ice. "And after that you'll own me, is that about right?" Tuttle smiled back, nodding.

"We might want you to do a job for us from time to time. Men of your caliber are hard to find."

Rising from his chair, Guinness thought about his own hotel room with a certain nostalgia. He wanted to be there right now; he wanted to be alone. He wanted to get himself his own bottle of firewater and to drink himself into a coma. He wanted to get away from Vlasov and Tuttle and the whole show—but of course that was impossible. You never get away. He had tried to once already this lifetime, and it hadn't worked out.

"By the way," Tuttle said suddenly, as if some vital final point had almost slipped past him, "how much did the British pay you? How much did you command a job?"

Guinness turned around from the door, slowly. "Two thousand pounds."

"What does that work out to in dollars?" Tuttle asked, smiling contemptuously. "About five grand? You'd be worth at least seven-five, maybe even ten, to us. Tell you what, you take care of Vlasov for us, and on top of that little assist with your legal problems we'll throw in ten grand, just as a gesture of good will. If you prefer, look at it as a retainer."

Guinness didn't smile back. Instead, his eyes rested on the small plastic bag on the motel room table.

"Keep your money, Tuttle. This one's on the house."

X

THE ROOM WAS pitch black and Guinness lay on his stomach in bed, trying to figure out why he was awake. He had the impression he had been asleep only a second or two before. Certainly he must have been asleep; his eyes were still closed.

Opening one of them cautiously, he saw the illuminated dial of his portable alarm clock, which read seventeen minutes after three—presumably in the morning. Guinness hadn't been awake at 3:17 A.M. since the day he went straight.

Then the phone rang.

Yes, well of course; the goddamn phone. What else in the middle of the goddamn night? Whoever was calling had better be prepared to announce that the hotel was on fire. He clawed the receiver off its hook and dragged it under the covers with him.

"Yeah?" The word came out as a kind of sleepy gasp, like something he had swallowed and that hadn't quite settled into place right. "What's the trouble?"

"Oh, not much." It was Ernie Tuttle, naturally. Cheery enough to set your teeth on edge. "Your pal Creon plans to bust you sometime this morning. A little bird told me he think's he's got enough to pull you down for Murder One."

Guinness was wide awake, now, and his feet swung

out over the edge of the bed and began feeling after his slippers.

"How much of a head start have I got?"

Tuttle laughed. "Look, you'll just have to ask him. His own people didn't know this was coming down until five minutes ago. I shouldn't think you've got too long, though—you'd better go get yourself lost." As he listened to the silent phone line, Guinness began absentmindedly working loose the three buttons of his pajama top. His memory was walking over every foot of the hotel. The elevators, the stairwells, the exits, all the hiding places, all the ways in and no ways out. He had known that finally it might come down to this, and he had made certain tentative plans.

"Guinness? You still there, man?"

"Sure."

"Well, listen. On your way to wherever you're headed, stop by the message desk at the Bayside Hotel on Mission Street in the city. The man there will give you an envelope containing a key to a locker at the Greyhound bus station—You see? We'll play it in reverse this time. Inside the locker will be a TWA flight bag with a few little items you may find useful.

"You know, of course, that this is going to force Vlasov's hand. He'll have to go for you pretty soon, or the police are going to be putting you out of his reach."

"Yeah, I know. Tuttle?"

"Yeah, what?"

"Just to satisfy my morbid curiosity, who've you got a handle on in Creon's office?" For a few seconds, perhaps as many as five, you could almost hear the wheels go round.

"A kid named Peterson," Tuttle said at last. "He's ambitious and he doesn't like his boss much. He wants to break this one all by himself, and I'm afraid I led him to believe I could help him do that. Why, you know him?"

Without answering, Guinness set the receiver back on its cradle.

He sat in the dark for a moment, wondering if perhaps he shouldn't simply go back to bed. He could just go back to sleep and not wake up until Creon tickled his ear with the business end of a .38 police special. Why the hell not? To go scampering off into the night would only put him out where Comrade Vlasov could take potshots at him.

But so what? Being in the can would simply delay matters. Vlasov would come for him if he had to burrow into the death house with a pair of chopsticks. Some things you just don't get to run away from.

So. How do we get out of this dump?

Not right away, though. There has to be a limit to just how spooked you can allow yourself to get. Especially by a meatball like Creon. No, you take your time. First a shave and shower; then you get dressed and split. No snickering down the fire escape in your jamjams.

Out in the hall there was, of course, a man standing next to the elevator. There would have to be; Creon would not relax his guard just because it was outside of normal working hours. He was dumb, but he wasn't that dumb.

Guinness had never seen this one before, but, just like all the others, he had "cop" written right across his nose. Probably a hotel dick—his shoes were too shiny to have seen much street use, and his hair was all slicked back like patent leather. And he had that respectful constable-on-patrol look that makes all the rich widows feel so secure.

He was a cop though, even if he did comb his hair. He had that cop way of standing, with his feet wide apart and his knees locked and his hands clasped behind his back. And he never looked at Guinness.

Hell, at three forty-five in the morning anybody would look to see who was getting on the elevator with him. Cops are always too damn blasé to be real.

Why was it, in God's name, that every cop he saw lately was all tricked out in a checkered sport coat?

Well anyway, they were on the eighth floor. Plenty of time.

The elevator door opened and Guinness stepped inside, positioning himself directly in front of the control buttons. The other man followed, coming to stand behind him.

"First floor?" Guinness asked, turning around and smiling. The other man only nodded. Guinness touched the button marked "lobby" and folded his arms across his chest, dropping his chin the way a man does while he waits for the elevator to begin moving down.

Just as the little green *4* lit up on the indicator panel over the sliding double doors, Guinness touched the button for the fourth floor and shuffled around a quarter turn, as though making room in that tiny space for the man behind him to get past.

"Your stop, I think," he said quietly as the doors began to spring apart.

In the next instant, before there could be any possible reply, he raised his knee as if to step over something and brought it down again, scraping the outside edge of his shoe along the man's shinbone and driving his heel into the top of the instep, with perfectly predictable results.

Soundless except for a sharp gasp, the man went down on one knee, wrapping his arms around his injured leg as he fell. Using his fist like a hammer, Guinness clipped him on the back of the neck and he slipped unconscious to the elevator floor, his head and shoulders out over the threshold.

He was a big slob and it took several seconds to drag him out into the fourth-floor corridor, where Guinness rolled him over on his back and patted him down, finding a snub-nose .38 revolver in a holster clipped to his belt over the right hip. In his jacket pocket was a small leather folder containing a badge and an Oakland Police Department identity card for Sergeant-of-Detectives Herbert L. Ganjeme; the word "Retired" was stamped in red across its face. Guinness returned the folder to its place but decided to keep the .38. It might come in handy sometime during the next several hours.

So, what does one do with unconscious former sergeants-of-detectives? It would be agreeable to have a little lead time before anyone turned in an alarm—so where could our friend Herb be stashed where he would stay out of mischief for, say, twenty minutes? Killing the poor bastard would accomplish that, but under the circumstances it seemed a trifle extreme.

There was a linen closet down the hall that looked like it would open up at a few hard words, so Guinness set about picking the lock. Inside was a big rolling hamper about a third full of dirty bed sheets—a nice padded environment into which to drop an unwanted house dick if he were suitably trussed up and gagged. Behind the relocked closet door he could kick and bellow indefinitely before anybody heard him. He might very well stay put until the chambermaids came back on duty at eight the next morning, over four hours from now. Yes, that would do nicely.

With Herbert taken care of, Guinness got back on the elevator and rode down to the lobby. The night clerk was not behind his desk—he rarely was past about 2:00 A.M.—so there was no one present to notice him leave.

At that hour the parking complex was also deserted, making it perfectly safe to hot-wire a car.

Under the circumstances, he didn't much feel like taking his own; after all, if Tuttle had his little sources of information, why shouldn't Vlasov? There probably wasn't much he didn't know—or anticipate—and he might just have gotten the idea to rig the ignition again, only this time with something a trifle more interesting than a gram or two of nitrogen triiodide.

After trying the doors of several cars, he finally found a Mazda that had carelessly been left unlocked, and he was on his way.

If you want to know what the end of the world will look like, take a drive at 4:00 A.M. through the business district of any small American township.

In Europe you were used to mummified cities, scooped out of the ashes of some antique disaster and lovingly preserved. But they were simply old—purple flowers grew between the stones of the Temple of Vesta, suggesting the continuity of life. And a hundred yards away, their hair covered by silk scarves, the laughing girls rode bicycles to mass.

And, of course, there had been the rubble left over from the war. Here and there in England, even as late as the first few years Guinness had lived abroad, where the money to rebuild was slow in coming; and all over Germany, protected from the *Wirtschaftswunder* lest their envious conquerors forget how they had been made to suffer, poor babies.

But this was different. Not a scar, or a memory—but annihilation. There wasn't a sign of life on any of the downtown streets. Not a neon sign, not even a parked car.

Could anything ever have lived here? Twice, three times a week, for five years he had driven up and down in front of these shop windows, had bought his clothes and had his hair cut, all right here. Could this have been the scene of his daily life?

No, impossible. That was someone else's life he was remembering—lived before the Armageddon was announced

Guinness turned off into the Alameda, into a residential area of small homes where here and there a forgotten hall light could be seen still casting an oblique orangeish flash, as if from the inner facets of some dark jewel, through an outside window.

In a few minutes he was back in his own neighborhood. Leaving the Mazda in a side street a couple of blocks away, he walked the rest of the distance.

Across the street from his house was a tiny white bungalow with an enormous picture window. The curtains were drawn now and the window was as gray and opaque as a sheet of slate, but the evening Louise had died he had seen the neighbor lady who lived there, whom after five years he still did not know even by name, peering out at all the excitement on his front lawn. He had seen her a number of times before, as she poked around among the flowers growing on either side of her door. She was a small withered creature of sixty-five or so, with glasses that could have been an inch and a half thick. She would always turn to watch you as you left, whoever you were, baring her upper teeth slightly as she tilted back her head for a better view.

That night she had been only a dim shape framed by the picture window, the only sign that she was alive being a flash from her glasses if she happened to move slightly. How long had she been there, he had wondered at the time. Hours, probably—from the arrival of the first fire truck. Just taking it all in, as a kind of alternative to the "Mike Douglas Show."

His own house looked pretty much the same as it had that last night. Of course, nobody had watered or cut the lawn in nearly two weeks and it was beginning to look like a wheat field. Someone had replaced the broken pane of glass in the dining room window with a piece of cardboard, but otherwise there was no evidence of the fire. There was still a padlock on the front door.

The back door didn't have a padlock, but the bolt, which didn't work off a key, had been thrown from inside. So Guinness got a hammer and screwdriver out of his tool shed and took the whole thing off its hinges. He did it carefully because it wouldn't do to wake up the neighbors and because the door's upper half was made of a latticework of little diamond-shaped panes of amber glass. He didn't want to break one; they were held in with woodwork rather than putty (another plot against the American homeowner), and breaking a pane would mean having to replace the whole god damned thing, and we couldn't have that. One new door in the lifetime of a rear entrance was enough.

"The kitchen'll be so much airier if we can let some more light in," Louise had said while they were making the rounds of the building supply places. "That old one is just awful, just two sheets of plywood on a little frame, and we can afford to replace it with anything we want if we can hang it ourselves." She had been cruelly disappointed when they couldn't find a pattern with more than one color in it, but the amber was better than nothing. In the late afternoon it would throw little patches of gold all over everything.

He leaned the door very carefully against the side of the house and went into the kitchen, which didn't seem to have been touched since the fire. The walls were blackened and smeared and the linoleum was discolored from water that had simply been left to dry on its own.

Huddled in front of the stove—an arabesque in thick lines of black grease pencil—was the rather schematic outline of a human form. It appeared as if Louise had been left lying on her right side, with her right leg drawn up and both arms thrown out in front of her.

Guinness stared down at the outline on the floor, trying to read it for some identification of what had happened there, but all he could perceive was the sound of his own breathing and of the blood pounding in his ears. He snicked off the light and passed on into the interior of the house.

On two of the steps leading up to the second story were thick-rimmed white circles of what felt like ground blackboard chalk, and in the center of each circle, like a bull's-eye, was a dark bloodstain. There was another, larger circle in the bedroom, and at its center was another stain, perhaps five inches wide. It had made the carpet matted and stiff and it still had that peculiar texture, at once brittle and oily, that dried blood loses only very slowly.

Guinness stepped into the bathroom and, without turning on the light, ran some water in the sink and began to wash his hands. He raised a double handful of cold water to his face, shook his fingers dry, and groped for the towel that always hung from a bar on the shower door. The towel smelled as musty as a length of shroud linen and almost made him gag.

It had been a mistake to come back here; he didn't need this. Dammit, he didn't want to feel anything. Hadn't he tried, all along, from the beginning, to look at it with cold eyes, the way he had looked at everything in the old days when he had been the best there was? Better to think of it as if it had been someone else's wife who had ended up a sketch in grease pencil on the kitchen floor; better to have left the whole thing in the abstract, where he could have puzzled it out like a problem in the calculus. Feelings would only get in the way.

But perhaps that was what Vlasov was counting on.

Guinness finished drying his face and went back into

the bedroom. After drawing down the shades of both windows, he turned on the night stand lamp.

The chair in front of Louise's vanity had been knocked over, but there were no other signs of a struggle. Vlasov must have caught her completely by surprise.

There was a flashlight in the drawer of the night stand; Guinness took it out, stuffing it in his back pocket, and turned off the lamp. He hadn't dared to leave any light on for more than a few seconds, just enough time to notice whether anything had been disturbed, but the darkness created no hinderance to his easy movement from room to room.

Perhaps it was a hangover from college, but he usually couldn't sleep more than five or six hours a night. So he had often stayed up to read long after Louise went to bed. It was impossible for her even to close her eyes if there was a light on outside her door and thus, as a matter of domestic necessity, he had gotten so he could move around the house blindfolded.

Sometimes he would close his book and simply listen to the quiet that was almost a presence, almost a personal possession. He liked it, the feeling of stealth and privacy, of having the world to himself. Every tiny sound was assignable—the crack of a ceiling beam as it adjusted to the change in temperature, the neighbor's cat in a faraway transport of sexual passion, the wind in the telephone wires.

The kitchen was on the other side of the house from his study, but in his stocking feet, and being careful not to step where he would make a floorboard creak, he could make it there and back as noiseless as a ghost. It was a kind of game—Louise didn't approve of late-night snacks. He had even perfected a technique for unscrewing the lid from a jar of peanut butter in absolute silence.

Not that it had made any difference. You could have fired a gun in the front room without waking Louise.

She was always asleep when he came to bed, so he would undress in the dark and come under the covers as quietly as he possibly could, and, without waking, she would always roll over toward him, putting her arm across his chest and burying her head in his shoulder. Sometimes her hand would creep up until the tips of her fingers rested against his lips; he would kiss them and her hand would settle back down on his chest and she wouldn't stir again. He would go to sleep finally, aware of nothing except the slow breath of her nostrils on his arm.

Now, in the darkness, he sat on the edge of the bed, trying to conjure up some physical sense of her. But the house, and their bed, had been empty a long time, and the room was like one of those rooms you see in museums—something from the past, roped off and containing nothing except the furniture. It was a lonely place now. One had the sense that no one would ever live here again.

Well, he hadn't come back to stroll down memory lane. He had come to find what the police had missed, what they wouldn't have recognized as being important even if they had seen it. It was his house, and he would be the only one to know what had a place there and what hadn't.

And Vlasov would leave something. He wouldn't have gone to all the trouble of so ostentatiously murdering Louise, of issuing his formal challenge, without giving instructions as to time and place, or at least as to place.

He didn't want simply to murder Guinness; God knows he had had plenty of chances to do that. No, he wanted a duel. Two gentlemen on the field of honor, or as close to that as a couple of middle-aged hatchet men could come.

Such had been the message of the nitrogen triiodide in his ignition slot: You see, I could kill you anytime I like, but that isn't what I'm after. One of us will live and the other will die, but it should have some meaning. More, at least, than we have customarily attached to such matters. Each of us will hunt the other, and this time the reasons will be personal. For once, let us concede to our homicides something of moral significance.

Only, of course, there wasn't much moral significance to putting an ice pick in a housewife's ear, just Raskolnikov and the moneylender all over again. But Vlasov was a Russian, one must remember. And apparently he was more than a little crazy.

Anyway, whatever it was—this inanimate second, this bearer of the white glove—it had to be around somewhere, and probably in plain view. Guinness started poking around the bedroom with his flashlight, looking for something that hadn't been there on that Thursday two weeks before when he had finished his lunch, promised his wife that when he returned from work he would take a look at the washer hoses, and gone back to his office to grade his way through a set of sophomore term papers.

He tried to imagine the problem from Vlasov's angle of vision. If you wanted to leave something in a man's house, somewhere where he would notice it and the police wouldn't, where would you put it? At the scene of the murder? No. Where you had left the body? No; the police would turn both places over and sift everything through fine wire. Even if they didn't notice it, whatever it was, they might lose it. And, besides, the bedroom wouldn't do in any case; the police were sure to have a field day going through the victim's private effects. Guinness's study was out for the same reason.

If you eliminated the dining area and the bathrooms, where anything unusual would stick out like a sore thumb, there wasn't much left beyond the living room.

In the first week after their return from Las Vegas, when they were looking around for a few nice things to replace some of the junk from their apartment, Mr. and Mrs. Guinness had happened onto a warehouse sale in a great barn of a place on Mission Street in San Francisco. Most of the stuff was terrible, right out of the Sears catalogue, but there was one thing.

It was an octagonal table, low to the floor and with a top made out of eight wedges of oak. The design, with eight carved legs and the slatwork running between them at the bottom, was very Spanish, and there was a rather striking pattern to the grains. The finish, of course, was in awful shape—otherwise they would never have been able to afford it—but with a little sanding and a little fresh stain and a lot of hand waxing it would look great in the living room.

In the center of the top was a circular hole, about twenty inches across, into which fit an immensely heavy wrought-iron pan with handles at either end. Tonight the pan contained two books of matches from a Chinese restaurant in Menlo Park, the program notice for a college guitar recital, and a picture postcard of a little blond-haired girl, about seven years old and in a blue dress, riding a carrousel. The postcard was the only thing Guinness couldn't remember ever having seen before.

He turned it over. Printed on the back, in the bottom left-hand corner, was the location. Griffith Park, Los Angeles, California.

Merry-go-rounds, for Christ's sake. Vlasov wanted them to tap it out on a god damned merry-go-round.

XI

So Jacob served seven years for Rachel, and they seemed to him but a few days because of the love he had for her.

What had Vlasov's wife's name been? Not Rachel, surely. Guinness turned back to the beginning of the file he was reading and ran his finger down the page of biographical data until he came to it—Raya Natalia. They had been married in a civil ceremony in Moscow on December 6, 1966. Vlasov would have been about forty.

Funny, Guinness had to think, it was very funny. He and Kathleen had tied the knot only five months before.

Seven years. Vlasov had been hunting him for seven years, and now they were ready for the showdown. Like a Western movie. Perhaps they'd climb on a couple of the horses at the Griffith Park merry-go-round and blaze away at each other until somebody got dizzy and dropped off.

No, it really wasn't the least little bit funny.

Guinness sat in the overstuffed chair in his study. His reading-and-sleeping chair, the only chair in the house in which he could be at his ease, with one leg thrown over the armrest, without Louise starting to scream bloody murder. His working notes on the Vlasov affair, pulled from the hole underneath his desk, were resting on his knee and he was reading them by flashlight. There wasn't much they could tell him that he didn't already know, but going through them again, like counting the beads of a rosary, set him free to think.

Nineteen seventy had been a lousy year all around. Kathleen lost a husband—or, more accurately, had walked out on one; both Vlasov and Guinness had lost their wives. And Raya Natalia had lost everything.

Kathleen. Well, it wasn't as if he hadn't been warned—not against Kathleen, of course, but against the whole idea.

"People in this profession simply do not marry," Byron had said, "not if they have any sense. When I'm feeling domestic, I go visit my sister's children in Cardiff."

Generally you couldn't get Byron above a stroll, but that day he had been just pounding along, his stick jabbing at the walkway stones as if he wanted to impale each of them in turn. And they were walking in London too, right out in the open, along the embankment of the Thames. Guinness had simply phoned him to let him know, and Byron had blown a gasket. They must talk at once, and the very devil with security.

"What the blazes do you think you're about, lad? If you're lonely, find yourself a nice, sympathetic little dark-eyed tart and take her to Bristol for a fortnight. For the love of God, what conceivable need have you for a wife?" Staring down in front of him, he rocked his head from side to side, too exasperated to listen to the answer, had there been one. "And I suppose you think you're in love with the lady."

"Yes," Guinness answered after a moment. It was odd how difficult the admission seemed, like confessing some shameful and diminishing secret. "Yes, of course I'm in love with her. Why would I take it into my head to marry her if I wasn't in love with her?"

Byron snapped around, throwing his stick angrily to the sidewalk. "Well, if you love her so bloody much, get rid of her," he shouted, red-faced and panting. "Send her packing back off to Seattle, dammit."

For a second or two Guinness wondered if the old boy might not be teetering on the edge of a stroke; Byron was given to fits of temper when people crossed him, but this was the hottest on record. Then, as suddenly as it had come, his anger seemed to flow out of him and his hands loosened and unclenched. He leaned over heavily and retrieved his stick, smoothing down the lapels of his overcoat as he straightened up. In one of those moments of self-collection with which he so frequently prefaced his little asides on life, he stared pensively down at the stick's silver handle, as if inspecting it for damage.

"Give her up, Ray," he said at last, his voice gentle almost to the point of pleading. "Do the poor girl a kindness and send her home."

But, of course, Guinness hadn't done that. Not him—no, he had been too smart for that. He could handle it, he could handle anything; wasn't he the smartest, the toughest, the most dangerous, most feared Lord High Executioner in Europe? Wasn't he just a holy terror? Wasn't he, though. No, he didn't intend to give up anything.

Instead, like a man who hopes to juggle both wife and mistress, he concocted a story to account for all those sudden trips to the Continent he was always taking. One minute to the next and he had to go. That needed accounting for.

Because, unlike Louise, Kathleen had been the type to ask questions.

He stuck as close to the truth as he dared, telling her that he was now and then employed by certain unnamed and unnameable, highly sensitive, bureaus within the Foreign Office, that he delivered messages of one kind or another to people whom those bureaus employed but could not contact directly without the most serious risks.

From the way he let it out, a little at a time, you might have thought he was imparting the gravest confidence instead of lying through his teeth, but what the hell. He didn't plan to stay in the assassination business forever, and when he got out the lies wouldn't matter anymore. God, what a fool he must have been to have thought he could pull it off.

And the worst was the Kathleen had believed him. But why shouldn't she, not being the type to imagine that her donnish schoolmaster of a husband could be anything worse than advertised?

Kathleen. After all these years she was still more of a sensation than a memory. A yearning that would still creep over him from time to time. Probably he had never known her very well.

All the way from the University of Washington she had come, with her B.A. in philosophy and her Phi Beta Kappa key and her Fulbright, to study Ordinary Language Philosophy at Cambridge. In the vague way one associates with semanticists and logicians, she was very bright.

She was also . . . Well, "beautiful" didn't seem to cover it, and "pretty" was well wide. But she was something, with her tall willowy frame and her dark-brown hair that ran all the way down to the small of her back in a thick, faintly waving mass. She was something fine.

The occasion of their first meeting had been a seminar on aesthetic theory that someone at London had put him on to, and that sounded arcane and richly pedantic enough to be almost irresistible. Lady Winifred Ireton, who had just finished what might turn out to be *the* book on Tolstoy, would conduct meetings once a week in her rooms at Girton College. Cambridge was quite a trip—over a hundred and ten miles, there and back—but the seminar was being touted as an event of sorts. So Guinness sent off his forms and paid his fees and enrolled.

Lady Winifred's parlor turned out to be small, dark, book-lined, and, perhaps because most of the furniture had been moved out to make room for several dozen collapsible wooden chairs, oppressive. Also, in spite of the fact that it was the beginning of the summer, the gas heater in the fireplace was turned all the way up, making the room as airless as a crypt.

Precisely on time, Lady Winifred, a mannish, middle-aged woman who chopped off her hair above her collar and wore a charcoal-gray suit with a lace hanky pinned to the breast pocket, took her place at the front of the room, in the only comfortable chair, and began working her way through *What Is Art?* Apparently the meetings were to be based on the premise that she was the only one there who had mastered the knack of reading.

While Guinness was sitting on one of the wooden chairs, thinking about how much his tail ached and if there wasn't some decent way he could slip off, he noticed this girl sitting just to one side of the fireplace. Apparently deliberately—there were a few unfilled seats—she had chosen the floor, and a spot to which the Turkish carpet didn't reach. Her hands were in her lap, resting on a book with a green cover, and she seemed never to move, or even to breathe, during the whole three hours.

Finally it ended. Outside, on the front walkway, Guinness tried to recall the times of the evening trains back to London. The trip took about an hour and a half, but at ten o'clock on a Friday night it didn't seem to matter much; there wouldn't be a thing in the world to get him out of bed the next morning.

Up and down the row of little grayish brick houses that made you think of Dickens, the doors were shut and bolted and the windows dark. The world where people lived and slept had closed itself off, leaving a street as desolate as a stretch of sand in the Gobi Desert. Guinness had been in Cambridge only twice before, and never for more than a few hours. He didn't even know where to go at that hour for a beer.

He struck a kitchen match on the sole of his shoe and lit a cigarette—he still smoked in those days; Louise hadn't talked him into giving them up. As he finished the operation, he noticed that the girl from the seminar had appeared beside him and was taking a pack from a pocket hidden somewhere in the pattern of her long peasant skirt. Guinness held out the match for her, cupping it between his hands, and she steadied it with her own. He noticed the almost transparent whiteness of her fingers, as long and tapering as you could wish.

"Did you enjoy that?" he asked quietly, shaking the match out and pitching it into the street.

Her eyes smiled a warm, enigmatic smile and she shook her head. It was as if they had known each other so long and so intimately that she wondered why he would need to ask.

"Then let's go get something to eat," Guinness ventured, raising his eyebrows. Her answer was to smile again, perhaps only at the non sequitur, but a wonderful smile that managed to say yes without implying maybe. "Well, this isn't my town; you'll have to show me where."

Then, without a word, she slipped her arm through his and they began walking away between the pools of light from the street lamps. It promised to be an interesting evening.

And it was. In her tiny Spartan flat they supped on bean salad and rose hip tea, which Guinness had never tasted before. He didn't get back to London until Monday morning, just in time to miss his first class.

For the month that followed he spent every minute he decently could in Cambridge, and by month's end he had decided. If he didn't marry Kathleen, then he couldn't imagine whom he ever would marry. If she would have him he wanted to marry her, and she would have him.

Of course, it never occurred to him that the collision between his marriage and what he did for a living—not the school teaching, for which she rather admired him, but what he really did—was inevitable. It never occurred to him that he would have to choose, and that by deliberately not choosing he was preparing a disaster.

But how much of that was Kathleen? Now and then, in the years following that disaster, he would wonder how much his hideous error had been simply his misunderstanding of who she really was. Perhaps he had never known her at all.

"These people," she had asked, after patiently listening to his lies about what he did on those trips to the Continent he would sometimes suddenly have to take, "are they spies?" Her tone was one of simple surprise, not the outrage and shock he had half expected.

"Yes, I suppose so; I don't ask." As he sipped his tea he watched her for a reaction, but there didn't seem to be one. She simply continued to sit in the precise center of his living room carpet, her feet drawn up under her and completely hidden in the folds of her dress and her hands lying open and palms up in her lap. Finally, she looked up from them and fixed a perplexed gaze on him.

"There really are spies?"

"Yes, of course. The British are very big on that kind of thing; except for maybe the Israelis, they have the best espionage network in the world."

She nodded—slowly, as if not quite sure whether she understood or not—and then asked if there was any danger in what he was doing. He told her no and then she allowed him to change the subject. They never discussed it again.

But how could he have possibly expected her to deal even with his lie? The British didn't have spies, not her British. Her British were Gertrude Anscombe and the Cambridge Platonists and the guards at the National Gallery. Everything he had told her was simply unreal.

Sometimes he wondered whether anything was real to her except making love and the subtleties of the *Tractatus*. In their purest forms, the life of the body and the life of the mind—that was it. Perhaps she accepted Guinness's confession simply because she didn't know what he was talking about, any more than if he had been speaking in Mandarin. Apparently, it posed no palpable threat, so she simply dismissed it. It was like explaining something to a child.

Only Guinness really didn't want her to understand. It would be easier as it was.

So they set up housekeeping. They took an apartment together in London, whither Guinness had persuaded Kathleen to transfer, and furnished it out in a compromise between his love of creature comforts and her indifference to them, as domestic as you could wish.

And in time Kathleen arrived at her fruition. Big-bellied and pregnant, she began the process of turning them into a family, and as if in sympathy, Guinness began to hang a few extra pounds on his normally spare frame. It was a nice marriage, for both of them, and they were happy. More than once in the years after, it occurred to Guinness that had he been run over by a truck the day after his daughter was born, had no subsequent history been allowed to touch him, his life would have been an enviable thing.

But of course it didn't work that way. It's only in the movies that you get to ride off into the sunset; the real world doesn't allow things to be rounded off so nicely.

Byron had been right. Byron had always been right.

"You're not likely to get away with it forever, sport. It's all very nice, the pipe and the slippers and the little lady at home in the flowered apron, but it just will not square. You've been playing at cowboys and Indians too long."

Guinness noticed the tired pouches under his eyes, but then Byron had never been one for the Regular Life; probably he had a new lady friend who was keeping him up nights. A week later the old boy had his coronary.

In violation of every conceivable rule, Guinness went to the funeral. There weren't more than eight or nine people present, and very likely half of them were there taking notes for the Warsaw Pact nations. It wasn't much of a send-off.

And, of course, Guinness had finally been forced to concede, his own disasters were no one's doing but his own. Everything that had happened was simply the sum of decisions he had made for himself, a karma rather than a destiny.

So on we worked and waited for the light, and one sunny April afternoon Guinness found an envelope in the post office box he kept under a false name. It didn't carry a stamp, just an address: Mr. Raymond W. St. Mary, London NW9. Inside was a blank sheet of paper, folded into thirds.

He went back to the apartment and took down from

his bookshelf a little blue-and-white paperback street atlas of London. The code initial indicated Wanstead, and there was a St. Mary's Avenue only a block down from the underground; presumably it would have a number 9. The kitchen clock told him he would have to hustle if he was going to make it by three.

They had used his first name. They only did that when it was a rush call, so he left a note threaded through the strings of Kathleen's lute: "Duty calls. Expect me when you see me."

A routine matter, as it turned out. Just a Polish colonel of intelligence who had decided to sell his country's secrets in exchange for a life of grouse hunting in Scotland. It seemed his greatest ambition was to mix with the British country aristocracy. Everyone in MI-6, it was reported, found that highly diverting.

He was frightened, though, and wanted the very best protection in transit, or no deal. Guinness was supposed to meet him in a forest outside of Oslo, where he was stationed at the embassy, and to shepherd him home.

It was raining in Oslo, enormous soft drops that spattered on your windshield in slow motion. Hell, it was always raining in Oslo.

Guinness had rented a Volvo, as he had been instructed, and had driven into the boondocks. The car was parked by the side of a certain specified dirt road, with the right taillight left flashing, all according to prearrangement. Guinness wasn't inside, however; he wasn't prepared to be all that good a boy.

McKendrick had told him that he was supposed to wait in the passenger's seat, that that was part of the recognition signal, but this whole deal smelled just a little off. If it had been Byron giving the orders, Guinness would have followed them to the letter, but Byron was a year in his grave, and Guinness just didn't know about this guy McKendrick. Byron would never have told him to do anything as dumb as that. The whole business had the faint odor of a setup.

So Guinness was off wandering between the trees. He kept moving, weaving silently over the spongy, grass-choked earth. He wanted to see who would approach the car, and how. And it was just fine with him if maybe they didn't know right where he was at any given moment.

After about twenty minutes, another car pulled up behind the Volvo. A heavier car, perhaps a Mercedes—yes, a Mercedes. Guinness could just make out the hood ornament. Black, or maybe dark blue or something; it was impossible to tell in the bands of diagonal light that seemed here and there to lean unsteadily against the trees.

A man got out from behind the wheel and stood with his hands thrust into the pockets of a tan raincoat. He wasn't wearing a hat and his hair was thickly blond and cut a little on the longish side; he really didn't look old enough to have made colonel. Guinness was across the road from him and the cars were between them, but he could see that the man in the raincoat hadn't closed his car door and that the window on the other side, on Guinness's side, was rolled down. He wished the sonuvabitch would take his hands out of his pockets.

Guinness drew his revolver out of his belt, where it had been sawing his backbone in half. He liked big guns when he had a choice, and this one was a .357 with a seven-inch barrel and enough weight to absorb the shock so you could keep your pattern fairly tight on the target. It would punch a hole through the bodywork of a car and still make a terrible mess of anybody unlucky enough to be caught inside. He stepped to the edge of the road and pointed it at Raincoat, holding it steady with both hands. The two men were perhaps twenty-five feet apart.

"Just one chance. Bring your hands out where I can see them."

The man said something in a foreign language, Russian or Polish or something Slavic. He seemed to be asking a question, but one had the sense that it wasn't addressed solely to Guinness—perhaps it was the way his eyes twitched toward the Mercedes. And he hadn't taken his hands from his pockets, so Guinness shot him through he neck. His head seemed to come unmoored, pitching violently over to one side, and he dropped forward fast enough to make you think for a second that he was being jerked down from below.

Then the dude in the car rose up from where he must have been crouched down on the front seat, bringing something to his shoulder that looked like a stubby rifle. At the same instant Guinness turned slightly to face him and emptied his revolver into the door and open window. In the blur of noise he couldn't tell if the other man had gotten off a shot, not until the shooting had stopped and he tried to take a step forward and toppled over on his face.

One bullet, right through the thigh.

But it could have been worse. It had missed the bone and the major arteries: it would hurt like hell for a while, but he wasn't going to bleed to death. It could wait until he got back to London—it would have to wait.

Guinness picked himself up out of the muddy earth and checked the Mercedes. The man inside wasn't very pretty to look at.

He had fallen off the seat onto the floor and was lying on his side, his head twisted up at a grotesque angle and his eyes wide open. There were two dark bloodstains on his shirt front, and a third slug had entered through the right cheekbone. From the mess in the car, it must have taken a fair share of the back of his head with it when it exited; there was even a spatter of blood on the windshield.

The other man, with about half his neck gone and his left shoulder soaked in blood, wasn't very appetizing either. His hands were still thrust deep into his pockets, even as he lay dead on the ground. Sometimes they die like that, without so much as a twitch.

No, Guinness decided, his own wound would just have to wait until he got home. He wouldn't care to take a bullet hole to a local doctor, not when the police would probably be finding this within a few hours.

Raincoat, or what was left of him, was the less chewed-up of the two, so Guinness swallowed hard and set about patting him down. In his right coat pocket was a small lugerlike automatic, probably a 7 mm, and inside his jacket was the red passport carried by members of the KGB. The stupid bastard—he might have made it if he had just answered in English. London would never have sent someone on a job where the contact spoke no English, not without special instructions. London had said nothing, so Raincoat couldn't have been their precious Pole. If he had ever existed.

A setup. What the hell had they wanted, to take Guinness alive or to kill him? He didn't know any state secrets, except for a few the KGB probably knew even better, so why would they want to rip him off?

Jesus, were they that mad at him that they would organize a special hit, just for him?

Maybe they had been willing simply to settle for pot luck. Well, he wasn't ever likely to find out now.

His mind kept going back to the Hornbeck job, his maiden voyage. Maybe it was like that; maybe they *were* that mad at him, as mad as the British had been at Hornbeck. As ye sow, so shall ye reap. It didn't bear thinking on.

Byron would never have sent him off into a thing like this. No one could have suckered Byron this way, not even the KGB.

Guinness kept the automatic, replacing it in Raincoat's pocket with his own gun. The police could make whatever they wanted out of the mess they would find, but there would be nothing to tie him in. One had to remember that in the real world this sort of thing was technically considered murder.

He bound off his leg with his nectkie, just to keep it from leaking all over everything, and attempted to clean himself off a little. In a way the road mud all over him was a good disguise; he could change in his hotel room. The sooner he was on his way, the better.

There were no real problems getting away. The elevator operator in his hotel gave him a funny look, but Guinness just lurched around a little and smiled fatuously. "Fell down," he said, laughing, making it all a tipsy slur. The operator just cast his eyes down to the floor and frowned. That solved everything; people are never much surprised at a muddy drunk.

On the plane he thought a few times that he might pass out; but you almost never really do pass out, not just because your leg hurts.

He was back in his apartment by the early afternoon. For a while all he could think about, was lying down, that and how freely he was sweating. Eventually he got around to phoning a certain "safe" doctor, and within twenty minutes he was having the slug taken out of his leg.

"You'll be all right," the doctor said. He was somewhere in his middle fifties, fat and seedy looking; you wondered where Services picked them up. He dropped the slug in an ashtray and smiled. "Keep it as a souvenir and stay off your feet for a couple of days." Guinness was glad when he had gone.

The problem, of course, was with Kathleen. "What *happened* to you?" she screamed when she came into the bedroom and found him with his trousers off and his left thigh all taped up. "You look white as a sheet. What the hell is going *on?*" It was the first time Guinness could remember that she had ever raised her voice.

After a second or two, her eye caught the shiny little brass-jacketed slug in the ashtray and she picked it up. She looked at him with the same questions, unspoken but in her face. Unfortunately, he wasn't sure what kind of answers to give.

XII

WELL, IT WAS no good pretending anymore that he was just a lowly courier, not with a bullet hole in his thigh. Even in the spy business they didn't generally shoot you merely for delivering the mail. She would have to be told.

"It gets sort of bouncy out there sometimes," he said quietly. He had pulled himself up into a sitting position—it didn't seem quite fair to discuss the matter from the supine—and he was resting his back against the headboard. I've been relatively lucky, I suppose. This makes just the second time I've been clipped, and the other was nothing but a scratch."

Kathleen was sitting next to the bedroom door, in the room's solitary chair. It was a bare little wooden thing and uncomfortable to begin with, but the way she sat in it—perched on the edge with both feet planted on the ground and her knees pressed together—made it look like an instrument of torture. Her hands were folded in her lap, one over the other, and her elbows were tight against her body; she gave the impression of wanting to occupy as little space as possible, of holding her breath in an effort not to stir.

The mere fact that she was using a chair at all marked the solemnity of the occasion. Why couldn't she just come over and plop down next to him on the bed?

He wanted to touch her hair, to rest his hand in the crook of her arm and enjoy that reassurance of contact.

"Do you kill people?" Except for the slightest trace of a quaver in her voice, you could have thought she was asking if he liked her lipstick. She wouldn't look at him, though. Her eyes seemed to focus on the carpet under the window ledge. She wouldn't look at him and she wouldn't come near.

"Sometimes."

"I see." A long, ragged breath escaped her, like a soundless sigh, so maybe she had been holding it in. Perhaps his answer, for all the ugliness it implied, had even been something of a relief. Very slowly, as if to illustrate her tranquillity, she drew the tip of her middle finger across her right eyelid. "Did you this time?"

"Yes. As it happened, I didn't have much of a choice."

There was no immediate reaction, at least nothing to which you could attach a meaning. She merely continued to sit on the edge of the chair for a while, abstractedly stroking her left elbow, lost in some private consultation. She might have been trying to remember when next the laundry would be delivered, but Guinness didn't really think so.

Then suddenly she stood up.

"You'll probably want some tea," she said, as if to herself, and left the room, closing the door behind her.

Apparently she forgot about the tea, because she didn't come back into the bedroom all the rest of that day, not even when it was time for bed. At long intervals he could hear her step as she moved from one room to another, but she didn't come back.

And that was that. Kathleen, it appeared, didn't think too much of having an assassin for a husband. Guinness sat staring at his hands, wondering why in heaven's name he felt so disappointed. Had he perhaps expected her to be impressed? That would have been dumb; she wasn't precisely the bloodthirsty type.

He should have known, of course. Kathleen hated anything like that, hated even to hear about it. All that winter the British papers had been full of this Manson business in California—running background pieces on the victims, and heaven knows what. They hadn't had anything like it since the Christie case, and they seemed determined to milk it for all it was worth. One paper even printed a special number containing the lengthy confession of one of the women defendants.

Kathleen had read the news after dinner every evening for at least as long as he had known her; it was a ritual of sorts. But the Tate killings had been too much for her.

"I don't know why people bother with such tripe," she had said at the time, turning past page one and refolding the paper with a rich, angry crackle. Guinness, who was sitting at the other end of the sofa, looked up from behind a library copy of *The Allegory of Love* and smiled.

"They didn't just make it up, you known. It happened."

Kathleen uttered a contemptuous little sound and pushed her glasses back up off the fleshy part of her nose. "God, here it is again," she hissed after a few seconds. A few seconds more and the whole paper was dumped in a wad on the coffee table.

Finally she had canceled her subscription, so perhaps she did believe they were making it up. People had believed that the moon landing was a hoax.

Everything like that—butchered starlets, gang killings, foreign service officers who got pushed under trains, all that stuff only happened in bad movies, not in the world. How could he possibly have expected her to accept it when it was just dumped in her lap like that?

There wasn't much doubt about it, he would have to quit if he was going to hang on to her. That was clear enough; he would have to break with it entirely. There was nothing unreasonable in that part of her attitude.

And it was time, anyway. Your life expectancy wasn't very long when people were sufficiently annoyed with you to think of setting up so intricate an ambush as the one at Oslo.

But he could still get away clean. It was still okay; the KGB still didn't have a make on him—they couldn't even know his name yet, or what would have stopped them from ferrying someone over to London and having him taken care of there?

It happened. You would simply go to the movies some night to see Steve McQueen's latest and be found dead in your seat when the theater closed for the evening. The civilian authorities probably wouldn't even notice the tiny needle mark at the base of your skull, just at the hairline. It happened all the time—nothing easier.

But they hadn't sent anyone to deal with him at home, where he would have been off his guard. Instead, they had launched a whole operation, complex and tricky, to flush him out into the open. And it hadn't worked.

So he still had his anonymity; he could still simply slip back into the mob and be lost from view. It wasn't as if he had dumped anybody really important to them, and the KGB had their cost accountants too. They wouldn't want him badly enough to start a manhunt that might very easily last for years.

He would just drop out of sight, and they would lose interest fast enough. What doesn't itch doesn't get scratched.

Still, it would be better if he could take Kathleen and the baby away from England. A nice circuitous route with a few changes of papers, and then home, just like Byron had mapped it out. They would all be safer back in the States. No one would ever find them there.

Guinness covered his face with his hands, trying to make his mind a blank. Such speculations weren't really very entertaining, and his leg was beginning to feel like it was on fire. It was getting dark in the bedroom, dark enough to leave visible only the outlines of things, but that didn't make it much past the middle of the afternoon. The room's only window faced into a tiny interior court, and they were only on the second floor—you had to stick your head out and twist almost the whole way around to see the sky.

He took one of the morphine tablets the doctor had left him and wished to hell Kathleen would come back, if only just that he could look at her. He wished a lot of things. He wished he had accepted the gracious offer of the American government that time when he was broke and had allowed himself to be shipped home. He wished he had never heard of MI-6 or the KGB or the CIA or any of the rest of the hoodoos under cover of which otherwise perfectly sensible people went around making precisely calibrated little holes in other people's skulls.

Serving the cause.

Of course he had never been that stupid. He had never been guilty of that particular piece of folly, not him. No, he had done it for the money. Just the bread, sweetheart, and none of your bullshit about duty and the old school tie. Not for Ray Baby. Not for him.

As he lay there on the bed, contemplating his lack of illusions and the moral sophistication it suggested, he had to blink hard several times to keep back the tears. He had been so fucking smart, as if any of that made any difference now.

He was getting hungry, that was all. Visceral spasms converting themselves into agonies of the spirit. In truth, he hadn't had a goddamn thing since yesterday afternoon, since before the fireworks had started, and it was a rule in life that one's personal arrangements always looked particularly bleak on an empty stomach. Nothing like a good meal to keep off the Dark Night of the Soul.

That sounded like something Byron might have said. Poor old Byron. Yes, he probably had.

Kathleen did finally come back in the morning. Of course, he couldn't swear she hadn't been in the room before then; after the morphine had taken hold, Guinness had slept straight on through. But he awoke still lying on the bedspread, and her side didn't look as if it had been disturbed.

She came only perhaps a foot over the threshold, and her hand never left the doorknob. Nothing could have been more tentative than the expression on her face.

"Do you think you'd like some breakfast?"

Guinness slapped the flat of his hand against his belly

and grinned. "I suppose I might be able to choke down a mouthful, yeah." God, that sounded corny.

Glancing down at her shoes for a second, Kathleen's only response seemed one of embarrassment. She looked drawn, as if the last several hours had worked on her like a vampire.

"I'll bring you in a tray then," she said and stepped back out of the room, closing the door behind her again.

Breakfast, when it came, consisted of two slices of lightly buttered toast, a poached egg, a small glass of orange juice, and a cup of clear tea. He wondered if perhaps Kathleen didn't think that bullet holes were like the flu.

She might have from the way she went around to the other side of the bed to set the tray down, where it would be within reach but she wouldn't. Her retreat was a curious mingling of graciousness and panic, in which, once again, she didn't speak before her hand closed over the safety of the bedroom doorknob.

"I'm going out for a while. Will you be all right?"

Again Guinness tried out his best boyish grin and again Kathleen only dropped her eyes, the way people do when they don't want to commit themselves. "Sure. And don't worry; I can hobble into the nursery if I hear Rocky fussing." There was a nervous little pause during which her hand stole off the doorknob to close over the fingers of the other hand.

"Not to bother," she answered at last, smiling tensely. "I'm taking her with me. She can use the airing."

Her voice was just a little too smooth, just a shade too reassuring. What was she afraid of, that he would carve their infant daughter into stew meat in her absence? God damn her, it was his kid too; she didn't have the right. He ought to do something, to put a stop to all this shit and reclaim his family. Once and for all.

Instead, he returned her smile, hoping his own was more convincing than hers, and nodded.

"Okay. Have a nice time."

The door closed again, and after a few minutes he

could hear Kathleen leaving. She didn't come back until late in the afternoon.

That night she slept with him, or at least in the same bed. But she stayed with her back to him, as far over on her side as she could. Once he reached for her under the covers, resting his hand on her arm; she didn't draw away, but there was no response and she was perfectly rigid, as if catatonic.

Of course, there could be no thought of an embrace.

The next morning Guinness got out of bed and started to walk the kinks out of his leg. After that, the normal pattern of their comings and goings resumed, but life together continued as a kind of charade. They almost never spoke, and they began taking elaborate care to stay out of each other's way. Like a couple of bitter enemies condemned for some reason to share the same rooms and conscious of the futility of quarreling about it.

What to do, what to do? If only they could have stopped being so maddeningly civilized about it; if only for a moment or two, things might have worked out differently. A good shouting, screaming, knockdown, drag-out battle and they might have been all right again. A little infuriated table pounding, some high-pitched raging, a few tears, and they would have made the baby cry and perhaps reminded themselves that they were human beings and not abstractions of good and evil.

But it hadn't happened that way. Guinness could perceive easily enough that his wife was under growing inner tension, that they couldn't possibly go on this way, but what to do?

"I've quit, you know," he said over one of their silent dinners. "I'm not going to do that kind of work anymore."

She just looked at him with large frightened eyes, as if his announcement had done nothing but remind her that her husband, the man with whom she had lived for three years and whose child she had borne, was covered in blood. Then, without a word, she put down her fork and left the room.

He hadn't yet told her that it would be necessary for them to leave England. It didn't seem wise to impress her with the possibility that he might have tracked some of his dirt into their marriage. Of course, she was a smart woman; it might already have occurred to her. You could never tell with her—at least Guinness couldn't, not anymore.

And then one day she was gone.

He had come back to the apartment after having been out for the morning and had found a note printed in dark-blue Flair pen on a piece of binder paper. It was pinned with a thumbtack to the bedroom door:

"I'm sorry. I just can't live with you any longer. It would be better if you didn't try to find us."

"Us." She had taken his kid.

A kind of madness overtook him at the idea, and he ran into the nursery, in his haste nearly wrecking the little latticework barrier they had put in the doorway against the time she would be old enough to start crawling. He tore the drawers out of the baby's tiny dresser and, as he discovered them to be empty, threw them down on the floor.

In their own room, not much was gone—only perhaps as many of Kathleen's things as would fit into one hastily packed suitcase. But her lute was missing; he couldn't find it anywhere.

So it was true. Kathleen had left him, and she had taken the baby.

Should he find them? He could do that; it was part of his work to find people, and he was good at his work. He could track her down if she went to hide in the jungles of the Amazon. He could hunt her and find her and make her come back.

No, he couldn't do that. He couldn't make her come back. He could find her; that would be easy. He could even kill her if he wanted to, but he couldn't make her love him again. She was lost to him, she and the child both. It was over.

When that simple fact had sunk in, he sat down on the bed, buried his face in his hands, and wept like a child.

The days following his wife's disappearance saw established a pattern of full retreat. Guinness packed his blue-and-white canvas suitcase and moved out of the apartment, locking the front door behind him. A week later he was strolling purposelessly along an embankment near the Tate Gallery and discovered the key in his pocket. He stared at it for a few seconds, almost as if he didn't recognize what it was, and then threw it as far out into the Thames as he could.

He had by then rented a room—the attic of a semidetached house in Holborn, not more than a ten minutes' walk from the British Museum. It was a dreary little hole, made even smaller by the fact that the ceiling slanted until on one side of the room it was only about four feet above the floor; and it had only one small window, not much larger than a man's handkerchief.

But none of that mattered. Guinness was never there except to sleep. The rest of the time was generally spent at the museum, where he daily inspected the Elgin marbles and the Egyptian mummies and the Viking jewelry from the grave-ship at Sutton Hoo. It was all totally familiar, of course. He had seen it all so many times before that now he hardly noticed it. The images registered on his optic nerve and he would pass on to something else, but still it had the effect of keeping him minimally distracted. Nothing more was either expected or desired.

When he was tired of the museum, he would find something else. For 3/6 he purchased a paperback book that described "250 places to visit in and around London," and he would pick one at random and visit that. The Imperial War Museum, Dr. Johnson's House, the Dulwich College Picture Gallery—it didn't matter. In Somerset House, he spent the better part of an hour reading Milton's last will and testament.

And malt does more than Milton can
To justify God's ways to man.

In the evenings, after all the museums and galleries and public buildings were closed, he would go to a pub near

Cavendish Square and drink stout; he would sit in a corner booth, propped up behind an unread copy of the *Times Literary Supplement* that he had been carrying around in his pocket for weeks, overtip the barmaid, and get smashed. Then, at about ten o'clock, just to prove that he could still do it, he would stagger down to one of the penny arcades on Oxford Street and play eight or ten brilliant games of pinball before going to bed.

That was the worst part. The absolute bottom line was going to bed every night in that wretched little attic room—not that the room made any difference.

Every night he would promise himself that the next night he would really tie one on. The trick, however, as he discovered fast enough, was to get just sufficiently tanked for dreamless sleep. No self-pity, no bad dreams, no memory. Nothing to wake you in the middle of the night, to make you tremble and sweat and wipe your face to see if it was really spattered with pale blood.

He tried keeping a bottle of Irish whiskey under his bed, but if you got too drunk the dreams were even worse and the hard stuff gave him heartburn. No, you had to strike a balance. You had to find that point of perfect equilibrium.

So he stayed in his corner booth and drank stout and kept rereading the same review of a book on the Scottish Chaucerians. And the barmaid would come with a full glass every now and then and take away his empties and five bob for her trouble.

But even with his overtipping, the barmaid didn't seem to care for him much. Fancy sitting around all night, just drinking himself insensible like that. Every night, just sitting there—as if he fooled anybody with his paper always open to the same page. Still, he was polite enough for two and talked like a gentleman; not that you could tell with these Yanks. Perhaps he had his troubles, but then, who didn't?

And at the end of the evening, Guinness would say his good night to the lady, leave a ten-shilling note on the table, and go home; never too late, because—you never knew—his escort might be a married man.

Because there was always an escort. MI-6 doesn't like it when one of its soldiers announces that he's quitting and then begins to come apart at the seams; it makes everybody nervous. Men do desperate and foolish things when they've reached the end of their tether and they bear watching.

Poor bastard, that kind of duty couldn't be worth too many laughs. Guinness would have liked to have stood him a drink sometimes, but of course that was impossible.

Perhaps, if he got flaky enough, they would call off his escort and do something really drastic. Perhaps one night he would be hustled into a waiting car and disappear into a peat bog in Northumbria. It wasn't as if that sort of thing never happened.

Curiously, the idea rather appealed to him.

XIII

BUT OF COURSE they didn't. Instead, they put him on a plane to Rome, where he was supposed to proceed by train to Florence and there do a number on a Russian string-handler by the name of Misha Fedorovich Vlasov. It looked like a pretty easy hit, and perhaps they felt a little light work in a warm climate would do him good; a kind of rest cure in the sunny South, with just enough going down to keep his mind occupied.

Anyway, it happened one morning that Guinness was having breakfast in a tiny pseudo-Italian restaurant in Bloomsbury—spaghetti and watered Lambrusco starting at around two in the afternoon, kippers and tea served anytime—when he chanced to look out of the window and to notice that there wasn't anybody in attendance.

Not many people in the Trade had any illusions about being able to keep an unnoticed tail on a fellow spook, certainly not for days at a time, and none of the people who were following Guinness around had even tried. Usually, they just waited around on street corners, making themselves nice and conspicuous, and Guinness had returned the courtesy by staying easy to shadow and taking pains that every once in a while everyone had a shot at the men's room. It was, considering the circumstances, a very gentlemanly arrangement all the way around.

Of course, they didn't know who he was—nobody had been that stupid—but they had eyes in their heads and this was no shoe salesman from Lambeth. The rumor mills were very busy.

Hadn't they all been ordered to carry I.D. and leave the weapons at home? I.D., for the love of God! One simply didn't carry I.D. in this line of work. Ergo, this one was a very heavy number, heavy enough to drop you in a dark alley, so, if you please, sir, he should know you were a friendly and not put a bullet in your shell-like ear.

The troops were justified in being a trifle skittish, more justified than they could begin to imagine.

"You really ought to read it, dear boy," Byron had said, pushing a flat manila folder across the desk toward him. "He seems to imagine that there's something mildly grotesque about you. But then he always was an old maid, our Dr. Conington."

Guinness had just gotten back from his training in Scotland, and Dr. Conington, who had had him interpreting ink blots and putting together wooden puzzles three mornings a week, wasn't very high on his list either. He didn't like people who asked him lewd questions about his dreams.

"If you think he's such a turkey, why was he allowed to use up so much of Her Majesty's valuable time? My firearms instructor was grumbling about writing you a rather pointed note on the subject."

Byron ignored the question and, when he saw that Guinness wasn't going to open the folder, slid it back to where he was sitting and opened it himself. For a long moment he seemed absorbed in its contents.

" 'Egocentric. Fundamentally unconstrained by conventional standards of behavior. Tends to view society as antagonistic to him. Capable of loyalty where he perceives support. Capable of any action he perceives to be in his own interest. In summary, a fairly classic example of the intelligent criminal type. Should not be trusted beyond reasonable limits of security.' My, my, my, Raymond; it seems you are a very bad boy. Lucky for you we found you when we did. Otherwise you might have ended up running the Turkish heroin traffic. Either that or the president of General Motors."

He laughed and dropped the folder into the wastepaper basket, where it hit bottom with a kind of muffled clang. It wasn't the sort of gesture Guinness entirely trusted. Odds were that report was out of the trash and back in Byron's files within two minutes after he left the room.

"Pshaw. That's why we keep the old badger. He could have used the same words to describe half the human race, and probably has. It might have been written about myself."

He might have kept Conington's report, but he never gave any indication that he believed it. Not Byron. Byron wouldn't have sicked all these goons on him just because he had handed in his walking papers. But Byron was dead.

And now there wasn't a soul out there.

They had obviously gotten the signal to withdraw, and that could mean any number of things, most of them reasonably ugly. Had someone at Whitehall decided he was just too damn dangerous in his present state of mind and that it was time to cut their losses? Well, if that was the way they felt about it, he wasn't going to go quietly. They could waste him if they had a mind to—hell, there wasn't anybody they couldn't waste—but he was going to see to it that they paid for the privilege.

Guinness paid his tab and took his raincoat from where it had been hanging on a peg near the door. As he put his arms through the sleeves, he could feel three or four pounds of gunmetal bobbing against his left thigh, and he smiled a grim little inward smile. It was only a dinky little Spanish automatic, not the .357 which good procedure had demanded be wiped clean and left at the scene of the late festivities, but there were eight rounds in the clip and one in the chamber and the action was fast enough to spray bullets like a fucking fire hose. It would do.

Outside the restaurant, he flagged down a taxi and, with his hand closed over the automatic in his raincoat pocket—you never knew who might turn out to be driving—gave instructions for the Tower.

It was a Sunday morning, well into the tourist season, so the place was jammed. They would have a fine old time trying to jump him there, but of course he didn't really expect them to try. They wouldn't be in any particular hurry, and he would have to go home sometime.

It was really more a question of testing their intentions; if nothing happened by closing time, then Guinness would know they were gunning for him. He chose a bench overlooking the barge entrance to Traitor's Gate and sat down to await events.

A little before noon, he watched a tall reedy-looking man in a black wool overcoat and a bowler hat that came down almost to his eyebrows buying a ticket to enter the grounds. While he reached into an inside pocket for his 1/6, the handle of his umbrella was hooked over his left forearm, something that at a distance of close to a hundred yards Guinness couldn't have hoped to have noticed but through the eye of long acquaintance.

Some men used their furled umbrellas as walking sticks, some carried them like bouquets, but McKendrick always hooked his over the left forearm. A convenient place for it, since arthritis resulting from an intended gunshot wound had frozen the elbow at a ninety-degree angle. Before then, back during the war and up until sometime in the middle fifties, McKendrick was supposed to have been one of Byron Down's most dependable boys; not brilliant, perhaps, but proficient. Afterward, he became his chief assistant and eventually his successor. Guiness didn't much like the sonuvabitch.

Winter and summer, he wore the same damn outfit, like a uniform: black wool overcoat, oversize bowler, and his bloody umbrella. Always the same.

McKendrick minced his way through the crowd and sat down on Guinness's bench. The two men didn't exchange so much as a glance for perhaps forty-five seconds, while the older man took off his bowler, set it carefully down beside him on the bench, and began smoothing back with his palm the thin, mouse-gray hair on either side of his head.

"Well, if you've finished pouting," he said finally, in the clipped accents of urban Yorkshire, "we have a piece of work for you to do."

He had unhooked the umbrella from his arm, and as he spoke he stabbed vaguely with the tip at the gravel in front of him. Nearby, a couple of squealing, plumply blond five-year-old boys were straddling one of the Tower's cannons, green with age and disuse; the bigger of the two was peering over into the muzzle. Twenty feet below them an emerald-green beer bottle, almost totally submerged, was making a clinking sound as the lapping of the Thames kept nudging it against the ancient stones of the embankment.

"Piss off."

They sat together in silence for perhaps another minute as McKendrick considered this response. He continued to stab at the gravel with his umbrella while Guinness watched the ponderous movements of the giant unloading cranes at work on the other side of the river; they looked like elephants, come down to the water's edge to bathe.

"You know, you ought to go inside sometime." McKendrick jerked his head back slightly, the way some men do when they wink coyly and tell you to, hey, check out the redhead at the next table. Only McKendrick wasn't winking; on his face was a cruel, wintery smile that had nothing to do with the contemplation of pretty girls. "You ought to visit the Bloody Tower," he went on. "They have the ax in there they used to cut off Sir Walter Raleigh's head."

"No they don't. The ax in the Bloody Tower is from a later period. So's the block." Guinness took a deep breath and let it out again, removing his hand from his raincoat pocket, where it had been resting lightly on the handle of his atuomatic, and folding it over the other hand in his lap. Nobody was going to shoot anybody. "And don't threaten me, McKendrick. I don't like it."

The two men turned slightly, just enough to catch

each other's eye. Neither of them smiled and both were wondering just how much the other one was bluffing.

Suddenly Guinness's face split into an irritating grin. "Besides," he said lightly, "I've retired, remember? We're all supposed to fall in the line of duty, I know; but then I'm not even putting in for a pension." The grin died, and the voice went low and icy. "If you want to send one of your goon squads after me, feel free. But make it your best effort, old man; anything less and I'll smear them and you all over London. Recent history would suggest I'm not all that easy to kill."

McKendrick, whatever his limitations, was not a fool. Guinness, he realized, wasn't bluffing. You can tell when a man is bluffing, when he's afraid and playing it for effect, and Guinness wasn't bluffing. He seemed almost to wish they would put out a contract on him so he could go down in a blaze of lethal glory.

It wouldn't do, however. The Foreign Office would have a perfect fantod.

"Would it make any difference if I told you that the man we want terminated is the one who set up the Oslo hit on you? Are you the vengeful type, Guinness?"

Guinness considered it. Oslo hadn't been the first time somebody had tried to kill him, but what the hell—business was business and nothing personal. If you made a hobby of collecting grudges, you wouldn't have much time for anything else.

Yet it did make a difference. It was childish, of course, but Oslo had indirectly cost him Kathleen. Since Oslo, his life hadn't been worth a tinker's belch to him, which of course was nobody's fault but his own. After all, the poor sonuvabitch hadn't specifically been trying to ruin his marriage, merely to kill him. Still . . .

Yes, he supposed that finally it did make a difference.

On the train from Rome to Florence, Guinness watched the Tuscan countryside slipping by and pondered that final conversation with McKendrick. The further he got from London, the less sense his own reasons for doing this last little thing made to him. Who really cared, anyway?

McKendrick did, of course. Jesus, did McKendrick care. Guinness remembered his instructions with distaste.

"We want this man mashed like an insect. We want him to die messily, and in a way that will leave no doubt that he has been the object of someone's special consideration. We want the Russians to know that they cannot order hits on our people and get away with it. Teach them a lesson, Guinness—one they won't so soon forget."

While he had said it, his eyelids had fluttered angrily several times and once or twice his Adam's apple had pumped up and down inside his gaunt throat. He really hated this guy Vlasov, whom he had probably never seen in the flesh and whose only offense was that he had been doing quality work for his own side. McKendrick was jealous, and like a fool he had allowed the issue to become personal. It was such a god damned waste of time.

Guinness stared out of the window at the fields of sunflowers and the pale pastel farmhouses that seemed to have taken on the color of the sunlight. He tried to keep track of the number of olive trees they passed, but after a while he lost count and began eavesdropping on a conversation between the two pudgy, flaxen middle-aged German women with whom he happened to be sharing the compartment. Evidently, they were on their way home from a combination religious pilgrimage and holiday in Rome, and their talk centered on the souvenirs they were bringing their grandchildren. They spoke in a heavy southern dialect he found rather tough sledding.

Finally one of them left to visit the W.C., and Guinness, left without distraction, took up again the thread of his not-very-inspiring self-appraisal.

It always came back down to the same question, more an inquiry into character than motive: What the fuck was he doing on this stupid train? He had been out of that line of work, 100 percent out; he didn't have a thing in the world against anybody named Vlasov and not the faintest interest in bumping him off.

Vlasov, it was true, had sort of loused things up for him with Kathleen—or, rather, had been the means of effecting a crisis that Guinness's own blindness and stupidity had made inevitable. He had been, in Aristotelian terms, merely the efficient cause, and even that, if under the circumstances the word was not wholly out of place, innocently. What sort of person, under the circumstances, would want to do a number on poor little innocent Vlasov? Who else but a total, irredeemable piece of shit?

So why not just pack up and go home? There would be a train back to Rome in the morning, so why the hell not?

No, he couldn't do that; he had taken the job, and now he had to see that it got done. It was perhaps only a point of professional pride, and at the moment that was the only kind of pride he seemed capable of summoning up. It would just have to do.

The train didn't reach Florence until the middle of the afternoon, so Vlasov and his outrageous insult to the integrity of British espionage would just have to wait until the following day. Guinness caught a bus to his hotel—the Astoria, if you can believe it—and, having tipped the bellman to take his suitcase up to his room, went into the tiny dining room for dinner.

Except for the necessity of evading the waiter's persistent attempts to sell him, at a ridiculous figure, an incredibly vulgar set of brass and enamel salt and pepper shakers, it would have been a pleasant meal. He had a table near the door to the patio, and after a couple of glasses of wine he was ready for bed.

He left an early wake-up call, and by five the next morning was dressed and tapping cautiously on the windshield of the only taxi he could find parked anywhere near the entrance of the hotel. The driver, a man of heroic paunch and mustaches, was asleep behind his wheel, and Guinness would have preferred to awaken him into a good mood.

But, alas, it was not fated to be. When finally the man opened one eye, he yawned widely, scratched himself on the breastbone, and with his thumb made a brusque movement in the direction of the rear seat.

Guinness handed him a slip of paper upon which he had written out an address, and they were off.

The address was for a house which, as it turned out, did actually exist. The street was in a fairly expensive but sparsely developed part of a suburb called Fiesole, but Guinness had picked the number at random. Fiesole went up the side of a hill that overlooked the city, and from the top Florence looked like a relief map of itself. You could see the Arno winding through town, with the grim tower of the Palazzo Vecchio and the great dome of the cathedral, its bricky redness obscured in the pale gray of predawn, dominating everything. It was quite a view.

Vlasov lived in Fiesole, about a third of the way down the eastern slope of the hill.

Picking a spot well away from the main road, in a field of dried grass, Guinness sat down under a huge oak, the shade of which would provide ideal cover, to wait. Vlasov's house was close to half a mile away but perfectly visible, and he wanted to begin clocking the man's routine.

If someone did the same thing at the same time three days running, chances were he would do it again on the fourth—and that was when you could hit him. The pattern was important, because if he varied it, and you screwed up as a result, he'd know he was being hunted. You had to know what the bastard was going to do. You had to know so you could be ready for him.

As he sat with his back resting against the tree trunk, looking at Vlasov's house, Guinness could scarcely credit his luck. The place was perfect; he couldn't have asked for more. A good two hundred yards from its nearest neighbor, it was a two-story affair with most of the windows facing off the second floor, so there wouldn't be much difficulty about approaching it unseen. There was a small L-shaped garden behind and on the far side, and, on the near side, screened from view by a row of low trees, an open carport. The carport was really intriguing.

At a quarter to seven, Vlasov came out of the house through the front door and went around to the carport, where for a few seconds he disappeared from view. Then a dark-blue sedan of some make Guinness had never seen before nosed onto the roadway and started on down the hill. Guinness stood up to follow the car with his eyes until it was swallowed up in the outskirts of Florence. Vlasov was on his way to work at an office which, according to the work sheet Guinness had read in London, occupied the third floor of a tiny building over the river, just two blocks or so down from the Ponte Vecchio. After a few minutes, Guinness started working his way down to the main road to catch a bus back into town.

For three days, and at as great a remove as he could manage, Guinness kept track of Vlasov's movements. He turned out to be a man of the most regular habits, driving to his office every day at the same time, working there until noon, eating lunch every day in the same restaurant off the Piazza della Repubblica, returning to his office at a quarter to one, staying there until he drove home again at five thirty-five. He never went out at night, although sometimes Guinness would catch a glimpse of him moving around in his garden. The lights went off in his bedroom every night at ten minutes to eleven.

Clearly, the house was the best place for a touch. It was isolated and provided maximum freedom from interference, and it wouldn't be crawling with cops within ten seconds of the first loud noise. The problems of trying to do it in the city, with its warren of little streets, were just too complex to bother with.

And Vlasov's area of maximum vulnerability in the house was clearly the carport. It was perfect, screened from view and yet accessible and out of doors; when he had a chance, Guinness always preferred to work out of doors.

There were only two practical ways of doing it in the carport: He could just wait there for the guy and plug him, or he could wire the car. What with the hilltop winds, trying to pick anybody off at several hundred yards with a rifle was a pretty poor bet. And Guinness didn't much relish the idea of hanging around in the carport for two or three hours with a pistol, so it would have to be the car. Besides, McKendrick had specified that he wanted something dramatic.

That night he broke into the supply shack of a construction site he had spotted near the railway station and stole two sticks of dynamite, some wire, and a couple of blasting caps.

The fourth morning found Guinness again sitting under his oak tree, this time with a pair of field glasses he had picked up in a camera shop the afternoon before. He was nervous as hell about this one—perhaps he was cracking up at last, just coming apart at the seams; and when it was over, MI-6 would gather him up and stash him in a nice, restful loony bin somewhere up in the Orkeny Islands, where he could wear out the rest of his life making paper dolls.

Anyway, he didn't want to miss anything; he wanted to make sure everything worked according to plan. Although he had gone through the usual training in explosives, it was the first time he had ever used any—somehow the idea of all that fuss and noise, the randomness of it, violated his aesthetic sense.

Dynamite, though, was supposed to be pretty reliable, and presumably two sticks would do the job. They were taped right up under the driver's seat cushion, with the wires running under the floor mats and the upholstery into the instrument panel. He hoped to hell everything was hooked up right.

It was ten to seven before Vlasov came out through his front door, five minutes behind schedule—and, god dammit, he had someone with him! It was a woman, a fucking woman, and she was dressed up to go somewhere! Arm in arm, they walked to the garage and disappeared behind the trees that screened off the carport. It seemed like forever that they were in there.

Then Vlasov came back out and started walking around the front of the car. Apparently he had opened the door for her on the driver's side and was going around to let himself in.

The whole thing was probably only taking a few seconds, but to Guinness it seemed like slow motion—

there was plenty of time for him to figure out everything, for the whole ghastly business to unravel itself before him. It was terrible.

Just as Vlasov got to the front of the car, the dynamite went up. With an appalling noise, appalling even from half a mile's distance, the car turned itself into a ball of red and black fire. The two sticks had been plenty.

Sitting in his office chair, in his house in California, Guinness could still remember every detail with a vividness that made his hands sweat. He could still remember the expression on Vlasov's face as he had begun turning toward the car to see what had happened. He could remember the car's hood, which had apparently been hinged from the front, popping up and off, doing a slow back flip until it slammed into Vlasov and knocked him down. The hood had probably saved Vlasov's life, protecting him from the full force of the explosion.

At the time Guinness had thought that they both must have been killed, though he didn't wait around to make sure. He had simply hopped a plane out, the first plane he could manage, which had happened to be bound for Zurich. From there he hadn't even returned to London but had put into effect the escape route he and Byron had so carefully devised. Screw it, the whole damn business; he never wanted to touch anything to do with it again, never again.

But seven years had not been time enough to forget. He remembered the way Vlasov and his wife had looked on their little walk to the car, the way he had smiled at her and touched her hand as it rested on his arm. The poor woman. The poor god damned woman. Where had they been going? Shopping? To the dentist? She had started the car while her husband went around to let himself in on the other side, and she had been blown to smithereens. No wonder Vlasov had been waiting seven years for the chance to kill him. Everything made sense now—the murder of Louise, the nitrogen triiodide in his ignition, everything.

Of all the jobs he had ever done, of all the people he

had killed and all the despicable little treacheries he had committed, this was the one he remembered. In seven years there had hardly been two days together when he hadn't thought of it. It came back to him in his dreams sometimes and woke him, cold and terrified, in the middle of the night. He should have known Vlasov would be alive. He should have expected him to come like this and demand his revenge.

Guinness put his files back into their hiding place, put the carpet back down, and left his house through the rear door, just as he had entered it. It was close to dawn by then, and the sky was a pale gray.

Out on the sidewalk, he noticed a car parked about two blocks up the street, just out of pistol range. He could just make out a man's shape behind the wheel, and then the glint of reflected light. It was Vlasov, of course, watching from a distance, just as Guinness had watched him all those years ago, watching to make sure that his challenge had been accepted. He couldn't have said how he knew it was Vlasov, but he knew.

Guinness fished around in the pocket of his coat until he found the postcard with the picture of the little girl on the merry-go-round. When he found it, he held it up at arm's length over his head. The lights of the car flashed on and then off again, as if in answer. Then there was the sound of its starting, and it turned around in the street and drove away. In a few seconds it was gone.

XIV

STAYING AWAY FROM the main arteries of traffic, where he would have been taking a chance of getting picked up by the police, Guinness made his way on foot through residential Belmont. For a while he followed the perimeter of the old Ralston estate, after the robber baron's time a lunatic asylum and now a Catholic convent school for the daughters of Bolivian silver czars—to all of which there was a pleasing continuity—and then he struck out over a low shoulder of land that in recent years had become a patchwork of housing developments, until he came back onto El Camino Real. He was almost on the border with San Mateo, the next town over, a fact indicated by a neon sign across the highway which, at a suitable hour, could be counted on to advise all interested parties that they were near the Bel-Mateo Motel.

It was going to be a nice morning, clear and cool, and Guinness was beginning to experience that rise of optimism that comes to those few who somehow contrive to be awake and out of doors just before a spring dawn.

But it wasn't only the morning. In spite of his unpromising circumstances—hell, there was at least an even chance he would be dead before the week was done—he felt almost immortal.

Maybe during all of the last seven years he had rather missed the cut and run. He had been happy with Louise—in all likelihood, he would never be happy again—but maybe, for him, it wasn't enough to be happy. Loneliness, fear, and at the end of it, tomorrow or next month or the year after next, nothing but a bullet in the back of the head and a porcelain slab in among the other John Does. These were all that could be left for him in life, but somehow it didn't seem to matter.

He was sorry about Louise, sorry she was dead and sorry that their life together was over. No part of him was glad to be free of her.

But, if not that, he was glad to be free of all the rest of it: the lawn, the house, one safe day after another. And wasn't she bound up in all of that? Whatever should happen now, whatever came to him, there would have been no place for Louise.

So be it. Right that moment, with the skyline turning pink and the long grass by the roadway still slick from last night's fog, if the angel Michael had appeared to him and announced, "Come, all's forgiven; we'll take away the flaming sword and you can go back to the life you've lived these seven years, and no one will ever bother you again," Guinness would have smiled and shook his head and begged off. He was of the devil's party, and he knew it.

He stopped and bought a newspaper on the corner occupied by the Belmont Theater, paused for a break in the traffic, and crossed over to join the throng waiting for the arrival of the Greyhound local to San Francisco. Screened behind his newspaper, he was perfectly safe; the express bus turned off at Ralston Avenue, several blocks back, to join the Bayshore Freeway, and if Creon was having any of the buses watched, which wasn't likely, it would be the express. That was the way his mind would work. He would expect Guinness to be panicked and in a hurry.

The ride in, naturally, took forever, and it was close to 10:00 A.M. before they nosed in at the Ninth Avenue bus station. Guinness was hungry enough to buy himself a corndog and a paper cup full of carbonated orange drink, and he stood leaning up against the wall of the concession stand watching the ritual duel between an old lady, the temporary occupant of one of the station's gray-painted slat benches, and two or three of the contingent of pigeons that called the place home.

She was a ferocious-looking old witch, immaculately turned out in a nylon dress of small white polka dots against a background of the most severe blue, a white knitted sweater with sleeves reaching down almost to her knuckles, and a small square black hat carefully positioned on hair the color of pewter. Around her neck, from which the muscles stood out like the cords of a rope, she wore a thin black ribbon, and she carried a walking stick with a silver head and tip.

Around her feet, within perhaps a three-foot radius, she had sprinkled some bread crumbs, and when the pigeons would make a rush for them, she would strike out with the tip of her walking stick. She wasn't trying to hit them really, just to keep them at bay. It made an odd spectacle, and Guinness wondered what moral the old gal must be drawing from it; for surely she would be the type to draw a moral.

His corndog and his interest in kinky games both being exhausted, Guinness headed off for the Bayside Hotel to fetch Tuttle's key. The round trip took him not quite three quarters of an hour, and the bus station locker into which the key fitted contained a red TWA flight bag, the contents of which would have to wait for some not-so-public place.

In the meantime, he thought he had better find Doris Lincer.

Doris was a bar girl whose vague aspirations for a better life had long kept her floating in and out of the state college system. She had begun to study half a dozen things—typing and real estate brokerage and dental technology—but always left them off just in time to keep her transcript blank. Once her restlessness had manifested itself in a yen for literary culture and she had found herself in English 262, Introduction to Poetry, at Belmont State. Guinness had, of course, been the instructor; he was fresh out of the graduate program at UCLA, still working on his dissertation, and as yet unattached.

He saw her throughout most of that year, although she quickly lost interest in the niceties of scansion. Even after his marriage she would phone him once in a while, but only once in a while. She wasn't the clinging type. He hadn't heard anything from her in almost three years.

In those days she had worked in a place just a block down from Union Square called the Board Room, so perhaps she still did. She still did.

It was an incredibly dark little room, long and narrow, with a bar and a tiny dimly lit stage along one wall. The stage was a little higher than the level of the bar, and on it, in a parody of dance, was a half-naked woman, possibly Latin, possibly not, with small breasts and arms that hung down limp at her sides, as if someone had severed the nerves. Even in that vague light there glistened on her underbelly the stretch marks of many pregnancies.

Presently, with the clumsy deliberation of an act performed underwater, she stepped out of her panties and hung them over a hook on the wall behind her. For perhaps half a minute Guinness watched her, wondering what had made the floor so sticky under his shoes.

When his eyes had adjusted to the absence of light, he threaded his way through the maze of tiny circular tables and plastic chairs and sat down behind one in the corner furthest from the jukebox, which was deafening. There he waited.

Doris was perched on a stool at the bar, talking to a customer, who, judging from the position of his hand on her thigh, was an intimate and trusted friend. It wasn't very long before she disengaged herself, dropped down from her stool, and, carrying a small tray, began swinging her way toward him.

Swinging was the word. Doris was a big girl, a good five feet ten, and generously built, a fact her working clothes did what they could to emphasize. She looked as if she had put on a little weight.

"Hello, Ray," she said, in a voice just loud enough to be heard in that din. "What are you drinking?" There was nothing in her manner to suggest whether or not she was pleased to see him as she took a small square napkin from her tray and set it down on the table in front of him. "Still beer?"

Beer—that was what was crackling inaudibly under his soles. Beer that had been jostled over the edges of these tiny round tables, to spatter equally on the linoleum and the trouser legs of middle-aged voyeurs. A more-or-less uniform film of it over the whole floor. He could smell it now, flat and faintly sickening as it mingled with the stale cigarette smoke and the odor of disinfectant.

He smiled and nodded, and she took her tray and went back to the bar.

She brought him back a glass and a seven-ounce bottle of some brand he had never heard of and sat down across the table from him, with her back to the bar. Guinness ventured a quick glance at the man she had left to join him, who looked as if he were trying to decide whether or not he should lodge a protest. Apparently, he decided not, because after a few minutes he finished whatever it was he had been drinking and walked stiffly out, leaving a dollar bill on the stage for the dancer.

"Aren't you still teaching, Ray?" she asked after she had settled into her chair and poured his beer for him. "It's the middle of the goddamn week." She smiled, or at least the distance between the ends of her mouth lengthened, and Guinness knew that she had heard about his wife. She was baiting him, just a little— daring him to tell some lie about passion and memory and old time's sake, and knowing that he wouldn't bother. Perhaps she half wished he would.

It was more with her eyes that she smiled, that she said she really was glad to see him and didn't care why he had come. They mirrored a weary cynicism that had learned to compromise with the frailties of human nature.

"The beer is going to cost you two seventy-five," she

said quietly, putting her hand over the back of his. Guinness let his breath catch in a tiny voiceless laugh and took her fingers between his palm and thumb.

"I'm in a certain amount of trouble, Doris; and I could use some extralegal help."

"Sure." She gave his hand a small squeeze, whether in sympathy for his trouble or in acceptance of his weakness as a man he couldn't tell. "I kind of figured that. Just tell me what it is."

"I need to disappear for a while. I need someone to ferry me down to Los Angeles—not you, kid; I'm not a very safe person to know right at the moment."

Very gently, she disengaged her hand and patted him on the back of the wrist. "Don't you worry. I wasn't planning to volunteer." It seemed a long time before she spoke again. "How soon will you need to go? Can it wait until tomorrow?"

"Yes. It can wait that long."

"Good." She nodded sharply and smiled a clever little smile. "Then you'll need a place to stay the night. I get off work at seven—come back here then and I'll have everything set up. You can buy me dinner."

Guinness rose from his cair, took a ten-dollar bill from his wallet, and dropped it on Doris's tray. "See you then," he whispered, bending down to kiss her between the eyebrows. "Will you take care of Miss Birthday Suit for me?" Without waiting for an answer, he worked his way down the narrow track between rows of tables and was gone.

The sun was hideously bright outside on the sidewalk, but that may have been nothing more than the effect of contrast. Guinness glanced at his watch and was a little surprised to find it was only eleven-thirty. There probably wasn't a fugitive warrant out on him yet, but somehow it still didn't seem like a hot idea to spend the next several hours walking the streets. Besides, he was tired. He hadn't had much sleep, having been under only a few hours when Tuttle phoned, and it had been an exciting day.

And he was hungry too; that junk at the bus station had simply started his juices flowing, and he hadn't touched his beer. No problem, though. San Francisco was lousy with places to eat.

After a chicken salad sandwich and a cup of tea at David's Kosher Deli, Guinness found himself a porno movie house on Sutter Street. There he would be protected by the surreal darkness of the place and by the fact that no one wished, under such circumstances, to appear at all curious about his neighbor. You could spend the day there, as he planned to, and not a soul would so much as look at you.

He paid his five dollars and decided that a visit to the men's room seemed in order. It would be the first safe chance he had had to inspect the goodies in his flight bag.

Tuttle, lord love the boy, had thought of everything. There was a nasty-looking little .25 caliber snub-nose revolver in a black leather clip holster, an envelope containing five hundred dollars in fifties, an Oregon driver's license, a social security card, and a Union 76 credit card, all made out to one Thomas S. Linkweather—the color photograph on the license was of Guinness—and a small, flat drug case just like the one he had found in Tuttle's motel room.

Inside were the three numbered vials of clear fluid, a syringe, and a note: "Number 3 puts you under for keeps. Happy hunting."

Guinness stuffed the cards and money into his wallet, which was already thick with twenty-five hundred from his own little nest egg, clipped the gun to his belt, and slipped the drug case into the left inside breast pocket of his coat. He left the flight bag, containing nothing now except Sergeant-of-Detectives Herbert L. Ganjemi's service revolver, inside the paper towel dispenser. Eventually, whoever around there was in charge of keeping things tidy would find it, open it up, and, being engaged in an enterprise in which you can always use a few extra Brownie points downtown, call the police. But by then everything with Vlasov would be settled and, one way or the other, Guinness wouldn't have a thing to worry about.

After rinsing his hands, he left the men's room, walking past the studied inattention of the guy who had sold him his ticket and pushing through the heavy curtained doorway into the theater itself.

Back when Guinness had been in college, they had called them stag films, and the ones the fraternities traded around among themselves were supposed to have been pretty hot stuff. But Guinness hadn't been a fraternity man, so the closest he had ever gotten was a thing that had been playing at a place in one of the seedier parts of Columbus. It had consisted of an hour and a half of the heroine walking her dog through what one could only presume was supposed to be Central Park, at the end of which the audience was rewarded for their patience with a fifteen-second peek at her tits. They had been very substantial tits, he remembered, but the black and white film hadn't really been able to do them justice. Guinness had left with the feeling that his two and a half dollars had been definitely squandered.

Apparently, things had changed a lot since then. He took a seat in a rear corner, away from the door, propped his knees up against the seat in front of him and folded his arms tightly across his chest, marveling at the amount of noise some people made in the act of coition.

Someone was standing . . . standing . . . standing . . . in the what? Where? In the doorway of his bedroom . . . back home in his bedroom doorway . . . standing there, looking at him. Was it Louise? Yes! It was Louise, standing in the light from the hall. He was home now, and it was nighty-night time, and the light caught Louise from behind, showing the outline of her body through her nightdress. Then the nightdress slipped to her waist . . . and then down to the floor . . . slowly, as if it couldn't bear to leave her . . .

Yes? She wants him to hold her in his arms. She wants him to hold her . . . heavy in his arms, there with him now and weightlessly heavy in his arms. Louise? Is the room too dark? . . . is it too dark? Why couldn't he see her face?

Guinness awakened with a start, slowly pulled himself up in his seat, and tried to read the face of his watch in the almost total darkness. Six-thirty. On the screen they were still at it, and he watched them with a dull resentment.

At five minutes to seven he was back at the Board Room, and the translation was astonishing. The noise was louder, if possible, and every table in the place was taken. The very spaces between the bar stools were occupied by men with one foot on the railing and both eyes on the stage.

Even jaded by an afternoon at the skin flicks, Guinness couldn't help but be impressed by what was going on up there; she was ripe and milk-smooth and perfectly gorgeous, facts unobscured by the smudgy reddish flush with which the footlights bathed her. Clearly, the management had saved its best effort for the evening crowd.

A touch on his coat sleeve made him aware of Doris standing just behind his shoulder, and, since they weren't more than five feet from the jukebox, he turned slightly and stooped so she could speak directly into his ear.

"I'm leaving now," she said. "Give me a couple of minutes and then meet me at the newsstand about half a block up." He nodded and she stepped back behind him and out of sight. It was as if she had been swallowed up by the elbowing mob around the bar. Guinness ordered a beer and forced himself to drink a third of it before he too departed.

She was buying a roll of butterscotch Lifesavers when he arrived, and she had her back to him. In her white plastic boots and her leather coat with the ratty fur trim around the edging and the openings of the sleeves, she looked like a hooker taking a break from the rigors of patrol. Perhaps on another evening she would have been; Guinness reminded himself that he really didn't know her very well, even if a long time ago they had been lovers.

She dropped the Lifesavers into the pocket of her coat and turned to go, passing her arm through his as they made the sidewalk. The other hand reached up to brush a strand of her shag-cut hair back away from her eyes. A passing stranger might have thought they met the same way every night of their lives.

"I have everything arranged," she whispered, pressing her head against his shoulder. "But the guy wants three bills for it. He says the round trip'll take him two days and he won't take a penny less. Sorry."

"It's okay. Did you nick him for a broker's fee?"

"No."

"You should have." They looked at each other curiously, as if each were trying to read the other's feelings, and then first Guinness smiled and then she did. As they walked along he dipped down and kissed her, thinking how nice it was for a change to be around a woman who didn't mind if sometimes you weren't a model citizen.

"Where would you like to have dinner?"

"My place." The way she said it and the way she smiled made the inside of his mouth feel suddenly very dry.

Her place was a good brisk three quarters of a mile from the Board Room, on the second floor of an apartment building that looked like a motel, all the doors on each floor opening onto a narrow walkway with an open stairwell connecting it to the one below. It was all perfectly exposed and there weren't any back doors; Guinness just hoped that Vlasov didn't change his mind about Griffith Park and decide to settle up early.

He had bought a bottle of wine along the way. Inside he set it down on the coffee table in the living room and looked around.

The last time he had been in Doris's apartment it had been a different apartment, one several blocks from this one. She must have been in the habit of renting them furnished, because there wasn't a stick of it he remembered, not even an ashtray. Perhaps he simply didn't remember as well as he had thought.

He tried to settle on just what it was about the room that struck him as so depressing. Perhaps it was that all the furniture was so low—he had had really to bend getting rid of his wine bottle; the damn table didn't seem to make it halfway to his kneecap—or perhaps it was the absence of any pictures or little knickknacks picked up on afternoon outings to Sausalito or Carmel. The room was astonishingly bare, a fact which seemed somehow to heighten your perception of its smallness. It made you feel like Alice in Wonderland, that perculiar sensation of finding yourself in a miniature world.

Catercorner from the front door was a tiny dining alcove and directly off of it, screened by a wall, was the kitchen. Guinness could hear water running and the refrigerator door opening and other busy feminine sounds coming from there.

There were a pair of matching chairs in the living room, square-cushioned and modern in design, with a covering of rough coffee-colored fabric. Guinness sat down in the one furthest from the kitchen and experienced a curious sense of injury. Somehow he had the overpowering conviction that he was fated to spend the rest of his private life in rooms like this one, one after the other—unpleasant and blasted and temporary. There would be no more small houses in residential areas where your neighbors were ROTC instructors and their wives, no more mortgages that would run well into the 1990s, no sense of permanence and possession.

In short, there wasn't going to be any more Louise. There would be Doris, or, more accurately, a succession of Dorises, stretching off until he was old enough and disengaged enough to have lost the appetite. Because that was all it was ever going to be anymore, merely the satisfaction of an appetite.

He had been married twice, each time happily by his own reckoning, but that was over. He had gotten over Kathleen, had come back to himself and started over, but he wasn't going to get over Louise. Not after the way she had died, after what, in his stupidity and selfishness, he had done to her. There would be no more wives; that aspect of his life was over.

XV

THREE FRAGMENTS OF NEWSPRINT, none larger than the back of a man's hand, limped along in a kind of spasmodic race down the narrow strip of broken and patched pavement behind Doris's apartment building. The wind came only a breath at a time, leaving them intervals every few feet to throw themselves wearily down like spent runners. It was a few minutes before six in the morning, and the gray mist that was just a little too thin to be called fog still hung weakly to the blurred edges of things. It was cold, colder than it should have been at that time of year, and Guinness stood with his collar up and his hands jammed down into the pockets of his jacket. He was waiting, and his eyes, which seemed to have taken on some of the morning's coldness, were watchful and suspicious.

"How do you like your steak, rare as an autographed copy of Kafka?"

He had stood in the doorway of Doris's tiny kitchen, his hand holding a can of beer and his eyes crinkled in a tender and remembering smile. It was a joke from the old days.

"Thank you, not quite that rare."

She had changed out of her tart's uniform into a pale-blue short-sleeved sweater, with a neck that didn't constantly tempt you to thrust your hand inside, and a pair of white slacks ending in cuffs that completely covered her bare feet. Her back was to him as she adjusted one of the racks in the oven.

"I heard about your wife, Ray." There was something casually gentle in the way she said it, something between compassion and simple curiosity, but containing no special invitation to imagine himself the unique victim of fortune. Death, and even murder, were, after all, common enough events. Guinness shifted his position slightly, making a vague answer that reflected that understanding.

"They don't say so," she went on, "but the papers seem to think you killed her." She was still facing away from him, but he could see how she had suddenly become very still.

"Are you asking me if I did?"

"I wouldn't care one way or the other." Rising back up from her crouch, she came around to face him with features set in an unreadable mask. Apparently, it had been that kind of a life.

"Then I didn't kill her."

"Did you love her?" she asked, smiling, as if she found the idea amusing. It wasn't a smile Guinness much cared for.

"Let's just say I didn't kill her and leave it at that."

The smile became just a shade broader, and then after a moment she nodded and turned back to her cooking.

She wasn't a bad cook, as it turned out. She wouldn't have won any prizes, but she wasn't bad. Of course she had never claimed to be a student of the domestic arts; it was the bedroom that she had taken as her special arena.

She had a way, after she had reached a certain pitch of enthusiasm, of suddenly hooking her pelvis an inch or so to one side. Each time, the movement would be accompanied by a little catch in her breath, as if you had suddenly somehow caused her a twinge of pain; but of course it wasn't pain. She would do it perhaps three or four times, several seconds apart, before she was finished. It was tremendously exciting. Perhaps more so because you never could be sure if it was passion or artifice—or perhaps because it seemed that the distinction had become blurred.

They had made love twice that night—each time brilliantly, like two highly accomplished technicians. But Guinness had been left with a sense of personal emptiness for which Galen's maxim did not seem entirely to account. It was as if the act no longer had any fixed place in the pattern of his life, as if the pattern itself had been violated to a degree admitting of no reconstruction.

For none of which, of course, Doris was in any way responsible. It wasn't as if the two of them had suddenly rediscovered Original Sin. And perhaps he was simply being melodramatic and things would eventually sort themselves out. He hoped so.

The mouth of the alleyway where he stood was suddenly blocked off by a blue pickup truck with an enormously wide aluminum camper in the payload. The truck seemed to hesitate for a second or two, and then slowly it finished its turn into the alleyway, the walls on either side of which it almost bridged. Guinness took one sideways pace, putting himself in the precise middle of the roadway, and the truck jerked to a stop a few yards short of him. The door on the driver's side popped open and the driver got out. He had to close the door again before he could get past the trash cans and to where he could put his foot up on the front bumper.

He folded his arms over his knee and stood balanced like that, looking at Guinness from under his eyebrows, for a long time without speaking. He was a big boy, only an inch or two taller than Guinness, but filled out. There must have been a good two hundred fifty pounds hung on that frame, and none of it looked the least little bit soft.

The impression of size was increased by a darkish blond beard and long hair that stuck out perhaps as much as three inches around the full circle of his face, making him look uncomfortably like an enormous bobcat. His thick forearms, where they were visible below the rolled-up sleeves of his Pendleton work shirt, were matted with the same darkish blond hair.

All in all, he was pretty impressive—the sort of man you instinctively wonder if you can handle, should it come to that. And he looked rather as if it might. He really didn't strike Guinness as the amiable type.

"You want a ride south," the bobcat said finally, with a faint down-home twang in his voice. "You got my three bills?"

Guinness said yes, he had the money, and the bobcat unfolded one hand from the pile on his knee, and thrust it out in front of him. "Then let's have it."

Guinness, for just a moment, contemplated how much he would enjoy twisting the sonuvabitch's arm out of its socket, just to teach him a decent respect for business etiquette. Once upon a time, in a burst of enthusiasm for polishing his professional skills, he had enrolled in a ten-week crash course in Gung Fu offered by the Anglo-Chinese Friendship League. They had met, for two hours in the evening every week night for ten weeks, in the basement of a Masonic lodge hall in Marylebone, and they had taught him how it was done. It was supposed to be easy, like pulling the drumstick off a Christmas turkey.

Of course, in the real world you couldn't dismember people just because they failed to display the proper deference. Not people you needed, at any rate, and at the moment our friend with the whiskers was a necessary person. Later would be time enough.

So Guinness did the sensible thing and took out his wallet, extracted six of Ernie Tuttle's fifty-dollar bills, and slapped them down in the outstretched hand, the fingers of which closed over the money like filaments of a meat-eating plant over an unwary fly. The bobcat held them in his closed fist for a moment, as if trying to decide if they felt like enough. Apparently they did, because when the moment was over, he pushed the fist into the pocket of a pair of elaborately shabby jeans and pulled it out again, empty.

His foot came off the front bumper of the truck, and

he wiped the hand that had held Guinness's money on the front of his shirt. "I don't want no trouble from you," he said with a kind of sullen rumble. "Money or not, you start gettin' cute with me and you'll end up by the side o' the road someplace, tryin' to flag down a ride with both y'r arms busted."

His head dropped slightly so that once again he stared out from under cover of his eyebrows. Guinness was suddenly struck by the idea that all this was probably meant to be intimidating—he was being threatened; good heavens, what a surprise!—and he smiled a ratty smile. These low-budget goons were all alike.

"Don't you worry, pal. God knows, I'd never want anyone to think I was getting cute."

The low-budget goon didn't seem entirely satisfied with his answer, and for a few seconds appeared to be meditating some response. Apparently, he thought better of it, however, and merely pointed back over his shoulder with his thumb.

"Get in the back. I don't want you seen on the way through town."

Guinness didn't particularly want to be seen, so he went around to the back of the truck and climbed in without further comment.

The inside of the camper was just a shade under six feet high, yet the light filtering in from tiny windows on either side created rather the impression of a cathedral in which the immense vaults are concealed in a gloom of their own fashioning. Lengthways against either wall were cots only slightly wider than park benches, between which ran a narrow little alley. On the left-hand cot lay an army fatigue jacket with the name Pfeifer stenciled in black over the right breast pocket. Guinness picked it up and read another name, this one embroidered in two-inch-high white letters on the back. Boyd. He set it down again and frowned. Boyd Pfeifer. Something told him most emphatically that he and Boyd Pfeifer would be having trouble before they were finished.

The truck lurched into motion, and Guinness drew tight the curtains in front of the windows before lying down on the cot opposite from the one occupied by

Pfeifer's jacket. The truck bounced around too much to make sitting in comfort possible—you got sick to your stomach. You got sick to your stomach anyway; apparently, the shocks were bad. If Vlasov didn't kill him, he must remember to have the shocks in his own car checked.

He folded his coat into a pillow and closed his eyes, keeping himself entertained by trying to puzzle out which streets they were taking from the way they felt through the mattress.

If the idiot had any sense, they would follow Geary right out to the ocean and stick to the coast road after that. The inland route would have been quicker, but they watched you closer.

It wasn't very long before he could feel them making the long, sweeping turn around Point Lobos Avenue that passed in front of the Cliff House and then fed into the Great Highway.

Once in a while Guinness was able to tune out the engine noises enough to hear the heavy pounding of the morning high tide against Fleishhacker Beach. He had come up there once in the summer to do a little surf casting, and the beach had been littered with small jellyfish. He wouldn't want to go swimming in those waters; things like that scared the hell out of him.

He tried to sleep, since there wasn't much of anything else to do, but it was impossible even to close your eyes with the truck lurching over every pothole like some drunk on his way home from a bender. Every bounce made him feel as if his stomach had been pumped full of raw sewage.

Objectively, however, on a purely rational level, he knew that he was hungry, and several times he attempted to calculate just how far south they were likely to have gone before his chauffeur would decide it was time to break for lunch; but each time the truck jolted he would lose the thread, and finally he gave it up entirely.

Perhaps it was just as well. Breakfast had been a skimpy business. Doris had been asleep when he got up, and he hadn't wanted to disturb her. He had dressed as quietly as he could and then checked the kitchen, but apparently she didn't even own a toaster. So he had had to settle for the inch and a half of orange juice there was left in a plastic pitcher in the refrigerator. He had stood by the sink, drinking his orange juice out of a highball glass, wondering if he would ever see Doris again. It didn't seem very likely.

Well, hell. Even if he did survive to the end of the week, there wouldn't be much point to picking up again with Doris. Not for either of them. Aside from an occasional spot of heavy breathing, they really didn't have much to offer each other; it was strictly a terminal relationship, and they both knew it. He would never be able to love her, not in any sense that could be said to mean anything.

Had he loved Louise? At all? Doris's mocking question came back to him, picking at his brain the way no doubt she had meant it to. Had he? Yes, he thought perhaps he had. Perhaps more than he had been perfectly aware of while she was alive. Perhaps even more than Kathleen, at least if love had anything to do with serenity. But probably the fine shadings of distinction he was attempting to draw were only functions of differences within himself. Probably he was a more loving person when he didn't spend a part of his time murdering people he didn't even know. God knows how he might have felt about Kathleen if his hands had been a little cleaner.

But he had loved Louise. Not that the affection of one Ray Guinness was much worth having, all things considered, but he had loved Louise. He would remember some trifle—the way she would sit talking to him while he had his lunch, with her sleeves rolled up above her elbows and her hair coming down in little wisps over her brow—and he would ache with the sense of what he had lost. He had loved her well enough.

Well, that sort of thing was all over with now, at least for the time being. Perhaps sometime again he might be up to it, but not now. Perhaps sometime.

He hoped not, though. God, he hoped not. His being in love was just too damned profligate of other people's lives.

He drew the pads of his thumb and middle finger over his eyelids and tried to think about something else.

It was about ten o'clock when they pulled into a Chevron station somewhere just north of Santa Cruz. At least so he gathered from a billboard on the other side of the highway: "Jct Rt 20& Hw 1, Santa Cruz, 10 min, Jim Stackman, Datsun." Guinness climbed out of the back of the truck and visited the men's room.

When he had finished, he bought a grape soda from a machine by the side of the building and stood drinking it as he watched Pfeifer pay off the attendant with one of his fifty-dollar bills. The attendant was the cautious type, turning the bill over two or three times and examining it carefully before he went into the office to make change.

Guinness shook his head ruefully. It was dumb to go around flashing a bill of that size; it made people remember you. Well, there was no point in worrying about it now.

Behind them, at the bottom of a slope covered with long yellowing grass, the Pacific Ocean twinkled in the harsh sunlight like a handful of colored sugar. He turned to look at it, sliding the by-now-empty bottle into one of the slots of a wooden case that was leaning up against the side of the machine. At that distance you could see the soft, feathery curls of the waves tumbling over one another, but you couldn't hear them. Guinness shaded his eyes with a hand and searched the water for swimmers, but there didn't seem to be anyone out yet. Perhaps they waited until the water was warmer; perhaps they swam somewhere else. It couldn't have looked any stranger to him if he had come there from one of the dead moons of Uranus.

For days now he had experienced this odd sense of being an alien among the familiar, of having suddenly discovered that he and the rest of the human race belonged to different species, even to different worlds. A gas station by the Pacific, the lobby of a hotel, the line of people waiting to board a Greyhound bus into San Francisco. He knew how they all worked, knew the decorums governing behavior, but knew them the way one knows the answer to a riddle. Eventually it would be the wrong answer, or the wrong riddle, and they would find him out. It seemed he was a fugitive from more than just the police.

The attendant brought Pfeifer back his change and counted it out into his hand. Guinness walked back to the truck, slowing as he observed how friend Boyd had taken up a position by the camper door. His fingers were resting tentatively on the handle, and as he watched his passenger's approach his eyes narrowed into puckered, speculative little slits.

"I don't want you gettin' out like that again," he growled. "You stay the hell in the truck."

Guinness tried not to let anything register in his face, tried not to let this being threatened and ordered about all the time reach him. After all, what did he really care?—it was probably the poor bastard's only mode of conversation.

"Right. When were you planning to stop for lunch."

Somehow the planes of light shifted slightly in Pfeifer's face, as if a new possibility had just opened for him. He seemed to make a deliberate effort at unhardening a little. But just a little. "I guess around Monterey sometime. Sure, you hungry?" With his free hand he stroked his chin whiskers. Somehow it wasn't a reassuring gesture.

"Not now, but I will be by then." Pfeifer only nodded and gestured toward the inside of the camper. Guinness took the hint, and they were on their way.

Once the truck was back on the highway, Guinness lay down again. He closed his eyes and laughed quietly to himself, thinking how upset old supercautious Boyd would be if he had any idea who might actually be trailing along behind them. Lucky little Boyd, all he was worried about was the police.

And, of course, Vlasov would be back there somewhere. A man who can track you all the way from Italy to California isn't likely to screw up between San Francisco and Los Angeles, not bloody likely. Not after seven years of finding his way from one shadowy little fragment of information to the next, sifting through them until they all added up to the same thing. Guinness tried to remember every slip he had ever made, everything that might conceivably have ended up in a KGB dossier somewhere. There couldn't have been many.

Then of course there was the cap on the bottle—it was obvious enough how Vlasov had managed that.

The name. Once he had had Guinness's name it would have been easy. In all those years of working for the British there had been two rules upon which Guinness had insisted: He had never allowed himself to be fingerprinted, never once in his life (the only ones on record anywhere would have been those at the police station in Belgrade) and he had never done a caper while traveling under his own name. Byron had made quite sure that the name had remained a secret.

Just to satisfy his own morbid curiosity, Guinness would have given something to have known for how much McKendrick had betrayed him. Probably not very much. Perhaps only the right to broker Vlasov's defection to the Americans.

"Certainly, if you want him he's yours. He buggered out on us, you know; so you can kill him with our blessing."

McKendrick had always hated his guts, even more than he had hated Vlasov's. And after Florence, Vlasov had probably ceased to be a major direct irritant.

It had to have been McKendrick. Sooner or later Vlasov's inquiries would have led him in that direction, and from McKendrick's point of view nothing could have been tidier than the deal Vlasov would have been ready to offer. Selling out Guinness would have been no skin off his ass, and God only knew how many debts to Uncle Sam he must have cleared by offering a prize like Misha Fedorovich Vlasov. It would have been irresistible.

So Vlasov was back there somewhere, bouncing along down Highway 1. So what? Vlasov would keep.

Guinness had by now become attuned to the erratic rhythm of the truck's bouncing and no longer felt sick to his stomach, which meant, he supposed, that you could get used to anything. It was a thought worth keeping in mind.

After a couple of hours, he could feel the truck slowing down and turning off the road. When it came to a stop, the door opened and Pfeifer stuck his head in.

"We got a Burger King here," he said, without noticeable enthusiasm. "What'll it be?" Guinness ordered a cheeseburger with fries and a 7-Up, if they had one. After a shorter time than one would have imagined possible, the camper door reopened and a white paper bag was set down on the floor. "You want to pay for that?"

Two dollar bills were produced and the door closed again without the subject of Guinness's change even so much as coming up. The truck was moving again before he had had a chance to open up the bag.

He sat on the cot to eat, bracing both feet up against the edge of the other cot and his back against the wall behind him. Plastic top or no, he didn't care to set the waxed-paper cup down, so he had to keep putting his cheeseburger back into the bag every time he wanted a French fry; it was rather like trying to extract your door key from an inside pocket when both your arms are full of grocery bags. But after all, you couldn't very well expect table service with a wine steward wearing white gloves.

It wasn't more than two or three minutes before he began to notice it, and then it came on very fast. His arms, his legs, and his tongue all started at once to feel as if they were doubling in size every five seconds, and he stared down at his cheeseburger and his cup of 7-Up, looking stupidly from one to the other, wondering which of them the creep had doped up, and what he could have used. Have it your way.

Jesus, how could he have been so fucking stupid? It was such an obvious move—he must really be deteriorating in his old age. And by a flake like Boyd.

He tried to stand up, not knowing precisely what he would have done if he had made it. Anyway, he didn't;

his knees buckled under him before he could even straighten up out of his crouch. On the way down he hit his head against the metal edge of one of the cots—he couldn't seem to decide which one—but the blow didn't quite manage to put him out. He made one more attempt to get to his feet, then said to hell with it and let unconsciousness come down on him like a broken wall.

XVI

GUINNESS WAS STILL lying on the camper floor when he woke up. The first thing he discovered was that his hands were tied behind his back, and the second that his right eye wouldn't open. Apparently, the blood from where the edge of the cot had cut his forehead had run down his temple and formed a crust over his eyelid. With a few seconds of frantic winking, however, he managed to work his lashes free, and finally to make the eye functional again.

The third thing he discovered was that he had a crashing headache, but that wasn't until he tried to move. He wondered whether it was from the crack on his head or a hangover from the knockout drops Pfeifer had put into his cheeseburger. He was reasonably certain it had been the cheeseburger—all that ketchup and pickle relish would have masked the taste of snail poison. Jesus, his head felt like it was full of rusty tacks.

A little feeling around his wrists with the tips of his fingers suggested that friend Boyd had trussed him up with cotton clothesline. That was a break; the knots would be large enough for him to have a chance of working loose.

Slowly, so as to keep himself from shattering like glass, he worked himself up into a sitting position. The truck was stopped, fortunately, and the door to the camper was open. When he had turned himself around enough to look out through it, he could see Pfeifer sitting on a fallen log about twenty yards distant, looking through what appeared to be the contents of Guinness's wallet. The guy displayed all the self-possession of a park bear leisurely poking around inside an expropriated picnic hamper.

Apparently, they were parked in the middle of a redwood forest somewhere. The only sound was the faint stirring of a breeze in the treetops—there probably wasn't another soul for five miles any direction.

"You find what you were looking for?" Guinness had tried to shout, but it came out as not much more than a reedy whisper. He sat down in the open doorway of the camper, swinging his legs over the edge as he tried to catch some air in his lungs. How far had he come, two yards? It felt like two laps of the Santa Catalina channel. He was going to have to rest up some before he would be in any shape for coming to terms with Mrs. Pfeifer's cherubic man-child.

As it turned out, though, he had only about half a minute's grace before Pfeifer crossed the distance between log and camper, took a handful of Guinness's coat lapel, and jerked him loose from his perch on the doorsill. The ground came up and smacked him painfully in the right shoulder, barely giving him time to develop enough turn to land rolling and with his collarbone intact. No, he and Boyd were just not going to hit it off.

Standing over him, Pfeifer was holding up in his right hand several small slips of paper. Guinness shook his head a couple of times to bring them into focus: They were the cards from his wallet.

"I never hearda nobody that had *two* social security cards." As it usually did with his type, having the upper hand had thickened Pfeifer's hillbilly accent. He was crouched down so that his face was about two feet directly over Guinness's. "Course, you got two o' everthing, don'tcha." He held up the two driver's licenses, both of which displayed the same photograph, so that

Guinness could see them. "Lickweather 'r Guinness—which is it, sport?"

"*Link*weather." Guinness spat out the first syllable as if he didn't like the taste of it. Certainly he didn't like the taste of whatever had been in there with the Bermuda onion; it was as if something had crawled inside his mouth to die. He hoped to hell he was reading his guy right.

He was, at least so far. Pfeifer's mouth opened into a cruel grin, displaying widely spaced teeth as square as bathroom tiles.

"Okay, Mr. Lickweather. Whatever you say." Once again he took hold of Guinness's lapel, this time pulling him up into a sitting position before he sat down himself in the now-unoccupied camper doorway. "You wanna tell me who y'r runnin' away from? Come on now, don't be shy."

Guinness glanced down quickly at his knees, giving it his best shot at looking cowardly and indecisive. Under the circumstances, it wasn't really very difficult; there is something profoundly unsettling about trying to provoke a man into kicking hell out of you, especially when you have your hands tied behind you.

"Suppose I decide not to," he ventured, after what felt like an appropriate delay. As with every illusion, if you want them to think you're bluffing, the timing is crucial.

His head cocked slightly to one side, Pfeifer made a number of disapproving little clicking sounds with his tongue as he hopped down from the camper. Guinness, who had managed to work himself around to a kneeling position, tried to prepare himself for what was coming.

The kick caught him just a little below the solar plexus, but by tightening his stomach muscles and turning enough aside at the last second, so that the blow glanced off at a slight angle, he contrived to keep at least some of the air under his ribs. It was a good kick, however, and several seconds passed before Guinness stopped making funny little grunting noises and could remember what it felt like to be able to breathe.

God damn the bastard. Damn—damn the sonuvabitch. It would just have to be with a pair of cowboy boots, wouldn't it? And ones with pointed toes. Never once sometime could it be maybe just tennis shoes or something. Just for variety.

Well, what else was new. His guts might feel as if they had been mashed to pulp back against his spinal column, but otherwise everything was going great.

There is a certain kind of man who never believes what he hasn't beaten the shit out of somebody to find out, and then he'll believe anything. Absolutely anything. Pfeifer was pretty clearly of that kind. It might momentarily be a little rough on the diaphragm, but ultimately it would make everything a lot simpler. Those kinds of men are generally pretty stupid.

But when the time came, Guinness promised himself, when the time came . . .

"Look," he managed, after perhaps three minutes of concentrated effort, "look, I can't. Please. They'll kill me."

Pfeifer just smiled. He was having such a good time.

"Well then, Mr. Lickweather, I'm afraid I'll just have to settle for what you got in y'r wallet and leave you planted under one o' these here big ol' trees." Still smiling, he pulled a familiar-looking revolver from the back pocket of his jeans. Then, using both hands to steady it, he lined up the sights on a spot just perhaps a quarter of an inch under the bottom inside corner of Guinness's left eye.

"Okay." Guinness had his eyes screwed shut and had turned his head away, as if trying to avoid the bullet. It was a realistic performance. He would have believed it himself except that Pfeifer hadn't bothered to draw back the hammer, something almost anybody would do if he really had it in mind to shoot. "Okay, okay. I'll tell you. Just put that thing away."

The story also was very good, full of those specific little details that add such an aura of authenticity. It seemed that Mr. Linkweather had been, until comparatively recently, an accountant for certain parties in Portland, Oregon, who controlled most of that city's gambling and vice. Mr. Linkweather had been skimming from the receipts and, when things got warm, had taken himself off and was now en route to join his mistress and the rest of his ill-gotten gains in one of the Banana republics.

Really, it was a very good story. It accounted for everything—the two sets of identification, all the cash he had on him, the gun. Guinness was very proud of it.

Of course, there was still the drug case, with its needle and its three little vials of colorless fluid—but it turned out that Mr. Linkweather was a diabetic.

Friend Boy bought it, the whole package from start to finish. Hell, who lies about being a bookkeeper? Guinness was beginning to experience that delicious feeling of power that comes when everything falls into place precisely as it should, when you know, positively know, that your brilliant plan has worked right down to the tiniest detail.

The poor simple bastard—you could almost hear the wheels turning as he tried to figure how Mr. Linkweather's troubles could be made to pay something. It was going to be such a pleasure stomping his ass.

"How 'bout I decide to sell you back to y'r friends up in Portland? How'd you like that, Mr. Lickweather? Hey, how'd you like that?" He laughed and shook his head and laughed again. He was feeling just fine, just fine and full of how diabolically clever he was.

Oh, he was a whiz kid, sure he was. He was on top of the world. He'd even put Guinness's gun away, back in his pocket. What the fuck, he didn't need any gun to take care of any little diabetic pencil-pusher with his hands tied. Not him. Not a smart boy like him.

Gradually, a little at a time, Guinness had made his preparations. He would have liked to have gotten his hands free, but it is never really practical to work knots loose right under somebody's nose. Besides, there was the tactical advantage that almost no one expects to be jumped by a man with his arms sewn together.

So he had settled for making it to his feet. Pfeifer didn't seem to mind. After all, he was the man in charge here; what did he have to worry about?

"You just go right ahead," Guinness said finally, with a short, brutal little laugh. "You just try shaking them down, sweetheart, and two minutes after they've finished with me they'll be converting your face into a sieve." Pfeifer's eyes narrowed, and Guinness knew that he had scored his point. "In fact, it might be a good idea if you just stayed out of this altogether."

They were perhaps fifteen feet apart now, which was perfect. If Pfeifer came for him, and he would, he would come in a rush—it was always that way. And by the time he had made half the distance, he would be too deeply committed to his own forward movement to save himself. It was obvious from the way Pfeifer was beginning to balance on the balls of his feet that he was at least thinking about coming over there and showing everybody who was boss, and when he did that he was a goner. When they charged you like that, all hot and careless with anger and dented pride, they set themselves up for you.

It wouldn't take much to get him to take those first few steps.

"Yes. Yes, you ought to stay out of this one, Boyd. A punk like you is bound to get carved into stew meat if he tries playing games with his betters, so you just cut me loose and I'll go on about my business and no hard feelings Maybe I'll throw you a bone after I've gotten to where I'm going."

He didn't announce himself, didn't start yelling or making threats—he just came. Guinness waited until he had crossed most of the distance and then stepped forward with his right foot and, continuing the counterclockwise movement until his back was completely turned, cocked his left foot up under him and let it shoot straight back. They say that if the person you're mad at lives through a kick like that, you haven't done it right, but Guinness had never made any claims to godlike proficiency in the martial arts and so was pleased with less.

It caught Pfeifer just under the navel and took him completely off the ground with a wheeze like that of a cork coming out of a half-flat bottle of champagne. After that, a carefully placed kick to the temple rendered him perfectly quiet.

Pfeifer never stirred while Guinness untied himself, or while he patted him down, retrieving his revolver and wallet, along with the drug case that, according to Ernie Tuttle, had in it the means of rendering the world forever safe from bearded hippies who preyed on runaway accountants from Portland.

Guinness weighed the possibility in his hand, and then decided to hell with it. Another time, should it prove necessary, he would have with the greatest personal pleasure put the sonuvabitch's lights out, but there was no pressing reason why right then and there he had to kill Boyd Pfeifer, and it wasn't his place to go around playing avenging angel. He was himself, according to almost any criteria, a pretty terrible person. The role of society's guardian should go to someone with cleaner hands.

So he contented himself with tying the still-limp form around one of the larger available redwoods. Pfeifer would awaken to discover himself embracing the trunk, his hands bound with the same length of clothesline he had used to tie Guinness and about a foot and a half apart. It would take him several hours, possibly on into the next day, to work himself loose, and by then even the soft bark of these trees would have burned and cut his face and bare arms until they looked like raw liver.

The keys to the truck were in the ignition. Guinness wasn't wild about driving himself all the way to Los Angeles, but events hadn't given him a second choice. Anyway, it was getting dark; no one would be able to see that clearly into the cab. And he simply wasn't an important-enough criminal to have justified an intensive statewide search. He was out of the Bay Area, and that was what really mattered.

His fingers were already curled around the door handle when he noticed that Pfeifer was beginning to stir. Guinness hesitated for a second and then picked the drug case out of the side pocket of his coat and went back over to where he had left him tied. Okay, so he wouldn't kill him; that didn't mean he couldn't have a little fun with the bastard.

When Pfeifer opened his eyes, the first thing he saw was Guinness, sitting on the ground next to him, loading up a syringe from the plastic vial marked "2." Guinness smiled at him, the way Browning's duke must have smiled at the envoy.

"Guess what, Boyd. I lied to you; this isn't insulin. Can you imagine what it might really be?" A yellowish light came into Pfeifer's eyes and he shook his head mechanically, as if the joints in his neck were gradually freezing shut.

"No?" Guinness raised his eyebrows, as if terribly surprised and disappointed, and then smiled again. "Well, that's all right; it'll give you something to ponder over while you feel your brains turning into jelly." He slipped the needle in just at the insertion of the neck muscle, and Pfeifer let out a short muffled little scream. "So long, pal."

He was out cold, even before Guinness could withdraw the needle. Somewhere, some government chemist had really known what he was doing.

It was the better part of an hour before Guinness could find his way back to the Coast Highway. One little dirt road looked pretty much like another, and at every fork you just had to guess. Eventually, though, he found a paved road with a sign that said he was in the Los Padres National Forest and could get to where he was going if he would only turn to the left and keep plugging along. The sign was correct, and within twenty minutes he was back on his way south.

Dinner was a rushed business at a Howard Johnson's in Morro Bay. It was well after nine when he arrived there, and he practically had the place to himself. They must have been in a hurry to close up and go home, because the waitress gave him the wrong flavor of ice cream for dessert—mocha fudge instead of choclate ripple—and slapped his check down before he had a chance even to touch his second cup of tea.

At about five minutes before four, he pulled into the parking lot of the Los Angeles International Airport.

He hadn't (so far as he could tell) been followed, but that wasn't very far. A child could have tailed Pfeifer, and after their little forest interlude anyone could have picked him up again and just stayed with him all the way down. How are you going to know who's behind you on the freeway?

There was a line of cabs along the curb in front of the loading area, but Guinness didn't take one until he had gone into the terminal, taken the up escalator to the ticket desks on the second floor, stood around for a few minutes watching the arrival notices change, taken the down escalator back to the baggage docks, and passed back out through the double glass doors to the outside. He didn't want to be remembered by anyone who might happen to be interested as the man who had hired a cab immediately after coming out of the parking lot. Nobody would be interested—at least nobody who wasn't already—but it was bad technique to exhibit unusual behavior, and sometimes bad technique can get you killed.

He paid off his taxi at the corner of Sunset and Vine, wishing he could simply find himself a bed and catch some sleep, but of course that was out of the question. Unless accompanied by a peroxide blonde, you couldn't check into a motel, not without luggage, and Guinness was a trifle short of blondes. Fortunately, however, it was a Friday night, and along Hollywood Boulevard there wouldn't be any problem about staying occupied and inconspicuous until daylight.

Walking the one block north, he found an all-night movie and sat through two and one half performances of *The Bedford Incident* before the department store across the street was open for business.

As soon at it was, Guinness bought himself some underwear, socks, two pairs of wash-and-wear trousers—one tan and the other black—two short-sleeved dress shirts, a black long-sleeved turtleneck sweater, and some toilet articles. All that, plus the canvas suitcase he afterward purchased at a luggage store next door, cost him a total of $137.64. Next time the police chased him out of town, he would have to remember to pack.

Using his Linkweather driver's license, he rented a car from a pretty little brunette behind the Avis desk at the Roosevelt Hotel and drove to a motel on Los Feliz Boulevard, not more than three quarters of a mile from Griffith Park.

Throwing his suitcase on the bed, he headed for the shower. Five minutes later, when he came back into the room with a towel wrapped around his loins, the phone rang.

XVII

WITHOUT LIFTING IT from its hook, Guinness held the receiver under his hand through nine rings. Two . . . three . . . His lips moved silently as he counted them off, one after the other (five . . . six . . .) the way felons at the post must have counted off the strokes of the lash. Finally, making himself a small private bet (eight . . . nine), he picked up the receiver and cradled it against the side of his face.

"Yes?"

"Mr. Guinness," answered a suave, indefinably foreign sounding voice. "You are no doubt fatigued from your travels. Would tomorrow evening be too soon?" Guinness frowned at the bare wall, counting at one the number of foreign gentlemen who would be likely to call him at a Los Angeles motel he had picked at random not more than twenty minutes earlier. Okay, so he had won his bet. Didn't that make him a clever fellow.

"That would be fine, Mr. Vlasov." His voice was under far better control than he had dared to hope.

"I am so glad. By the way, were you aware that you have been followed?—I mean, of course, by parties other than myself. I leave it to you to deal with them as you think best. Pleasant dreams."

The line went dead, and Guinness replaced the receiver. For a long moment he simply stared at the motel room carpet, trying to decide why he wasn't a whole lot more sacred than, in fact, he was.

Oh, he was scared; anybody would have been sacred. But he should, by rights, have been terrified. Vlasov was a pretty terrifying person.

In their line of work what made the difference was command of technique, and Vlasov had that. Jesus, to tail a man for over four hundred miles, a man who knew you by sight, who would be expecting you, looking for you, and not to be spotted once. You had to be very good to do that, and Vlasov was very good. All the time Guinness had known he was back there somewhere—the whole trip down he had had that funny feeling in the back of his neck that invariably meant he was being followed—but there had never been a single sign.

And in thirty-six hours Vlasov wanted to play hide-and-seek amid the eucalyptus trees in Griffith Park. Any sensible man would be scared green.

"He's a constitutional fanatic," Tuttle had said, "a man given to causes and holy crusades. Nobody could figure out why he had defected—it's the sort of question that has to be answered in a deal like this—and that was all the shrink who looked at Vlasov's interrogation films could tell us. 'This is not a man who turns traitor so he can raise fruit trees in Oregon. No way.' "

And yet he had defected. In response to a higher loyalty perhaps—but he had broken faith. With the KGB, the Party, Mother Russia, you name it. For all of which there would have to be an atonement. That streak of fanaticism, which for those outside the profession might go under the name of moral decency, would demand no less.

And what of that higher loyalty, the late Raya Natalia Vlasov? She would demand her revenge; it was only a question of how wide a net she would use, of how many little fish would have to be dragged in before she would consent to rest quiet in her grave.

One's wife, what would she not demand of her murderer, of the one who had put her in the line of fire? Guinness understood the ethics of the thing as clearly as did Vlasov, although perhaps he did not feel himself bound to them to quite the same degree.

Who the hell wouldn't be scared?

Somehow, though, he was only bored. The whole thing had come to seem so inevitable, so outside the control of either of them, that it seemed pointless to worry. One way or the other, it would sort itself out.

For some reason, Guinness found himself thinking not about Vlasov, but about the basement of a schoolmate of his in Newark. He hadn't been down in that basement in, hell, probably thirty years. Probably it didn't exist anymore.

In the basement had been a train set, an enormously complex business laid out on a huge sheet of plywood. The trains had belonged to Guinness's friend (whose father, unheard-of luxury, had laid out the track for him), and sometimes Guinness had been invited down there to help him play with them. There had also been, on a wall shelf that was otherwise cluttered with gardening tools and mason jars filled with preserved peaches, a set of about fifteen of the Tom Swift novels. Guinness had always meant to borrow a couple of them sometime and read them, just to see what they were like, but he had never gotten around to it, and then his friend had moved to Indiana and had taken the train set and the Tom Swift novels with him, and that had been that.

Guinness wondered what Tom Swift would have done about Vlasov, foreign agents having been something of a specialty with him. But then Tom Swift wouldn't have incinerated Mrs. Vlasov in the garage of her Florentine villa (you don't do that to ladies, not if you're Tom Swift), so perhaps the complexities of the situation would have been beyond him.

Anyway, Tom Swift, Mrs. Vlasov's husband, the Armies of Infernal Justice, and whoever the hell else was lurking around out there in the shadows—they were all just going to have to wait until Raymond Guinness, expert on murder, treachery, and the intricacies of Jacobean poetry, had had himself a couple of hours sleep. Guinness drew back the counterpane on the bed furthest from the bathroom door, climbed in, and was gone before he had time even to remember to pull down the shades.

By a quarter to three that afternoon, nap time was over and Guinness was headed north along the Pasadena Freeway. He had reached no firm conclusions yet as to who was following him, but the field had narrowed itself down to three cars.

The freeway shot up a little ramp and abruptly terminated in your typical downtown warehouse district, with tangles of traffic signals and telephone lines overhead and gas stations and electrical generating plants and truck-tire dealerships on either side of the street. One of three possible tails made a right turn, heading off on God only knew what innocent mission, and the second passed Guinness on the outside and was soon a good two blocks ahead of him.

That left just one late-model dark-blue hardtop to worry about. Just to make sure, Guinness continued on up until he hit Colorado Boulevard, stopped in at a coffee shop and bought himself a roll of orange-flavored Tums at the cashier's desk, and continued on his way. Of course, within half a mile his friend in the dark-blue hardtop was back there behind him again. There was no mistake.

How could he have missed the guy all that morning and the night before? He must be losing his touch, getting sloppy in his twilight years. Four hundred miles of highway, plus the whole length of Los Angeles, and he hadn't spotted him.

Well, he could forgive himself the four hundred miles—he hadn't been driving through half of that, and it had been dark the other half—but the city! All those stop signs and turnoffs: It was embarrassing.

Anyway, Guinness promised himself, he would make up for it with the smooth professional polish of his takedown.

Because the guy had to be taken down. It had to be established just who was in on this phase of the game besides Vlasov and himself. What neither of them needed now was some hideous new complication, so whoever he was, and whosoever's interests he was in there to protect, Guinness was just going to have to get rid of him.

The Huntington Library had been one of those places Guinness had haunted while he was in graduate school. It was a tidy drive from UCLA, but he had made it perhaps as often as once a week for the eighteen or so months before he was far enough along on his dissertation to be able to take that job at Belmont State and move north.

The place was a bookish paradise, almost as good as the Bodleian, and with a little help from his director he had obtained permission to use the reading room, spending many happy hours there at work at a desk from which he could look up and see before him the complete *Dictionary of National Biography* nestled in between Johnson's *Lives of the Poets* and a two-volume set of the *Alumni Cantabrigiensis*.

Today he parked his rented car in the visitors' lot just at the side entrance. Inside the reading room he hitched a stool up close to a window from which the main driveway was completely visible, opened a volume of Partridge's *Dictionary of Slang*, and pretended to read until he saw a familiar dark-blue hardtop—a Chevy, as it turned out—moving tentatively through the ornate wrought-iron gateway and up the gravel roadbed. It pulled into a space on the left-hand side of the almost perfectly square parking lot, just about as far away from Guinness's car as the dimensions of the area allowed. Whoever was inside seemed, for the time being, prepared to stay there.

Guinness couldn't see much of him; just the lower half of his face was visible through the side window. All you could really tell was that he had on a moss-green jacket and wore his sideburns down almost to the corner of his jaw. That would probably be enough, though.

There was a back door that led through a series of corridors into the main display hall, where they kept the Ellesmere Chaucer and the holograph copy of "Lycidas." That emptied into a covered walkway leading to the gallery, the entrance to which sported a little semicircular terrace with giant ferns shading you from too vulgar a contact with the afternoon sun. It was the sort of spot Henry James would have hit upon for the big scene in one of his later novels, if you can imagine such a thing as a James novel set in Los Angeles. Guinness only tarried long enough for a glance back through the greenery to make quite certain before he went inside that there was nobody immediately on his tail.

On the wall at the end of the main gallery hung Reynolds's *Mrs. Siddons As the Tragic Muse,* to which, because of a fancied resemblance to his first wife, Guinness had always been drawn. The figures in the background were ludicrous, of course: What had the eighteenth century known about tragedy? But the calm melancholy of Mrs. Siddons's eyes, or perhaps simply the looseness of her hair or the way she held her hands, reminded him of Kathleen.

"Look at the expression on that face," Louise had sputtered on the one occasion when he had taken her to see it—they had snuck off, at her insistence, for a few hours of relief from her father's reminiscences about life in the stationery business. " 'Now where could I have left the car keys?' You have funny taste in paintings, Ray," and they had gone out to sit in the garden until it was time to go back to paying their honeymoon visit to the mausoleum at Autumn Years.

Perhaps, in one of those uncanny flashes of intuition women are reputed to have, she had suspected something of the reasons for his absorption in what, after all, was not really one of the supreme achievements of Western art. But then, how could she have? She knew nothing about Kathleen apart from the bare fact of her existence.

Now, all these years later, Guinness once again stared up at the Tragic Muse as if hoping she might reveal to him the wellsprings of his destiny. Perhaps in future he shouldn't teach his sophomores quite so lively a contempt for the English Augustans.

When he turned around there was, sure enough, a fairly tall man with longish sideburns, wearing a moss-green sport coat. He was standing by the main stairway and gazing with rapt attention at a small Watteau.

Guinness began a slow circuit counterclockwise around the room, stopping for a few seconds before all of the larger paintings, until he was directly across from the other man, who had not moved. There were perhaps fifty feet between them then, and Guinness undid the button of his coat to give himself access—should it come to that—to the .25 caliber revolver that was tucked into his belt—Tuttle's holster, for some reason, had been right-handed.

He walked right across the room, knowing his friend with the sideburns wouldn't dare to turn around, and stopped only about a foot behind him. Fortunately, there was no one else in the gallery who seemed interested in that particular Watteau, so there was no one to overhear Guinness's melodramatic opening.

"Don't move, pal," he breathed into Sideburns's ear. "The first time I see your elbows wobble I'm going to burn you, right here in front of the tourists."

There was one of those pregnant silences that you read about in books. Since it is normally rather difficult to see a person's face through the back of his head, Guinness couldn't be sure just exactly how his little caution had been received.

"So now what?" the man said at last. Sensible fellow, he was going to be reasonable and not force Guinness to prove in public how tough he was.

"So now you clasp your hands together behind your back—nice and relaxed, nothing showy; just like you were taking a little stroll to ponder on the mysteries of art—and you walk on out of here and into the garden, where we'll find a quiet little nook and talk things over. And remember, I'll be right behind you. One bad move and you'll miss your birthday."

Sideburns did as he was told. The hands came around to the back slowly, and the fingers knitted loosely together. And then they both started moving slowly toward the door, Guinness about ten feet behind and a little to the right. It was nice to be dealing with professionals again; Sideburns had probably been through this routine, on one side or the other, half a dozen times in his life, and he knew enough to stay calm and do as he was told. An amateur would have started screaming bloody murder; he wouldn't have been able to help himself.

Once out in the garden, the two of them found a nice little out-of-the-way cement bench, screened off on one side by a thickly overgrown grape arbor. Before letting him sit down, Guinness subjected his prisoner to a quick frisk that came up with nothing beyond a Western-style stitched leather wallet, complete with carvings of bucking broncos and longhorn steers. There were no guns, no lethal-looking pointed instruments, nothing particularly sinister at all. Guinness took his first close look at the man who apparently had been following him all the way from the San Francisco Bay Area, and he didn't add up to much either. Just a man, perhaps in his mid- to later-forties, with dark-brown hair and that puffy, rather seedy complexion suggestive of too many five o'clock Happy Hours, of too much time fueled by salted peanuts and beer.

The wallet did contain a number of business cards reading: "Harry Spignaldo, Confidential Enquiries," with an address and phone number in Oakland.

"Sit down." The man sat down on the cement bench and Guinness held up one of the cards. "Is this you?" Harry Spignaldo nodded his head three or four times, as if anxious that the gesture should not be missed.

"Now, Mr. Spignaldo, if you want to get any older, you're going to tell me why I keep seeing your face in my rear-view mirror."

Driving away from the Huntington, after having left Mr. Spignaldo unconscious and leaning restfully against the grape arbor, Guinness considered the answer he had received to his question. He had taken up his position behind the bench, just touching the back of Spignaldo's head once in a while with the revolver muzzle, which had rendered that gentleman only too eager to provide any information he could. Mr. Spignaldo had, in fact, maintained with some heat that "a lousy seventy-five bucks a day, plus expenses" didn't oblige him to ornament the library lawn with his brains.

"Look, man," he had said, and Guinness, through the

muzzle of his revolver, could feel his trembling, "look, man, I don't carry any heat—you patted me down, so you know I don't carry any heat. I'm just a guy trying to make a buck, that's all."

"Tell me how you were supposed to make it, Harry."

"This guy comes to my office and pays me a week in advance. That's over five hundred—I ain't seen that much together in one place for months." His hands touched the bench on either side of him and then sprang nervously back into his lap. "All I was supposed to do was to follow you and let this guy—this guy who comes to my office—let him know about anybody you have anything to do with. That was all."

That was all. Anybody he had anything to do with. And that, so far, would hang it all on Doris. Guinness closed his eyes, and for a fraction of a second he thought he saw her face, the way it would be while she was being slapped around by some thickset goon who wanted her to tell him things she didn't know. It might not happen that way, but it could. There was no rule to say it couldn't, and she would know who to thank for it. Terrific.

"Who was it, Spignaldo? Who is it you're working for?" He pressed the gun muzzle a shade harder against the back of Spignaldo's skull. "Spill, Harry, or it comes off right this very minute. What did he look like?"

"Look, man, I don't *know* who he was. Just a guy with five hundred bucks. Why should I ask?"

"You want to die, Harry? What did he look like?"

"Okay, man, okay. Around six feet. A dark suit, double breasted; looked like he must have bought it second-hand from Harry Truman. Maybe fifty years old; maybe a hundred and ninety, two hundred pounds. A big guy. Lightish hair, but not blond. Foreign from the sound of him."

"Foreign from where, Harry?"

"How should I know, man? I never finished the tenth grade."

"GUESS!"

"Okay, okay. I'm trying." Spignaldo's hands came back out of his lap and pressed palms down against the surface of the bench on either side of him. Guinness noticed how white the nail beds were. "He sounded like that guy in the old movies—the one that was supposed to turn into a bat."

"Dracula? Bela Lugosi? You mean he sounded like Bela Lugosi?"

"Yeah. That's right. Like Dracula."

"How were you supposed to get in touch when you had learned something? You were supposed to report, weren't you?"

"Yeah. By phone. He gave me a number to call."

"Tell me."

"Eight two seven, three seven nine five. In the City."

"Good boy, Harry. And when you wake up, just remember that you did, in fact, wake up."

With that, he quickly transferred the revolver over to his right hand and used the side of his left to give Spignaldo a sharp crack at the top joint of his neck, just where it ran into the base of his skull. Spignaldo started slightly, but then went limp and began falling forward from the waist. Guinness caught him by the nape of his collar and leaned him against the arbor.

"That's right. Like Dracula." Dracula in an antique, double-breasted suit. Guinness stared grimly over his steering wheel as he drove back along Colorado Boulevard, unable to restrain a certain sneaking admiration for Comrade Vlasov's imaginative daring. Because in his position it took guts to con the Russians into providing you with your stalking horse. They must have been sorry to lose him; the man was obviously a tactician of genius.

What had he done? Phoned up the San Francisco consulate at a quarter to three in the morning, ranting hysterically into some undersecretary's ear about how he was going to cancel the ticket on a certain Raymond Guinness of 1427 Avon Street in the obscure hamlet of Belmont, California, and how they'd never be able to stop him? Something like that, probably.

Not that the Russians would care, even if he did throw in that said Guinness was the gentleman mentioned on such-and-such a page of the Bluebook. But

Guinness would be their first solid lead to Vlasov, and they would care about that. Those people took a very dim view of treason.

So they would put a tag on Guinness, just to see if he would lead them to Vlasov. They wouldn't dare use any of their own personnel, not when there was such an excellent chance of Guinness ending up messily murdered. No, they would use outside help. Some innocuous slob like Harry Spignaldo. And Vlasov, who clearly had his ways of finding such things out, would just tag along behind. Spignaldo would follow Guinness, Vlasov would follow Spignaldo, and Guinness would be spared the sight of any uncomfortably familiar Slavic faces. It was very tidy. Very tidy indeed.

XVIII

GUINNESS USED HIS fork to turn over the cherry tomato in the center of his small green salad. The other side didn't look as shriveled, but he decided not to eat it anyway and lifted it out and onto the glass ashtray just in front of the napkin dispenser. The dispenser was at the wall end of his table, which he had picked because it was away from the windows and allowed him an unobstructed view of the main entrance.

In addition to the salad, he had before him an "extra-cut" rib-eye steak, a baked potato that came with a little paper tub of sour cream, a small steel pot of hot water in which to steep his tea bag, and a slice of Boston cream pie. The condemned man enjoyed a hearty meal.

Except that he wasn't enjoying it. He ate with the glum determination of a twelve-year-old playing scales on the piano. The food, though objectively tasty, sat like lead on his stomach, and he felt almost ready to gag with every swallow. He had only bothered with dinner on the assumption that it would steady his nerves.

They needed steadying. Guinness had devoted the entire previous four hours, ever since he had left Spignaldo sleeping peacefully in the gardens of the Huntington Library, to making absolutely certain that no one was following him.

Staying away from the freeways as much as possible,

he had made his cautious way to the downtown area of Los Angeles and parked on the roof of a five-story garage just catercorner from the Times Mirror Square. It was probably silly of him, but he didn't really much care for the idea of riding around in a car that Vlasov and anybody else who cared to play would by this time be able to spot in a second. It made him feel naked. There was an Avis office just three blocks to the east, so what the hell.

For the rest he just kept on driving through into the evening. He didn't dare go back to his Los Feliz motel room, and it wasn't necessary anyway. He hadn't even bothered to unpack.

The old fuddy behind the desk had decided to take it as a personal affront when Guinness checked out after only four hours, but life is hard and you can't please everyone. If Spignaldo had a relief man—hell, he would have to have had a relief man; nobody can tail you for days on end by himself—the motel would be where he would have to go. It would be about his only chance of picking up the trail.

But as he sat in the Lariat Steak House in Santa Monica, picking over the contents of his salad bowl, it wasn't any crushing anxieties about Spignaldo and his confederates that were disturbing Guinness's digestion. No, in all likelihood, Spignaldo was at that moment on his way back to Oakland, pondering over the merits of some other line of work. No, he was safe enough from Spignaldo; it was Vlasov who presented the danger.

But then, ever had it been so.

Vlasov was brilliant and apparently in perfect control, both of the situation and himself. "Would tomorrow evening be too soon?" He might have been issuing an invitation to play bridge.

And this was the man who was planning to kill him, who had apparently lived through the last seven years with no other purpose. Seven years of planning and hatred, and it was all aimed right at Guinness's head. Seven years, and they were but as few because he loved her.

She must have been quite a lady, Mrs. Vlasov; she

would have to have been to have inspired such a revenge. A grand passion apparently, the real thing. Guinness wondered what it must be like to love like that. It had to be neurotic, that kind of love; it had to be.

As if physically to disengage himself, Guinness let his fork drop with a clatter onto the little sterling steel plate on which his half-eaten steak rested, and rose to leave. The huge menu board that you faced as you slid your tray along to place your order and pick up your dessert and hot drink had said, "No Tipping," but he left a dollar for the busboy anyway, folding it once and placing it underneath his cup and saucer. He had been overtipping now for some time, as if in a series of small acts of contrition.

Outside, with the breeze from the ocean just catching at the side vents of his open jacket, he felt better. Vlasov shrank in his imagination back down to human scale; after all, like Guinness, he was merely a man. He could be killed. And for all his enormous virtuosity as a tactician, he was pretty obviously off the wall.

Sane men didn't go around slipping ice picks into housewives just to satisfy some private whim. They didn't scare the shit out of you by stuffing your ignition lock full of nitrogen triiodide and then issue elaborate challenges to come shoot it out with them in back of the merry-go-round at Griffith Park. The guy was a nut.

Guinness closed his eyes for a moment and tried to think about something else.

Where was he, exactly? Probably somewhere near Venice; he knew that if he looked behind him he would just be able to make out a smear of light from the cars on the San Diego Freeway.

For a brief while in grad school he had kept company with a girl who lived in Venice. She had worked in the records department at city hall, sorting traffic tickets or something, but in her free time she had been very into ceramics and little theater—that sort of thing. After a couple of months she had decided that Guinness just didn't have an artistic soul and they had split up.

The luckiest break of her life, as it had turned out.

Otherwise it would have been her body they found on his kitchen floor.

And, merciful God, what about himself? Even if by some miracle Vlasov didn't kill him tomorrow, that wouldn't exactly turn him into a preferred risk. How long could he last? The KGB knew who he was, knew all about him—Vlasov had seen to that—and he would be a sitting duck any time they decided they wanted to balance the score.

And then there was Tuttle to deal with.

Tuttle would be after him to take up his old line again; that had almost been part of the deal. And Tuttle would have his ways of making it difficult if he tried to refuse. Guinness wasn't even sure he wanted to refuse.

A sitting duck, a goddamn sitting duck. He'd be lucky if he lasted out the year. Vlasov could almost save himself the trouble.

Guinness unlocked his car door, having decided he needed to find himself a nice noisy crowd. He wasn't the best company for himself tonight, and he needed distracting.

The Baskin-Robbins in Westwood was like a fish-bowl—brightly lit, with three walls almost entirely of glass—but so what? No one was dogging his trail, of that he had abundantly satisfied himself, and it was just the sort of place Vlasov would most wish to avoid. Hell, half the adult population of the world was out looking for him—so while he wanted to live, Vlasov would keep his head pulled in. And on a Saturday evening every sidewalk and store in the area was packed with Dionysian undergraduates from UCLA, which was within walking distance.

Guinness knew, or at least had once known, precisely how far it was by shank's mare from the English department offices to this part of the downtown, if you could talk about a place like Westwood as having a downtown. He had walked it, back and forth, almost every day during the year and a half he had lived in Los Angeles and spent his hours pouring over volumes of early seventeenth-century meditative verse.

It had been a strange period in his life, those eighteen

months—or at least the first three or four—far worse than what he was going through now. This was a cake-walk; all he had to deal with was the probability, shading off into certainty, that he was for it. It was over—this week, or sometime. But it was over. If Vlasov didn't get him, they, whoever they would be, were coming for him, and it would be his turn to be found one night in a seat at the movies, with a needle mark hidden by the hairline at the base of his skull. Big deal—nobody lives forever.

But back then, Jesus. If he had dinner at the Tia Maria, he would spend ten minutes sifting through the chili, looking for the slivers of glass; walking down a city sidewalk, he would study the faces, wondering which one would be his man and where the bullet would hit.

But that wasn't the worst. Perhaps you will be more sensitive to it one day than another, but the feeling that you are a target never leaves. A person can get used to anything.

It was the living over of every touch he had ever made, night after night, while he tried to sleep. Very specific memories—the precise geometry of Janik Shevliskin's fall, the patterns traced through the air by his arms and legs as an ounce and a half of copper-jacketed lead turned his brain into blackberry cobbler.

Everything. The powder loads in the cartridges, the times of the trains, the room numbers of hotels in Munich and Amsterdam. Like a little boy who has mucked up his homework and has to stay after school to write it out a hundred times on the blackboard.

Not guilt, exactly. Simply the burden of a past. The past is the one constant—it and the fact that its ghosts always find you out in the end.

But this too passed away—everything does. Guinness learned how to sleep again, and the bogeymen didn't come to get him after all. He knew that they would, but they didn't. So he survived and took a degree in British literature and a job up north and, eventually, a wife. There had been plenty of time to lull him to sleep. And then Vlasov had come, who was enough of a bogeyman for anybody, and proved him right after all.

Guinness sat at one of the little desk-seats Baskin-Robbins provides its customers with and slowly worked his way through the hot butterscotch sundae with French vanilla ice cream (no nuts and no cherry) he had purchased for ninety-five cents. All the other little desk-seats were filled along all three walls, filled with little clusters of two or three people identifiably together. It was an unpleasant shock to realize suddenly that he was the only one there alone, and the only one there over the age of twenty-three or so; all the rest were in some variation of the Student Uniform: jeans and polo shirt or jeans and nylon windbreaker or jeans and army fatigue jacket. All the boys—and they were mostly boys for some reason—sat bunched down with their legs thrust far out in front of them, as if their chairs were runaway soapbox racers and they were trying to brake them with their feet.

The girls didn't seem to have any feet at all; their legs were drawn up under them, giving them rather the appearance of nesting birds.

Male and female, they all seemed engaged in the same vast, shapeless, intensely jocular debate, which would spill over from one little cluster to the other as people got up or sat down or left or came away from the counter with their arms full of various combinations of ice cream and heavy syrup and carbonated water. It was a familiar phenomenon, for which the appropriate metaphors were tribal rites and feeding time at the zoo.

Behind his eyes, where he could be reasonably certain it wouldn't show, Guinness frowned slightly and decided that perhaps he wasn't being entirely fair. It was, of course, easy to be disdainful of what one of his colleagues—a man who had himself at around age sixty shed his tie and wife and tweed jacket for beads and a Pendleton shirt that never seemed to get buttoned above the navel—called "The Young." It was especially easy if you weren't a captive of the Mr. Chips Syndrome, and Guinness wasn't.

Of course, he had been once; or at least he had contrived to think that he was, which comes to the same thing. All along, their respect and regard, which probably he had never had, had been important to him, even at that upper-crusty public school in London into which Byron had somehow managed to smuggle him.

All those skinny, pimpled, pale-faced adolescent boys in the upper forms, to whom he had solemnly assigned "research" papers designed to arrive at profound conclusions about Longinus and Romanesque art and the origins of the Punic Wars in three to five typewritten pages, due Monday. God, how he had worried over them and browbeaten them and invited them to tea on Thursday afternoons so they could talk about their plans for university and their terror of their parents and stare hopelessly at the curve of Kathleen's thigh muscle under her long peasant dresses.

Even for them he had experienced compassion and a certain contemptuous fondness, symptoms that grew more noticeable after Kathleen had been brought to fruition and had put him squarely in the parent racket himself. And something had survived and followed him to California and the corridors of Belmont State.

But of course he had outgrown it.

And even that was a lie. What he really felt at that moment, as he perfectly well knew, was envy. Again, envy.

Across the room from him was a girl of perhaps twenty, dressed in a pair of skin-tight elaborately faded denims and a yellow tee shirt that showed off her breasts to the best possible advantage. She had soft blond hair that perhaps hadn't even come out of a tube, and she was laughing and talking with appropriately adorable gestures and now and then coyly closing her lips over the straw of her pineapple milkshake. The boy toward whom all this was directed was also blond and ruggedly handsome in a solidly midwestern sort of way—he rather reminded Guinness of the kid who had been his roommate during his freshman year at Ohio State.

The two of them had so much future ahead that it probably never occurred to either of them to think about it. They would never be old or afraid or intimate with pain and death; everything to come would be part of an unbroken series of triumphs. And tonight they would lie in each other's arms, after making wonderful, prelapsarian love, and dream no dreams. So it had been destined from the first star swirls.

XIX

THE PARK, WHICH according to Guinness's map had a circumference of several miles, was surrounded by a chainlink fence. Thank God there weren't the customary three angled strands of barbed wire at the top—the stuff that had made his life miserable all over Eastern Europe—so getting over wasn't going to be a big problem. He figured the height at about ten feet.

It was two-fifteen in the afternoon and a taxi had dropped him off on Los Feliz Boulevard, within walking distance of the southeastern corner of the park. On the other side of the fence was a stand of medium-sized scrub oaks that seemed to go on up the rising ground forever, providing plenty of cover.

Besides, who was going to notice? Why, after all, would anyone break into Griffith Park in the middle of the afternoon when he could just as easily drive through the main gate without even having to pay admission? Why indeed?

Because for once in his life he might like not having his every move anticipated and observed by one Misha Fedorovich Vlasov, formerly of the KGB. That was why. It seemed like a good enough reason.

He climbed over in the approved manner, first throwing his jacket up and over the top and then picking a spot where the chain was anchored to a post—it wouldn't rattle so much that way, and it wasn't as likely to buckle under the strain and make you lose your toe-hold—and then just crawling straight up, like a lizard up the face of a hot rock. The trick was to do it fast, so the thought of how the wire seemed as if it would cut your fingers straight through to the bone wouldn't make you shift weight back to your feet. You couldn't walk up a fence like a goddamn flight of stairs; the purchase was lousy.

He jumped down onto the other side, landing with his knees well bent and catching himself with his hands as the shock of impact tried to send him sprawling.

Not too bad. Ray Guinness, former boy wonder of the cloak-and-dagger set, could still manage a ten-foot fence without putting himself in the hospital. That, at least, was a start. He picked up his jacket, dusted it off, checked to make sure that the drug kit in the inside pocket had survived intact (perhaps it would have been better to have kept it with him, but all he needed was to slip and he would have stood a better-than-even chance of ending up with a butt full of curare-soaked glass), and headed off into the trees. It was a long walk from there to the merry-go-round.

He felt better this afternoon. But then that was the way it always happened—you got the jitters the night before every touch, regular as clockwork, and they translated themselves into self-loathing and *Weltschmerz*. The more dangerous the job, the more you felt like slashing your wrists, or taking a vow of silence at the door of a Trappist monastery.

Once in Liège, in 1964, he had spent the entire night, right on through from dusk to dawn, drafting and redrafting a letter to his mother, with whom he had held no contact in almost ten years.

It had taken the form of an extended apology for his having been such a prick as a kid, for it seemed that Mamma, with her beer bottles and her doorknob-sized knuckles, had actually been a poor thing. He should have understood, it became apparent in the harsh light of his desk lamp, that her indifference to him had grown out of the dead-end quality of her own life. For those ten or so hours he had lived through every detail of her imagined history, and he realized what must have been the precise nature of her despair. But of course he hadn't realized it at the time and, in consequence, of course, had failed her. Everything, it seemed—her misery and his own—was his fault.

But such things pass, and the next morning, with a tight disapproving little smile at his own apparent flair for the melodramatic, he had burned all versions of the letter—there had been five, if he remembered correctly—one page at a time in the wastepaper basket of his hotel room, and that afternoon one Georg Kleutgen, himself an assassin noted in the trade for his flawless, if perhaps excessively brutal, methodology, was found in the basement garage of his apartment building, slumped over the steering wheel of his Citroën with a bullet hole about the diameter of a lead pencil in front of his left ear. The attendant hadn't seen anybody leave or enter except his regular tenants, and Kleutgen's employers were at a loss to explain how their man could have allowed himself to be polished off so neatly.

By the time the body had been discovered, Guinness was already on a plane back to London. That night he slept like a baby.

The afternoon sunlight flickered through the branches of the scrub oaks as they stirred in a faint breeze that must ultimately have come from the ocean. Guinness walked slowly, enjoying the coolness of the mottled shade and the sound of the leaves crackling under the soles of his shoes. There was no hurry.

After all, what difference did it make? Raymond Guinness and Misha Fedorovich Vlasov, both former government employees and widowers, and both, if judged by any reasonable standard of conduct, evil men. Ray and Misha, the Katzenjammer Kids, Tweedledum and Tweedledee—as alike as clones. One of them would die and then, eventually, the other would die under circumstances that were predictable but ultimately beside the point; they were the twin horsemen of their own private apocalypse. Ray and Misha, the Katzenjammer Kids, Tweedledum and Tweedledee.

And where was Tweedledee this bright afternoon—oiling his dueling pistol? Making peace with his Marxist god, or grieving over the long-dead Raya Natalia?

It would be nice to indulge the luxury of remorse, but it was something Guinness was painfully aware that he simply could not afford. In that respect, Vlasov had been lucky.

Or perhaps it was simply that Guinness had been able to set private feelings aside in order to be about the business of surviving, and perhaps Vlasov had not. Perhaps that made Vlasov better—having that capacity for surrendering even his life to the act of mourning.

In his advance, Guinness startled a chipmunk, who ran hurriedly up the trunk of an oak tree, and Guinness smiled and noticed how much the bark of oak trees looks like the fractured surface of dried mud and wondered, quite dispassionately, whether or not he would be alive the next day, the day on which he had contracted to return his rented car to the Avis office in downtown Los Angeles. Well, perhaps if he asked him nicely enough, Vlasov would do it for him.

Maybe it was simply part of his technique—Guinness had never really bothered sorting it all out—but somewhere along the line, somehow every bit finally ended up looking like a particularly kinky kind of suicide attempt. You study a man, you study his routines and his preferences and his patterns of thought, you get so far inside his head that you sit down in a restaurant and, as you run your eyes over the items on the menu, catch yourself thinking, "No, I can't have that; he probably doesn't care for it."

His image and your own become so blurred together in your mind that it no longer seems possible, or particularly worthwhile, to try separating them. Perhaps that, and not the fear of death, is what gets to you the night before you're supposed to drop the hammer. Or perhaps it's more complicated than that.

Or perhaps it really doesn't matter, because by the next morning the success or failure of the thing, the question of who is going to live and who die, has begun to appear perfectly academic. Am I the same person I was yesterday? And if I'm not, did I kill that other person in order to become me?

Of course, Vlasov had killed Louise out of motives that were purely personal; it wasn't as if the Communists had put a contract out on her. Vlasov had put himself outside of all law, had turned his back on everything and gone out entirely, irrevocably, on his own. That did seem to constitute a real moral difference between them.

Oh hell, who did he think he was kidding? Hadn't he gone out to nail Vlasov because of Kathleen? Vlasov had created a few marital problems for him, so he had gotten all huffy about it and trotted off to Florence to try barbecuing the guy in his garage. And the fact that, like a good little soldier, he had done it with the encouragement and in the name of the British Foreign Office did not, after all, constitute much of a defense. Some jobs should be left to other hands.

They had both of them violated the one absolute commandment of a profession not noted for honoring ethical mandates: Thou shalt not go around snuffing people just because they happen to have pissed you off.

Tweedeldum and Tweedledee.

Jesus, to throw it all away like that, to kiss a lifetime of service to the Party goodbye just for the exquisite pleasure of doing a number on the man who inadvertently had killed your better half. Vlasov had to be off the wall; it was the act of a lunatic.

And yet, somehow, rather grand. Confronted with that kind of passion, Guinness suddenly couldn't help feeling rather paltry. It was so outside the range of his simple Anglo-Saxon soul; perhaps you had to be a Russian.

According to the map he had picked up at a gas station in Santa Monica, it was, as the crow flies, probably a good three miles from where he had climbed the fence into the park to the little picnic area near the main entrance. Guinness was sure that was the spot Vlasov meant; they don't move merry-go-rounds around much, and he thought he remembered the thing from a time he and a friend from grad school and a couple of girls from the College of Nursing at USC had gone there to lie on the grass and drink beer.

And, since he wasn't a crow, it wasn't an easy three miles, either. Overland all the way, because he couldn't risk using the roads. All he could do was to keep the sun over his left shoulder and plod on.

Once, he made a vast detour to avoid disturbing a couple who had parked their Volkswagen off the road and were stretched out on an army blanket, apparently just getting ready to make love. Or perhaps they had finished already; it was impossible to tell. Guinness only just caught sight of the girl, who was just facing away from him, sitting up with her hands behind her back either to hook or to unhook her brassiere. As soon as he saw her, he dropped down to a crouch, where he waited perhaps ten or twenty seconds, just to make sure she hadn't noticed him, before starting back the way he had come. It would have seemed monstrous to have wrecked their little moment, and what woman wouldn't have been deeply unsettled at being discovered three quarters of the way out of her clothes? It was a tough life, but one tried to keep civilians away from the combat zone. He came away as quietly as he could.

It was close to four o'clock when he saw the Golden Gate Freeway in the distance. He saw it first, even though it was furthest away, and then the main gate and finally the picnic area. He made a wide arc to the left, traveling on rising ground for perhaps half an hour, before he had a clear view of the merry-go-round.

He was just below the crest of a hill. A good spot, he decided, well concealed but with plently of visibility. And there were plenty of underbrush and dry leaves; if he kept his ears open, nobody was likely to be able to sneak up on him. So he sat down, with his back against the trunk of one of the larger scrub oaks, and began to wait.

The cars started heading out through the main gate by about five-thirty. At a quarter to six a blue Volkswagen, indistinguishable from the one belonging to his pastoral lovers, wound around the bottom of the hill and was gone. Perhaps it was them. Perhaps they were students anxious not to miss dinner at their college union. They seemed about the right age, and students can be poor enough to want to save a few bucks on the price of a motel room. God, didn't Guinness know that.

Perhaps it was somebody else—completely different people. And what difference did it make anyway?

The picnic grounds weren't completely empty until close to seven, by which time the sun was almost directly at Guinness's back. Finally, at a little before seven-thirty, a truck drove through and parked just beyond the gates and someone climbed out to swing them shut and stitch them together with a padlock and a length of chain. After that, it was perfectly quiet, and before long the only light was from the cars out on the freeway. Guinness wondered how long it would be before Vlasov decided it was time to begin.

It was after ten before he got his answer.

Almost on a line between where Guinness was sitting and the merry-go-round, there was a narrow little dirt path of perhaps a hundred yards in length. On the left was a grassy shoulder that sloped down to the picnic area and on the right a stand of eucalyptus trees that stretched on out past the clearing occupied by the merry-go-round and covered altogether perhaps as much as three quarters of a mile square. The path ran from the asphalt roadway that skirted the bottom of Guinness's hill to the merry-go-round. Probably, from the air it looked like the stick of a lollipop.

At the far end, on the left, was a little unpainted shed, from which, presumably, the merry-go-round was controlled and powered. At seven minutes after ten an electric light over the shed's one-and-only doorway popped on.

Well, it would have been something like that. Vlasov was no kind of an idiot; he wouldn't have been expecting Guinness to just drive right up to the front gate. No, he would know that his man would sneak in hours ahead of time and find himself a nice safe place from which to watch developments. Neither of them was going to walk blindly into anything, and it wouldn't have been good form to expect it.

Vlasov had just issued his invitation to the dance.

Guinness began working his way down the hill—not straight down, but at an angle. He didn't have any illusions about Vlasov not having guessed his approximate location, and he didn't particularly want to walk into his arms; so he took it careful, changing his direction every two or three dozen yards and stopping every few minutes to listen. That sort of thing takes time.

He made it to the roadway without anything ugly happening, so he took his jacket off, with the drug kit still in the inside pocket, folded it carefully, and jammed it in behind a fallen log. Then he waited a few seconds before running like hell for the eucalyptus grove on the other side, staying low and rolling for cover when he made it across. Nobody shot at him.

Okay, so apparently Vlasov had decided to be a sport and play by gentlemen's rules. Wonderful. So here he was, Raymond Guinness, in the middle of the Great Outdoors, all set to take on an experienced and clever, if slightly daft, Russian agent—and without so much as a fucking tailor's needle for protection.

Oh yes, he had left his gun back at his motel room. And on purpose, no less.

The plan was, you see, that he was going to psych friend Vlasov out. Vlasov, so the theory goes, had to be hanging onto his self-possession by a thread, so what would it do to him to realize that the man he had centered his life around destroying wasn't even frightened enough to bother about coming armed? Anyway, that was the plan.

Besides, it was impossible to believe that the issues between them could be resolved on so crude a basis as their relative firepower. You do not aim guns at mirror images of yourself. Whatever Vlasov might think, they would have to fight it out on some other level than that. One suspected, one hoped, that the upper hand would be a state of mind.

The drug kit—well, that was for later. When the time came for shooting hypos full of curare into people's veins—if it ever did—there would be all the time in the world.

A quick search turned up a sizable eucalyptus branch, about eight feet long and reasonably sound, lying on the ground. If you plan to strike a gong, you need a mallet. Guinness took the branch in both hands, like a baseball bat, squared off against the biggest tree he could find, and cut loose. Branch broke across trunk with a satisfying whack, loud as a pistol shot, that after bouncing around through the eucalyptus grove for a while would sound from a distance as if it might have come from anywhere.

R.S.V.P. Now the next move was up to Vlasov.

After several minutes—he would need plenty of time to make up his mind; this wasn't precisely charades they were playing—the merry-go-round light went on. Guinness took a cautious survey and through the trees was finally able to make out a human form sitting on the turntable, just at the foot of the path. Perhaps if he had brought a gun . . .

But no. Vlasov was well out of range, and there was no way he was going to sit there like a good boy until Guinness could get close enough to draw a bead. It was because they both understood things like that that Guinness had left the damn thing behind.

He stepped out into the middle of the path, and the figure on the merry-go-round turntable never moved. Guinness could see him quite clearly now; it was Vlasov all right, little changed in seven years.

"You should have seen him, cool and unreachable, slouched down in a chair with his head back, his elbows on the armrests and his knees crossed, holding a Turkish cigarette between thumb and first finger and looking for all the world like a character out of a Fitzgerald novel." That was how Tuttle had described him, and there he was, to the life, his back against one of the brass merry-go-round poles, smoking a cigarette.

One step at a time, very slowly, Guinness started down the path toward him. Each step constituted an individual act of will.

Vlasov, of course, didn't even seem to notice. He just sat there, occasionally taking the cigarette from between his lips and exhaling a feathery plume of white smoke that would rise through the night air to swarm around the overhead light like a cloud of angry bees. There was a pistol lying beside him on the turntable, but he never looked at it. Why should he? He knew it was there.

Finally, when Guinness had stopped at a point just outside the sixty-foot distance beyond which not many men in the world can be expected to hit a moving target, Vlasov brought down his gaze and smiled. The light caught his rimless glasses at a peculiar angle, etching two dark smears of shadow down his cheekbones.

"Good evening, Mr. Guinness. It was gracious of you to come."

XX

It was a warm night and the crickets were busy. The air was heavy with the competing odors of eucalyptus oil and smog, and in the extreme distance, really only as a gray suggestion of sound, was the muffled throbbing of traffic.

They were quite alone. Possibly nowhere else in Greater Los Angeles could they have contrived to be quite so alone. Somehow, it really wasn't a very encouraging thought.

Guinness tried hard to remember what it had been like the only other time in his life he had been genuinely afraid, afraid with no compensating alloy of excitement, no surging of adrenaline and heroic passion. What he wanted was to recall the texture of that fear, to see if he could bring back how it had felt.

That had been Hornbeck, of course. The first man he had ever killed for money. The first man he had ever killed, period. Climbing out onto the shoulder of that lonely stretch of English roadway, and smiling and saying, "Can I give you a hand?" It had been the bravest thing he had ever done in his life, and he had been scared to death.

But it didn't compare with this. There could never have been anything like this.

Vlasov. The way the light from overhead turned his

rimless glasses into shining impenetrable disks behind which it was impossible to imagine there could be eyes. Then he would move and the face would become human again.

He had lost weight, it looked like. In seven years he had lost quite a lot of weight. Guinness could remember, seven years before, thinking how slender, how ascetic he had looked; but now there were hollows in his temples and the skin over his jawbone seemed as thin as paper.

He looked like a death's head, like Dr. Donne in his shroud. The man reeked of death; it seemed to surround him like a private atmosphere. Surely, anyone who touched him or spoke to him or even breathed the same air would have to die.

Come on, Guinness, you're letting him get to you. Stay loose, man. Stay loose and don't let him psych you—that was going to be your gambit, remember? What the hell, he's just a man, not a visitation.

Guinness hooked one thumb through the front belt loop of his trousers and forced himself to grin. He tried to make it a good grin, full of easygoing contempt, but it didn't seem likely that he was fooling anybody.

"It was good of you to ask me. I take it that we're alone here?" The question was purely rhetorical. If there had been anything else alive there, any living thing at all, Guinness would have known about it. It was a sense that you developed in The Business, if you lived, or perhaps you were born with it. A kind of private radar.

The cigarette dropped from between Vlasov's fingers onto the asphalt walkway, and his shoe pivoted slightly on its heel to cover the spot where it had landed. With the thumb and first finger of his left hand, he reached into his shirt pocket and extracted a nearly empty pack. His right hand never moved from where it was resting lightly on the side of his thigh—just a spasm of movement away from the pistol, the make of which Guinness couldn't seem to place but which looked to be small, no more than 7 mm.

For some reason, it seemed worth noticing that the cigarettes were Camels, the kind without the filters.

Vlasov shook one out and placed it between his lips. He crumpled the pack and dropped it on the turntable beside him before going back to his shirt pocket for a lighter. The shadows down from his cheekbones disappeared as he clicked on the tiny point of flame.

"We are," he said quietly, drawing on the cigarette. "Now. There was a watchman, as it turned out, but . . ." The meaning was completed in a tiny shrug as the lighter flame went out with a snap. "He is in the shed."

Guinness didn't find it necessary to inquire what had happened to the watchman. He shifted his weight from one leg to the other, but the grin never wavered.

"Okay, so be it. Now that there's only the two of us, what exactly did you have in mind?"

Just like Eric Von Stroheim on "The Late Show," Vlasov took the cigarette out of his mouth, pinched backward between first finger and thumb. He waved it around in a languid faintly theatrical circle that made you wonder if he wasn't deliberately trying to distract your attention away from the other hand, the one that sooner or later was going to make a dive for that gun.

"Eventually, of course, I have it in mind to kill you." There was nothing particularly remarkable about the way he said it, except that when he said it he moved his head slightly and his eyeglasses lost the glare from the overhead light. For just a second, then, you could see his eyes, and his eyes were as eloquent as you could want.

This, Raymond M. Guinness, in case you hadn't noticed, is a man who hates the insides of your bones.

Well, that was his problem.

"But there is, after all, no great need for haste." Vlasov readjusted himself, and once again his eyes were lost behind their blank disks of yellow light. "We have time to talk."

"Maybe I don't feel like talking."

Vlasov only smiled his weird death's head smile and turned his hand slightly on the end of his wrist. It was a gesture that conveyed his indifference to what Guinness maybe didn't feel like—that and a profound confidence that he could afford to be just as indifferent as might please him.

Well, something would have to be done about that, the sonuvabitch.

And that was the great thing at this moment—to break his confidence, somehow to put him off his stride. At the moment the initiative was Vlasov's.

"Oh come now, Mr. Guinness. A man must surely be interested in the reasons why he is about to die. So much curiosity is only natural."

Somewhere high up in the eucalyptus trees a night bird was singing a peculiar, restless, tumbling sort of song. Perhaps there were two of them and they were having an argument—the air was too hot and windless to allow you to tell. Guinness laughed softly, but not too softly to be heard.

"If I remember, you've tried to kill me once already. Just what possesses you to think I'm going to let you do any better this time?"

"I take it you are referring to Oslo?" Vlasov shrugged slightly and might even have been smiling behind his clouds of cigarette smoke. "Yes, that was a sadly mismanaged affair."

He seemed for a second to have lost himself, to have surrendered entirely to the thought of just how sadly mismanaged it had been. If it had worked, after all . . .

But he was back an instant later, and with his cigarette he made a slight pointing gesture in Guinness's direction. He made it once, and then, as if driving some conclusion home, twice more.

"But, you see, you were the difficulty. You were nothing more to us than a code name on the index tab of a dossier filled with dates and speculation, and it is less than simple to assassinate a ghost.

"And then there was the problem of subordinates; no plan is better than the people one chooses to carry it out. Those two, I knew they were not 'up' to it, as you Americans say. 'Up to it'—such a curious idiom."

Again the cigarette made its slow circle, and again the death's head smiled.

"But you are no longer a ghost, Mr. Guinness, and, as you see, this time I have taken the task upon myself. Perhaps before I simply did not want you badly enough."

"And you want me badly enough now, you think?"

"Oh yes, Mr. Guinness," Vlasov half whispered. And then he laughed. It was an ugly sound. "Yes, I want you very badly now. Now, you understand, the matter is personal. I should imagine that it is now for the both of us."

Without moving his eyes, Guinness began to study the ground fall to his right. The eucalyptus was particularly thick just there and, away from the overhead lighting around the carrousel, it was dark as the inside of a bat's ass hole.

Very slowly, he brought his left hand up to the side of his face and scratched the bottom edge of his sideburn with the nail of his little finger. It was a gesture he had seen Byron Down make perhaps a hundred times, and with Byron it always suggested the same refusal to be intimidated, to grant something too much importance.

"You refer to the ladies? Vlasov, you shouldn't be so sentimental—it impairs the judgment."

"Let us say, rather, that it provides a motive." Again Vlasov let his cigarette drop to the asphalt and stamped it out. His hand felt at his breast pocket for a moment and then dropped to his lap when, apparently, he remembered that the pack had been empty and he had thrown it away. "We have each suffered an injury that demands retribution. For each of us, then, revenge is a duty we owe to the dead and to ourselves. It is a categorical imperative."

From the tone it was impossible to tell whether he was serious or joking. Another man would have been joking—would have had to have been. The whole idea was so unreal. People in their line of work simply didn't steer by those kinds of coordinates. A categorical imperative, Jesus. It took a few seconds before Guinness could even remember what a categorical imperative was.

Yet it never crossed his mind that Vlasov could be anything except serious, and in that seriousness Guinness saw his chance.

He let his hand drop back down to his side. Vlasov didn't start, which was a good sign. Apparently there were some things he was concentrating on harder than he was on staying alive.

"Well, if you feel that way, it seems like you've caused everybody a lot of unnecessary trouble. Why couldn't you have just stayed home in Moscow and blown your brains out there without inconveniencing anybody?"

Vlasov didn't reply. In fact, for a long moment he didn't do anything, didn't even move. Which, by itself, was reply enough. Guinness was pretty sure he had hit a nerve.

"That's right, isn't it, Vlasov? I wasn't sure before, not dead sure, but I am now—all this about how bad you want to do a number on me is just so much self-hypnotizing horsehit, isn't it? Hell, you've had a dozen chances at me, but I'm not what you're really after, not really. I'm just part of the mechanism. You go through the motions, but what you really want is for me, or somebody—anybody, really—to cancel your ticket for you and take away all the pain. Isn't that right, pal?"

Still, Vlasov did not move. And yet, without changing, his whole carriage seemed to have undergone some subtle change. As if in not moving he had lost the capacity to move. There was about him a tension, a terrible rigidity, as if he were frozen in place.

Then, slowly, he began to shake his head. And the borrowed light from his spectacle lenses flashed off and on like the warning signals from an oncoming train.

"No," he said finally, almost to himself. "No, it was by your hand, not mine." He raised his bent arm slightly from his lap, and the hand closed into a fist. Perhaps he had wanted to point an accusation, but the fingers, in their individual wrath, refused to open. It seemed so.

Then he allowed the arm to sink back down into his lap, and he raised his head. The voice, when it came, was hoarse with almost overmastering emotion, and the words seemed directed at no one at all.

"It was you. She was . . ."

With the clarity of an hallucination, Guinness suddenly could remember pulling away the sheet that had covered Louise's face. He could remember the way her eyes had been half open, and the smell of her burnt hair. It was, at that moment, a sustaining memory.

"Sure, Misha. It was me. I killed her. I wired the dynamite to your ignition switch; I did that. But who put her in the car, Misha? Who handed her in like she was Cinderella going for a little ride in her magic pumpkin? Who married her, hey, babe? And put her right square in the line of fire. Who did that to her, hey, sweetheart?"

By the end, he was shouting. It was all supposed to be calculated; just a technique, like the tongue lashings he would sometimes give his classes of freshmen when too many of them were late with their homework. But by the end he was seething with a hatred that seemed born out of more grief than just his own. It was just crazy. And then Vlasov was shouting too.

"You did this," he half sobbed, his fist, still apparently not able to unclench, shaking in the air. "You murdered her. She never harmed a living thing, she would never . . . and you murdered her. My wife, my wife." And before his, Guinness's wrath evaporated.

"No, you poor silly bastard, you did it yourself. It was my own wife that I murdered, but that's my problem.

"Don't you see, even now? Wives and clear consciences and the right to call ourselves human beings, we don't have any business with any of them. That's all for other people, not for you or me or the rest of our kind; it's what we gave up our share in when we went into our line of work."

For a long moment neither of them spoke. Then Vlasov's fingers, where they were resting on his right thigh, spread slightly. It was probably as close as he would ever come to a start.

"You are not armed," he said at last. It was as much a statement of fact as a discovery, like something at once a surprise and obvious. Guinness smiled wolfishly.

"That's right, sucker. I'm not."

He was already most of the way across the path before he saw Vlasov's hand begin to drop down for his gun. The shot, when it came, was already perhaps as much as a half second too late and smacked harmlessly into the trunk of a eucalyptus tree.

Two hundred yards through the fucking trees, downhill and in the dark. Twice he caught his foot on something and pitched over like a drunk in a vaudeville skit, but with all the bobbing and weaving he was up to, he was probably lucky he didn't plow straight on into a nice, solid, foot-and-a-half-thick trunk and knock himself cold. The gods were with him, at least so far.

Finally he threw himself down and listened. Not a sound. Not enough light to zip your fly by. Vlasov hadn't come after him.

But then, of course, Vlasov wouldn't. Not a dumb thing like that. You do not come charging after a man like that, not through a forest, not in the pitch black, gun or no gun. If you use a light, he can find you easier than you can find him; and if you don't, what the hell good is the gun? No, Vlasov might be crazy, but he wasn't stupid. He would find himself a spot somewhere just out of the light and he would settle down to see what happened. It was what Guinness himself would have done.

Or maybe not. Maybe Guinness would have just decided that the moment was not propitious and would have gotten the hell out of there. Would that be what Vlasov would do?—after all, the man wasn't stupid.

But he was crazy. And at that moment, crazy mad. Mad like a swarm of bees. He had been teased into a rage by the man who had killed his wife, who had burned her to a cinder right in front of his eyes. He had built his life around his revenge, and no way in the world was he going anywhere until he had had himself the satisfaction of cutting Guinness into inch-wide strips with a dull knife.

And that was his weakness, the poor tormented sonuabitch. That was his one weakness.

But in the meantime, he had the gun. One must not forget the gun. Guinness brought himself up to a low crouch, his eyes nervously searching for a point of light among the trees. There was none. No light, no sound, nothing. Pity, he almost might have preferred it if Vlasov had just charged in after him, hardware blazing. It would, at least, have settled everything.

But no. Vlasov had fired once, and he couldn't afford to fire again unless he had Guinness in his sights. One shot, two maybe, you could get away with; but make it sound like the battle of Culloden and somebody sitting on his back porch three quarters of a mile off is going to phone the cops.

"Hey, them kids is at it agin over thar in th' park," and in ten minutes a couple of squad cars would be nosing in through the main gate.

No, Vlasov wouldn't want to be disturbed before he had his business finished, so he could be counted on to be careful about how he popped off his little hand-cannon. There might be some small comfort to be drawn from that.

This wasn't really an OK Corral—type situation, which was another part of the reason Guinness had left his arsenal under the mattress in his motel room. That and the fact that Tuttle and his people had specified that they wanted Vlasov to just disappear from the face of the earth. It's no cinch to dispose of a body with several large, conspicuous bullet holes in it.

Slowly, Guinness began to make his circling way through the trees. With the merry-go-round as the center, he wanted to make as big a sweep as he could in hopes of finding out where Vlasov was laying for him. He went counterclockwise to keep from running into the road—try to get across that open space and you would probably end up a dead man.

The grove, so far as he could figure, was spread out like a fan, covering perhaps two hundred degrees of the circle, and Vlasov would be in there somewhere. He would want the cover too; and on the other side was a picnic area, with nothing but a lot of two-inch-high grass you couldn't have hidden a grapefuit in.

The grove and the merry-go-round, then, were to be their little theater of operations, in some dark corner of which friend Vlasov would be sitting on his heels and waiting for his chance. He would stay put for the time being, until he got restless, hoping for Guinness to come wandering into range.

It was with some satisfaction that Guinness remembered having read somewhere that eucalyptus trees were evergreens. He did not, therefore, have to contend with a two-inch carpet of dead, brittle leaves. The ground was reasonably soft, in fact, and if you paid attention to staying clear of the occasional tangles of fallen branches, you could move around quietly enough. A breath of wind to provide a little cover noise would have been nice, but you can't have everything.

As it was, it took him a little over forty minutes to find where Vlasov was laying in wait.

He had picked himself a pretty good spot, but then he would pick himself a pretty good spot—the KGB didn't make you a full colonel for standing around with your thumb in your mouth. It was about sixty feet down a slope from the merry-go-round, just beyond the penumbra from the flood lamps, so he had plenty of shadow to hide in and the light was close enough to give him something to shoot by. There were large tree trunks just behind him and to the right, and that particular area happened to be very bushy. It was a very good spot. Guinness might have stumbled right up to him if Vlashov hadn't just happened to have picked that moment to move, and if his glasses hadn't picked up and reflected a faint twinkle of light. Probably after all this time crouched over like a back-alley crap shooter, his legs were beginning to give him trouble.

The two of them were perhaps as much as fifty yards apart, and all Guinness had to do if he wanted to bring on Armageddon was to step on a dead branch. It might as well have been fifty miles.

Well, that was hardly a big surprise. It's only in the movies that you can sneak all the way up on the guy who's waiting in ambush for you—not unless he happens to be deaf, dumb, and blind.

There was nothing for Guinness to do but make himself comfortable, because it was going to be a long wait. Close at hand was a large rock, approximately the size and shape of a beer keg that had been tipped over on its side and gotten itself half buried, and one end of it was about four inches from the trunk of a tree that probably you couldn't have closed your arms around. Guinness lay down behind them, resting his head on his crossed forearms so that he could look out through the gap between. From there he could just make out the corner of Vlasov's left shoulder.

Time. It was close to one in the morning, and time was on Guinness's side. If your primary interest in enterprises of this kind is simply to stay alive, then you can always wait. But Vlasov was less interested in surviving than in revenge, so time was against him. Eventually, the high-school dropouts and the winos and the bored, dispirited mothers with their five-year-olds would be back. Someone would come to turn on the merry-go-round and collect the tickets from the people who wanted to ride on the unicorns and the pink swans. And long before any of that happened, Vlasov would have to have his business settled. He had lost now whatever advantage he had enjoyed from being the hunter. Who could tell—if he walked out of here alone in the morning, the job undone, what would keep Guinness from starting to shadow him? One annonymous phone call to the local Russian consulate and Vlasov would never make it to dinnertime.

So it was now or never. This was his last chance, and Vlasov would know it.

He would assume, of course, that Guinness was out there somewhere, looking for him. Guinness wouldn't have come, wouldn't have exposed himself like that, just to go skipping off again into the darkness.

But could he count on that? Might not Guinness just leave, and then make his call? Wasn't it just possible? And that would put Vlasov in a box.

The thought would have occurred to him, and eventually he would leave his little nest and go looking for Guinness. He would have to, just to find out. He would have to know for sure, no matter what the risks.

Of course, Guinness would never leave it to another man to pull Vlasov's chain for him. The hell with the Russians, and for that matter with Ernie Tuttle; it had to be something he did himself or nothing would make any sense at all, as if it ever had.

But Vlasov wouldn't know that. Would he think that he was the only one with a score to settle? Hadn't Guinness told him that that kind of nonsense was for suckers?

Screw it. It would have to wait, Guinness thought to himself. He could sort it all out once his head was off the block. Now was the time to concentrate on staying alive.

Every once in a while, not more than three times in an hour, Vlasov's shoulder would move in the darkness. Usually up and then down again, as if he might be getting ready to leave the protection of his hiding place and go on the prowl. And every time, Guinness felt his insides turning into ice water.

He wondered sometimes what must have been going through the poor bastard's mind, but that was something else that could wait. Tomorrow, if he lived, he could feel all the compassion in the world, but not now. Tomorrow he could yield himself to wave upon wave of sad and sentimental regret, he could rage at life's injustice and the fatal coils of the gods, but it would have to wait until tomorrow.

Right now he had to want to kill Misha Fedorovich Vlasov. He didn't have to hate the guy's guts—excesses of that sort can get in the way too. It would be enough simply not to like him very much.

Guinness thought perhaps, for now, he could manage that.

Finally, at a quarter to five, only an hour or so before the sky would lighten enough to let you make out the line of the horizon, at what he must have judged to be the very last allowable minute, Vlasov began to stir. Keeping his back against a tree, he edged himself up very slowly into a standing position.

He took his time, peering cautiously into the darkness behind and to either side of him. For a long moment he stared right at the spot where Guinness lay hidden, but then he turned away.

When apparently he was satisfied, he cleaned his glasses with a handkerchief drawn from somewhere Guinness couldn't see and pressed them back on the bridge of his nose with a delicate gesture of his middle finger. Grace under pressure.

Now Vlasov would have to come down into the grove, away from the flood lamps, down where he would have little to shoot at except sounds. And perhaps a little less cautious than he might be, knowing that the dawn was coming and his one chance was slipping through his fingers.

Guinness waited until Vlasov's back was turned and then pulled himself up as quickly as he dared. Crablike, he made his way down the sloping ground. Knowing that Vlasov would come down and then begin working his way to the right, since there would be nowhere else to go except out onto the grass, he went that way too. Eventually, Vlasov would come within range, and then they would both see what would happen next.

The spot he settled on was about fifteen feet above a natural trail that in this dark Vlasov would almost have to follow. There was a good-sized tree for cover, and he would have the advantage of the slope.

A few minutes later Vlasov came. Guinness couldn't bring himself even to breathe. It seemed forever before Vlasov came even with where he was waiting—and then a little further, just a little. Just enough that Vlasov would have him at his back.

It was a distance a running man could cover in only a few steps: not more than about twenty feet. He hadn't gone five before he knew that Vlasov was beginning to turn. In what seemed like slow motion, Vlasov's right elbow began to come out from his body and he began to step backward with his right foot. They were no more than six or seven feet apart when Guinness could see the gun. It circled around on the end of Vlasov's arm, as the arm seemed to turn faster than the body. And then it fired.

XXI

THE SPRING SEMESTER had ended and summer school wasn't scheduled to begin for another week, so there were no students on campus. Even at the multilevel parking structure where Ernest Tuttle left his car there was no one in the booth to give him a ticket with his entrance time stamped on the back or to collect his money when he would be ready to leave. Having been out of college long enough to have lost touch with the life cycle that begins in September and ends in June, he was a little surprised.

From the central quad he looked around at the buildings, mostly flat-roofed and modern, with brick façades and tiny oblong windows that made you think of the arrow slits in medieval castles, and wondered which of them was likely to be the Humanities Building and what could have gotten into a man like Raymond Guinness to have made him want to bury himself in a dump like this.

He shrugged imperceptibly and wandered over to a soft drink machine jammed in under the outside staircase of a thing called McCoy Engineering Hall, and for thirty-five cents he bought a can of Sprite. Lunch had consisted of two tacos and a cup of black coffee, and it had left him thirsty.

After the first swallow, he made a face and dropped

the can into an adjacent trash barrel; the stuff was flat. Well, that figured.

Tuttle was a practical sort of man; he did not believe in astrological signs, tea leaves, pyramid power, or the efficacy of consulting one's biorhythms. Things had simply not been going his way of late, that was all. A string of lousy luck that was bound shortly to reach its end.

In a year or two, with just a few decent breaks, he might be all finished with this back alley stuff and have himself a nice, safe desk job in the planning end of things, possibly even a regional directorship. It wasn't impossible.

Over the last three or four years, and especially after a nasty screw-up in Vienna, after which he had spent ten weeks in the hospital having shrapnel fragments pulled out of his legs, he had come to see that there was no percentage in fieldwork. How many guys did he know who were doing that kind stuff and had made it to fifty? How many did he know who were dead or basket cases in some veterans hospital somewhere? If you were smart, you got out while there was still time and lined yourself up a soft spot in administration, where you could go home at five o'clock and not worry that some clown might be waiting around the next corner to shoot your ass off.

And he could do it, too. He had a good record and his papers were on the coordinator's desk this very minute. If everything had gone precisely as planned on the Vlasov caper, he might have been on his way home right now, with a month's extra leave in front of him and his own little gig going right in the Washington office the first Monday back. As it was . . .

Damn California, land of the crazies. Go to the best seafood restaurant in San Francisco and you couldn't get soft-shell clams for love nor money. He wouldn't be sorry to leave; there seemed to be something in the climate that turned people off their heads.

If he could have come back with Guinness on a silver platter, they would have been ready to give him the world, and he had halfway promised Prescott in Operations. A shooter of that standing was hard to come by.

But so far Guinness was being very unreasonable.

To give him his due, though, in points of technique he was as reliable as a Swiss watch. Tuttle had to admit that the man knew what he was up to, even if he did make everybody around him jump through hoops. This latest thing had been beautiful, like he had never been away.

It was all a question of velocity and impact, as if they had been weights colliding in a vacuum, and not men. How far apart had they been when Vlasov fired? A yard, perhaps two—and Guinness closing fast. He might not ever have seen the flash, let alone felt anything. Anything less than a clean kill—the heart or the brain—would not have mattered. There would have been no time for a second try.

He had grabbed Vlasov's arm, just above the elbow, using his grip to pull himself in even faster and to keep the gun away from him, punching out with his right hand into the man's thorax. That was when he felt it for the first time, the terrible scorched wrenching, as if every sinew in his arms were being torn loose. The pain shot through him, through the whole length of his body, it seemed; but by then Vlasov was already stunned and helpless.

They went over together, tumbling and rolling down the gentle slope, further and further into the darkness. Guinness contrived to bring his knee up so that it came down into Vlasov's solar plexus the first time they made contact with the ground, and then his own momentum pitched him free. He managed one turn on his shoulder, trying to protect the injured arm, and then landed on his back with a shock. It was a second or two before he was sure he could still move.

Then came a moment, only a flicker, of blind panic. What about Vlasov? Where was he, the bastard? That gun, that damned gun.

But no problem. The gun hadn't landed two feet from Vlasov's right side, but he couldn't have picked it up, couldn't have squeezed the trigger if it had been lying in the palm of his hand. He was too busy dying.

Guinness brought himself up to where he was resting on his knees and looked at the dim outline of his enemy, knowing that it was over, that he had won. Vlasov lay on his back, his hands down at his sides as they trembled mechanically against his trouser legs. He seemed to be concentrating every shred of his will on trying to breathe, but he couldn't—the only sound he made was the gurgle from his smashed windpipe as he suffocated in his own blood. It was over for him. Without the glasses—they had been lost somewhere in all that bouncing around; Guinness would have to find them—his was already the face of a corpse.

Just to be on the safe side, Guinness picked up the gun: a nasty little thing but of small caliber, which was a blessing. In a minute or two he would take a look at how much damage it had done and then decide if he was likely to live or not, but just then the question didn't strike him as very interesting. All that seemed permanently important was that Vlasov was dying.

And he was taking his time, the poor bastard. He might be getting a little air, just enough to draw the process out another fifteen or twenty minutes; he might be at it for another half-hour. It probably wasn't much fun.

Guinness brought the gun to level, resting the muzzle directly against Vlasov's temple—Vlasov didn't seem to notice—and then thought better of it. No bullet holes. Just in case something went wrong, just in case the disposal people messed up and Vlasov somehow managed to become police property, there couldn't be any bullet holes. Nothing absolutely inconsistent with accidental death.

And besides, guns make noise.

Until they were hanged for it in 1829, an enterprising pair of hoodlums named Burke and Hare had kept the medical school at Edinburgh supplied with fresh cadavers, no questions asked. They had developed a technique: finding a vagrant in the streets at night, then covering the mouth with the palm of the hand and pinching off the nose between first finger and thumb. It left no mark, no sign of violence.

Guinness wiped his hand on the front of his shirt and then covered Vlasov's face with it. Vlasov didn't even struggle, never lifted his hands, never tried to twist away—perhaps he was already unconscious; perhaps he had simply stopped caring. After three or four minutes, when he pressed his thumb against the side of Vlasov's neck, there was no heartbeat, and Guinness gently closed the blind eyes. The war between them was over; they would both simply have to be satisfied with the result. The night had suddenly become very cold, and haunted with the spirits of the restless dead.

On the fourth morning after Guinness's disappearance, the phone in Tuttle's motel room in Belmont rang, waking him up. The message had been brief and very much to the point:

"That package in which you were interested is buried under a pile of branches in Griffith Park. Take the main road in about a half mile past the merry-go-round, then get out of your car and head into the trees on your left. About fifty yards should do it. It won't stay hidden forever, so I wouldn't linger."

Tuttle was scribbling furiously. "Where the hell is Griffith Park? Listen, Guinness, are you okay?"

"Los Angeles, stupid. And I'll live. I'm coming home this evening. When I get back to my hotel room, I plan to have about three drinks more than is good for me and then go to bed, and I'll be very angry if at any point along the way I'm arrested. So that gives you the rest of today to do your little number with the cops. Any trouble, and all bets are off."

Then the line went dead.

Tuttle didn't like it, not at all. The man sounded very ragged, like maybe the first badge that came near him might just get itself blown away. Guinness didn't strike him as the type to make idle threats.

Tuttle frowned and replaced the reciever. Ten minutes later he was dressed and standing in a phone booth next to the entrance of a Safeway—which, except for the neon tubes in the dairy cases, was still dark inside—dialing a number you simply didn't call from your motel room. It wasn't done.

The phone at the other end rang only once before Tuttle heard the familiar voice of a middle-aged woman whom he had never seen and probably never would.

"Yes?"

They ran through the current security procedure and then Tuttle gave his instructions for having Vlasov's body retrieved. Whoever was sent was to keep his eyes open and call back between twelve and one that afternoon with a quality report. Tuttle would be in his room.

What he heard had scared the hell out of him.

"We borrowed a station wagon from the City Recreation Service and got there a little after ten. You should have seen the joint—we almost decided that we had better forget the whole thing and wait for dark.

"Cops all over the place. I asked some old guy who tended the peanut machines what the fuss was, and according to him they'd found the night man in a shed over by the merry-go-round, very dead. A length of electrical extension cord was still twisted around his neck.

"Anyway, the office had led us to believe that you were reasonably hinky about clearing this one up, so we decided to risk it. We found your stiff right where you said he'd be.

"Whoever iced him was the tidy type: All the papers were gone from his wallet, no weapons, no personal effects, even the labels had been torn out of his clothes—your perfect John Doe, or as perfect as you can make one without cutting off his hands and pulling the dental work out of his head. There was an ugly-looking bruise on his throat and the cartilage in his windpipe was all smashed up—enough to kill him, but we don't think he died of that. We also found a trace of blood in his right ear; everything else was consistent with death by smothering. Somebody doesn't mess around.

"We wrapped him up in a plastic tarp and put him in the back of the wagon and got out of there, fast. He's stashed now where he'll keep for the time being. You want an autopsy?"

"Thank's just the same. Just take his prints and lose him."

Jesus. Think of the fun if the cops had found him first. A double murder, right in the middle of a public park, in all likelihood with Vlasov's face staring out from the front page of every newspaper in the state. Oh, the fine times the Russians could have had with a little disaster like that—no wonder Guinness had hauled the body such a distance, and on foot.

With a car he could have left the damn thing in the middle of the Nevada desert, so he had to have been on foot. Better than half a mile, carting a corspe. Very considerate of him, especially since he had had to manage it with a bullet in him. It must have taken forever.

From about 4:00 P.M. on, which was as soon as he could get away from the coils of the law, Tuttle had met every plane coming into the San Francisco Airport from Los Angeles. Guinness was on the nine o'clock PSA flight, and he really looked like hell.

At first Tuttle had thought he might be carrying a package or something under his coat, but then he noticed that there was no arm in the sleeve. The arm was in a sling that seemed in some way immobilized against his body.

In basic training they always told you the story about the Spartan boy who concealed a fox under his cloak and then, rather than make a spectacle of himself, let the thing claw his guts out. You were supposed to be very tough in this business, very much the hardnose, and every once in a while it did prove necessary to go walking gamely past a hostile guard with your leg broken in four places; but one wondered what Guinness could think he had to prove.

Behind the casualness of his gait there was a willful precision, a care that every movement should stay in control, as if it were beneath him to suffer. His eyes looked weary, though, and his face was the color of wet paper. Tuttle's presence didn't seem to register at all until he was almost directly in front of him.

"What the hell happened to you?" he asked, putting out a hand. Guinness didn't take it and didn't answer. He only frowned slightly, as if Tuttle had cracked some tasteless joke. He didn't say anything, as a matter of record, until they were in the car and going over the cloverleaf that fed airport traffic back onto the Bayshore Freeway. And even then he wasn't precisely what you could call chatty.

"Will you watch it?" Guinness had snapped as they went around the curve, perhaps a trifle faster than necessary. "I don't much care to have my arm smashed flat just because you feel like burning rubber."

"Sorry." Tuttle eased his foot down a little on the brake pedal and began to check for cross traffic as they came out of their turn. "Vlasov get a shot off?"

"One."

He didn't go back to his own hotel—Tuttle didn't think he was in any shape to be left alone and so talked him into spending the night on the extra bed in his motel room—and Tuttle, as usual, did most of the drinking. But gradually Guinness's disposition began to improve and Tuttle found out what had happened. Or, at least, as much as he was going to.

The bullet, it seemed, had entered just to one side of Guinness's breastbone and had bounced merrily along over his rib cage before it exited and finally buried itself just below the right bicep, flush up against the bone. Guinness had been lucky: The bone was bruised but unbroken, not even cracked, and none of the major arteries had been touched. Otherwise, out there alone in the middle of the night, it was a pretty safe bet he would have bled to death.

Jesus, a half mile carrying a dead body slung over his shoulder and all shot up like that. Guinness said he had had to put Vlasov down and rest every few hundred yards to keep from fainting. Not good for too many laughs, that kind of thing, not with a bullet in you.

"You should have said something—we have our connections, you know. How the hell did you get yourself pieced back together down there without bringing the cops in on it?"

Guinness only shrugged. And, true, it had been a stupid question; hell, the man had lived in L.A. for over a year. No doubt he knew half a dozen doctors who would forget their civic duty for an extra hundred bucks.

In The Business it was considered a breach of etiquette to inquire too closely into how a job had gone. If Guinness had wanted to talk about it, that would have been one thing, but he hadn't. So it seemed unlikely that Tuttle would ever find out precisely what had passed between Vlasov and the man who had killed him. It would have been worth something to know.

But, God knows, Guinness wasn't going to tell him. Guinness had hardly talked at all, and what he had said didn't precisely make worlds of sense.

"Vlasov wanted to die," he had almost whispered, as if he were saying it to himself. And then he had looked up at Tuttle, as if noticing his presence for the first time, and had smiled a peculiar ironic little smile. "If he could have killed me first, that would have made everything perfect, but I wasn't the main target. He brought all of us—you, me, the Russians, every player in the game—all down on him at once, and one or the other of us could be counted on to take him off. He planned it that way; he was too moral a man for it to have had any other ending. You have to admire that kind of integrity."

Maybe Guinness did, but as far as Tuttle was concerned it was strictly off the wall. It made you wonder how Guinness had managed to survive as long as he had, this not really being a line of work that was very kind to the philosophical type.

Anyway, the next morning, having refused all offers of breakfast, the former front-runner on San Mateo County's Most Wanted Fugitives list walked out through the door of Tuttle's room at the Casa Belmont to resume what one supposed had to be called "normal life," or what from now on would have to pass for it.

But at least he was no longer an object of official interest to the police. It had taken some doing, but finally Creon had been persuaded of the wisdom of canceling his a.p.b. and regarding the investigation into the death of Louise Harrison Guinness as concluded. He hadn't liked it much, even after Tuttle had produced the ice pick with the blood that would type with the victim's and the fingerprints that belonged to somebody whom he was rather pointedly told was none of his affair.

It seemed he had had his heart set on busting Guinness. And even forgetting the murder rap, there was still the small matter of assault, grand theft firearm, and possibly even kidnapping, all committed against the person of one Herbert L. Ganjemi, late of the Oakland Police. Ganjemi, for all of being a dumb shit, was a friend and a brother officer, and you just didn't drop a friend of Creon's into a laundry basket, steal his piece, and then go on about your business. After all, there was the dignity of the Law to be considered.

"Look, pal," Tuttle had answered, rising up out of his chair and leaning over his hands on Creon's desk, their faces not more than half a yard apart, "the government is not interested in having its citizens hassled by every small-town cop who happens to think he's Matt Dillon. If Dr. Guinness is in any way molested, if he gets so much as a traffic ticket any time in the next hundred years, you are going to find this two-bit department of yours picked over like the underwear in Macy's basement. You don't know what harassment is until you've gone a few rounds with us, and when we're done you won't be able to find a job as a warehouse guard in Hermosillo, Mexico. We want the man left alone, you got that?"

Well, Creon had toughed it up a lot and yelled about how nobody, but nobody, could tell him how to do his job—as if an asshole like that would have the faintest idea how to do his job—but eventually the message had filtered through. Guinness was off the hook. There would even be an item in the local papers about a new official theory that the murder had been committed by a transient, whom the police had every hope of eventually apprehending.

And that was that. Guinness had taken an apartment not far from his office, his house was unpadlocked and up for sale, and he was back at his job. Everything seemed to be back to normal.

Except, what was normal anymore? Guinness was behaving like a zombie. For the past two weeks he had lived his life in precisely three rooms: his apartment, his office at school, and the mausoleum in Colma, where his wife occupied a space in the next-to-the-bottom tier of the south wall. He would sit there for hours, four or five times a week, staring at the blank square of marble to which the little steel plate reading "Louise Harrison Guinness/1944-1977" had not yet been bolted. It was a grief that seemed too large for the exclusive use of just one little mortal, and God knows what else the man was mourning beyond his late missus. He was like someone haunted by ghosts, willing them up from their several graves out of a recognition that he deserved to be tormented.

The night Guinness came back, he had crawled onto the spare motel-room bed and lain there in his clothes, not even bothering to take down the spread. It made Tuttle nervous; every few hours he would wake up and every time Guinness would still be awake, lying on his back and staring at the ceiling. You could see his eyeballs glistening in the faint light that came in through an open space between the curtains. Guinness might not have slept at all that night.

Was he sleeping at all now? It was a safe bet Tuttle wasn't; his buddy Prescott had seen to that.

"Listen, Tuttle," he had said over the phone, in that maddening Harvard Yard accent of his, "we made a deal. You want me to go waltzing into the Old Man's office and tell him that you're the only man to fill the slot he's owed me since Kaufmann's heart attack? You want me to ooze all over the place about how we just can't live without you another second? Then you deliver Guinness. I want him, Tuttle, and I don't care if you have to wheel him in trussed up like a turkey. We've got lots of shrinks around here and it won't take them any time at all to put his head back together enough so that he can hold a gun. After all, how sane does he have to be?"

Tuttle made a face at himself in the glass wall of the telephone booth, thinking about Kaufmann's heart attack and wondering if the actuarial figures for people in Prescott's department were likely to be all that much of an improvement.

"I keep telling you, Al. You can't rush a man like this. Four days now, and every damn day I've asked him the same question and he's given me the same answer. He says that he doesn't want to spend the rest of his life having to look over his shoulder, and it might even be that he means it. What the hell do you expect me to do? I can't hang around out here forever; the Vlasov business was cleared up a long time ago."

On the other end of the line there was silence, broken only by the faint sound of a pencil eraser being tapped against the surface of a glass-topped desk some three thousand miles away.

"Tuttle?" came the answer at last. "Tuttle, he hasn't slammed the door in your face or anything like that, has he? I mean, he hasn't threatened to string your guts out to dry; he's still talking to you, isn't he?" Tuttle had to admit, yes, Guinness was still talking to him. They were almost—well—almost friends.

"Well then? Isn't that answer enough for you? You said it yourself: Once a shooter always a shooter. He'll come around. He just wants to stew over his grievances a while longer. Ten to one, by now he already knows he's coming back and just isn't ready to admit it.

"Don't you have some vacation time coming, Tuttle?"

"Yes." Tuttle nodded sullenly at his reflection in the glass. He could see what was building. "Yes, I've got two weeks."

"Then enjoy yourself in sunny California. Have a big time. Ride the trolley cars and eat all the Chinese food you can hold. When you come back, I'll expect you to have a beautiful tan and Raymond Guinness with a ring through his nose."

The line went dead. Tuttle hung up the receiver with a shade more violence than is strictly good for the equipment.

That had been—what?—ten days ago? Tuttle fed another thirty-five cents into the soft drink machine and pushed the button for grape soda. Grape soda turned out to have been a judicious choice. A little sweet, perhaps, but it was cold and this time they hadn't left the gas out.

"Come on, man," he whispered under his breath. "It's your karma; you can't hold out forever".

And what Prescott had said was perfectly true: As long as Guinness continued to allow himself to be approached, he had not really said "no." He had merely said "not yet," which is not the same thing. If the pressure were kept up, it would only be a matter of time.

Tuttle shaded his eyes with his left hand and looked off down the slope of the hill into which most of the college's buildings had been embedded, on down to the tennis courts and the playing fields that occupied a narrow strip of flatland. Perhaps it wasn't such a bad life to be a professor and spend your time correcting essays; in a sense, he could see Guinness's point. After all, wasn't it his own ambition to come in out of the cold and join the charmed circle of the paper pushers?

In a way, it made him feel a little guilty, what he was trying to do to Guinness—but not very. He was tired of all the rough stuff; he had never been anything beyond merely proficient at it, and it was only a matter of time before he would meet another somebody like Guinness behind a gas station men's room, somebody who had been born a thug the way Paganini had been born to play the violin—and that time it would probably be for keeps. Guinness was his ticket to safety, and if one or the other of them had to go out into the cold, cruel world and get shot at, then it was damn well going to be Guinness.

And who could say, in his present temper, that it might not be the best thing for him? He needed something to keep his mind occupied; perhaps it was necessary for him to begin risking his life again in order to be reminded that it was worth living.

Sometimes, in the evening, they would sit together in Guinness's room (Tuttle had gotten into the habit of inviting himself and Guinness hadn't objected, hadn't even seemed to notice), and for periods of twenty or thirty minutes Guinness would not even move. He would stare at some object in the middle distance that only he could see, hardly seeming to breathe. What it was that he thought about, whether it was simply the death of his wife or the neurotic little tragedy of Misha Vlasov or the whole ugly coil of earthly destiny, he never said. Perhaps he didn't think about anything; perhaps his mind was too numb with what had happened for him to think at all.

So perhaps it would be the best thing for him. God knows, if he kept up like this much longer, he'd either blow his brains out or end up in one of those loony bins that seemed to line the south side of Ralston Avenue. There might be no limit to what a man could stand, but there was to what he could bear to brood about.

So perhaps, for Guinness, getting back in would be what getting out was for Tuttle: a way to survive. It wasn't absolutely out of the question.

Anyway, Guinness was a big boy. At one time he had been at the very top of their highly competitive profession, so it wasn't as if anyone were seducing the innocent. If he went back—and he would go back—it would be because that kind of life was something he needed the way other men need air, something finally impossible to evade.

If not today, then tomorrow. Finally, however, it would happen, just the same. In three days Tuttle would take a plane back to Washington, so that was the deadline for both of them. Guinness might hold out until the last possible moment, but in the end, like a man of sense, he would perceive the necessity of the thing.

Room 244, Humanities Building. That was what the little girl who answered the English Department phone had told him, and she should know.